More praise for

WHERE THERE'S A WILL

"Solid . . . Oliver's deductions will remind classic mystery readers of archetypal scientific sleuth Dr. Thorndyke, and his three-dimensional personality and humor will continue to attract first-timers."   —*Publishers Weekly*

"Fabulous A-quality level forensic investigative tale."
    —*Midwest Book Review*

"A diverting . . . mystifying vacation."   —*Kirkus Reviews*

Praise for

GOOD BLOOD

"First rate! Elegant, ingenious, and beautifully crafted."
    —Sue Grafton

"Elkins has long been a top-rank writer and it's always pure delight when he brings out another book."   —Earl Emerson

"Elkins's eleventh mystery shows the forensic anthropologist in fine form . . . the forensic facts Elkins chooses to include and the brisk pace of the plot make for a total success."   —*Publishers Weekly*

"Aaron Elkins's 'skeleton detective,' Gideon Oliver, can't even take a vacation without bumping into bones. Thank goodness. Otherwise we would not have *Good Blood* . . . Mr. Elkins never fails to enlighten and entertain . . . His only failing is that he makes us wait too long between books."   —*The Washington Times*

"Vintage Elkins: well-drawn supporting characters, lovely scenery . . . a bit of interesting science, [and a] cast of colorful characters."   —*Library Journal*

continued . . .

WHERE THERE'S A WILL

AARON ELKINS

BERKLEY PRIME CRIME, NEW YORK

THE BERKLEY PUBLISHING GROUP
Published by the Penguin Group
Penguin Group (USA) Inc.
375 Hudson Street, New York, New York 10014, USA

Penguin Group (Canada), 90 Eglinton Avenue East, Suite 700, Toronto, Ontario M4P 2Y3, Canada
(a division of Pearson Penguin Canada Inc.)
Penguin Books Ltd., 80 Strand, London WC2R 0RL, England
Penguin Group Ireland, 25 St. Stephen's Green, Dublin 2, Ireland (a division of Penguin Books Ltd.)
Penguin Group (Australia), 250 Camberwell Road, Camberwell, Victoria 3124, Australia
(a division of Pearson Australia Group Pty. Ltd.)
Penguin Books India Pvt. Ltd., 11 Community Centre, Panchsheel Park, New Delhi—110 017, India
Penguin Group (NZ), Cnr. Airborne and Rosedale Roads, Albany, Auckland 1310, New Zealand
(a division of Pearson New Zealand Ltd.)
Penguin Books (South Africa) (Pty.) Ltd., 24 Sturdee Avenue, Rosebank, Johannesburg 2196,
South Africa

Penguin Books Ltd., Registered Offices: 80 Strand, London WC2R 0RL, England

This is a work of fiction. Names, characters, places, and incidents either are the product of the author's imagination or are used fictitiously, and any resemblance to actual persons, living or dead, business establishments, events, or locales is entirely coincidental. The publisher does not have any control over and does not assume any responsibility for author or third-party websites or their content.

WHERE THERE'S A WILL

A Berkley Prime Crime Book / published by arrangement with the author

PRINTING HISTORY
Berkley Prime Crime hardcover edition / April 2005
Berkley Prime Crime mass-market edition / February 2006
Selections from *Gunshot Wounds*, Second Edition (1999) by Vincent J.M. DiMaio are reprinted with permission from CRC Press, Boca Raton, Florida.

Copyright © 2005 by Aaron Elkins.
Cover art based on Omnia Vanitas, Dutch School (18th century) / Private Collection © Bonhams, London, UK / Bridgeman Art Gallery. Interior text design by Kristin del Rosario.
The Edgar® name is a registered service mark of the Mystery Writers of America, Inc.

ISBN: 0-425-20852-4

BERKLEY® PRIME CRIME
Berkley Prime Crime Books are published by The Berkley Publishing Group,
a division of Penguin Group (USA) Inc., 375 Hudson Street, New York, New York 10014.
The name BERKLEY PRIME CRIME and the BERKLEY PRIME CRIME design
are trademarks belonging to Penguin Group (USA) Inc.

PRINTED IN THE UNITED STATES OF AMERICA

10 9 8 7 6 5 4 3 2 1

Acknowledgments

As usual, Professor Oliver needed a bit of help before he finally sorted things out. On his behalf, I would like to thank the following people:

- For continuing education on planes and flying: my friends, former airline pilot Bill Benedict; Captain (ret.) Ivory Brummett, United Airlines; and Captain Norm Hapke, American West Airlines.

- For freely sharing their expertise and experience in the forensic sciences: Professor Emeritus Ted Rathbun, University of South Carolina; Professor Emeritus Stan Rhine, University of New Mexico; Professor Steve Byers, University of New Mexico; Professor Alison Galloway, University of California–Santa Cruz; Paul Holes, Supervising Criminalist, Contra Costa County, California Sheriff's Office; and pathologist Alexey Nicolaevich Zolotarev of Russia.

- For an introduction to Hawaiian cattle ranching and a great day on horseback riding the Kohala range: Jeanette Rutherford, Barn Manager, Ponoholo Ranch, Hawaii.

- For their guidance on the law and on law enforcement: Lieutenant (ret.) Alicia Lampert, San Diego Police Department; and Andy Slater, Assistant State Attorney, West Palm Beach, Florida.

- For a hands-on education on handguns: Bob Lampert, former photojournalist, McGraw-Hill, Inc.

- For reconnaissance on the Big Island of Hawaii: Major General (ret.) Dave de la Vergne.

ONE

November 4, 1994, Latitude 16.28N, Longitude 161.06W

SILENCE, as sudden as a stopped heart.

After the monotonous grind of the engine for the last three and a half hours, and then the brief stuttering and missing, it seemed to Claudia that the absence of sound had a physical presence, a doughy mass that filled the cockpit, pressing on her eardrums and stopping her nostrils.

"The fuel's run out," she told the old man.

"So that's that, then," he said. He'd had plenty of time to get used to the idea, and he spoke as much in resignation as in fear. In the red glow from the instrument panel, his weathered face, even the billy-goat scrap of beard, might have been a carved mask, all stark planes and angles. On his lap, his left hand gently cradled his heavily bandaged right. The bleeding had slowed down to an ooze now, or maybe it had stopped altogether. For a while it had been pumping steadily, soaking the gauze and staining his pants.

He'd fainted a couple of times, and she'd thought he might die on her, right there in the cockpit.

As if it would have made much difference.

"Yup, that's that," Claudia said in the same emotionless tone. "We're going down."

She thought she heard him sigh, very softly.

A light plane that has run out of fuel at an altitude of 10,500 feet does not plummet to earth like a safe falling out of a window. It drifts down, slowly and silently, borne on the wind, gliding two or three miles for every thousand feet of altitude lost. To descend more than ten thousand feet takes twenty or twenty-five minutes, and once the trim is adjusted there isn't much to do, especially when there is nothing below to look for—no beacon light to aim toward, no obstacles to avoid—nothing but the cold swath of stars above and the black, vast, empty Pacific Ocean below.

There is plenty of time to think.

IT seemed to her now that she'd known in her heart from the beginning that they weren't going to make it. She should have said no in the first place. She was a daytime flier, a visual-flight-rules pilot, and she'd never claimed to be anything else. Did the boss want to go to the Hawi airport? Fine, let's go. Fly north along the eastern slope of the Kohala ridge with the coast on your right and keep an eye out for the runway, nothing to it. Hana? Just point the nose toward Maui and go; you couldn't miss it. Even Honolulu, where they'd gone for the Cattlemen's Expo—fix the bearing and keep flying until you see Diamond Head and the airport. But this instrument-flying, this flying in the dark, wasn't for her; she wasn't used to it. And a rushed, crazy flight like this—with barely enough time to do the chart, four hundred miles over empty ocean to some rinky-dink, flyspeck island in the middle of nowhere—that was plain stupid.

Still, she had done everything right, everything by the book. Scared or not, she'd used the North Pacific navigational chart to locate the damn island in the first place, find the distance, and plot the bearing. She'd contacted the flight services center for the wind conditions and adjusted the bearing accordingly. She'd checked everything three times. The plane was fully fueled, newly maintained, and ready to go. The destination was well within the Grumman's range, especially if she flew high and kept to fifty-five percent power, which was her plan. Fortunately, the whiskey compass was as reliable as it could be, having been adjusted on the compass rose only four days earlier, and as they'd taxied slowly down the runway of the deserted Waimea airport she'd carefully set the gyrocompass to it and rechecked it against the correction card. And, day-time flier or not, she was a damn good pilot; she had a feel for flying, she could do this.

All the same, fifteen minutes into the flight, as the airport beacon shrank to a fading spark in the blackness, her courage failed her. "This is impossible. I can't do this," she said abruptly. "We have to go back." She was already easing down the left rudder and beginning to turn the yoke to circle back toward the Big Island.

"We're not going back," Torkelsson said curtly. "You know I can't."

"To Honolulu then. You'll be safe there, and you can take a plane anywhere. We can lock in—"

"Claudia." With his uninjured hand he reached across to stay her arm. "They'll be looking for me there, too. If we land in Honolulu it'll be the end of me." Pleading didn't come naturally to him, and he seemed to realize it. His clutch tightened, grinding her wrist bones together, an old man's claw. "And I'll see to it that it's the end of you, too. I promise you that. I'll tell them everything."

But threats weren't his style either, and with a grunt of embarrassment he let go of her arm. "It's not something I want to do," he said. "You know that. But so help me, God, if you drive me to it . . ."

"Okay, okay," she said grimly and found her original bearing—what she hoped was her bearing—again. On to Tarabao Island.

Just as the Torkelssons had given her back her life, they could take it away again. It had been Magnus Torkelsson who had first seen something in her four years before, when she was a neurotic, dope-addled twenty-one-year-old on the fast track to self-destruction. What she was doing in Hawaii, exactly how or why she had come there from East Texas, she didn't know—literally could not remember—but someone had gotten her a seasonal job clearing brush at Hoaloha, the Torkelssons' big cattle ranch, and the rugged outdoor work had suited her. She was a big, strong girl who knew a little about ranching, a willing worker with a mechanical bent, and inside of a year she was on their year-round windmill and pump maintenance team. Then, when their regular pilot started talking about moving on and she had expressed some interest in flying, they had sent her to flight-training school in Hilo. For a while she had shared piloting duties with one of the Torkelsson nephews, but when he got tired of it she had taken the job over completely, flying somewhere, usually just to another part of the island, three or four times a week. She'd enjoyed it, too.

They were good people, people of the land. They had been straightforward and open with her, and she had responded the same way. And there lay the problem. Torkels-son knew all about the sad mess of her teens—the dope, the psychiatric hospitalizations, the expunged record of juvenile crimes, even the two outstanding warrants. All he had to do was go to the FAA, and goodbye to her commercial pilot's license. Her flying days would be over, the law would come down on her, and more than likely she'd wind up back in East Texas, maybe in jail, or worse yet, living with her parents.

Trying to find Tarabao Island in the dark was better than that.

As frightened as she was, Claudia's instincts told her that they were staying pretty much on course. The gyro-compass was reassuringly steady and undeviating. Checking it every few minutes against the whiskey compass, there was never a need to adjust it. And the night was crystalline. She'd be able to spot the airport beacon and runway lights—they'd be the only illuminated objects for two hundred miles in every direction—if they were actually turned on as promised. And, of course, if she came anywhere within visual range of Tarabao. But that much she was certain she could manage. Almost certain.

They flew for more than three tense hours during which Torkelsson rarely spoke. The first time was to ask, timidly: "Why do they call it a whiskey compass? I've always wondered." He was trying to make amends.

"Because the fluid the needle floats in is supposed to be alcohol," she barked, unwilling to let him off that easily. *Who gave a shit why they called it a whiskey compass?* "But it's not, it's some kind of kerosene or something. Who cares?"

The next time, about an hour later, staring fixedly out the window at nothing—there was nothing to see—he said: "About where are we now, would you say?"

"About halfway there, probably."

"Yes, but where, exactly? Can't you check it on the chart?"

She laughed, a nasty, grating laugh that hurt her throat. How could he have flown so many hours beside her, and beside Gus, and beside his nephew, and know so pathetically little? "What would looking at the chart tell me? What good is it over an empty ocean? There's nothing to see. And if there was, we couldn't see it anyway. It's dark out there, if you haven't noticed."

"I was merely asking a question, Claudia," he said stiffly. "I just wanted to know where I was."

And something inside her, whatever it was that had been holding her together, snapped. She began ranting, screaming at him in the small cabin. *If he hadn't been too cheap to buy a goddamned GPS, they'd know where they were, and more important, they'd know where Tarabao Island was and how to get there. How many times had she asked them for one? What did they cost, a lousy couple of hundred bucks? But no, the used Grumman Cheetah had come without a GPS in 1986—and without an ADF as well—and Gus had flown it just fine for eighteen years without seeing the need for them, and they'd never had a problem, and what was the point of wasting money—*

The stricken look on his face made her stop. It was the first time she'd ever spoken to him like that. "I'm sorry," she said. "I guess I'm a little tense."

"I understand, Claudia," he said mildly. "I'm a little tense myself."

She groped for something to say. "How's the hand?"

He smiled at her—a sweet, achingly wistful smile. *What does it matter how my hand is?* "It throbs a little, that's all. It'll be fine once I get it taken care of."

"Sure, it will."

Again they fell silent. Ten minutes passed. "Claudia," he said pensively, "do you like wood?"

"Do I what?"

"Do you like wood, working with it?"

"Sure, I guess."

"I love wood. Love the smell of it, love the feel of the curls that come off when you plane it down. In Sweden I was apprenticed to a furniture maker, did you know that?"

His voice was dreamy, his mind a million miles away. "You know what I'm going to do when I get settled? I think I'm going to make furniture for people—chairs, cabinets, that kind of thing. Everybody needs furniture. In Australia, I was thinking."

"I thought you were coming home when everything quieted down."

"No . . . that was the plan, but I don't really think that would be the best idea," he said, almost as if they were talking about something that might actually happen. "I've got some money socked away in a mainland account; more than enough to set up shop, and I wouldn't have to make very much—wouldn't *want* to make very much—just enough to live a nice, quiet life. Wouldn't that be something? No more hoof-and-mouth, no more blackleg, no more pinkeye, no more cattle stink—just that clean, fresh smell of pine, of oak, of fir . . . they all smell different once you know them, did you know that?"

"That sounds nice," she said.

"Well, I was wondering . . . do you think you might like to work for me—with me? It'd be good to have somebody I trust. You're a strong, smart girl, you'd pick up the craft in no time, and then, after I'm gone, you'd have a real profession. You'd be surprised, there's a lot of pleasure that comes from turning out a quality piece of handmade furniture. We could maybe share a house, or I could live in back of the shop and you could rent somewhere if you'd like that better. We could take jobs or turn them down, whatever we feel like. What do you think?"

She smiled at him. "Sure, Mr. T. I'd like that."

"We'll plan on it, then."

Her throat was aching. "You bet."

After that, they flew on without speaking, deep in their own thoughts, their own regrets, until the last of the fuel ran out and the Cheetah had started its final descent.

YUP, that's that. We're going down.

She had known for the last twenty minutes that they had missed the island. Since then they had flown in expanding circles, hoping somehow to find the beacon. But she had little hope of finding Tarabao or anyplace else. It was a minuscule island, and the Pacific down this way was very empty. In going on four hours since they'd left Hawaii they'd never seen a single light, not even from some lonely freighter.

She trimmed the tabs slightly back for as long and slow a descent as possible—*funny how, even now, you did whatever you could to give yourself maybe two more minutes aloft, as if it made any difference*—sat back, and slid open the window to let in the cool night air. She took two deep breaths, shivered, and closed it again.

"What do we do now?" Torkelsson asked.

"First get your life jacket on. And you know there's a raft stowed right behind us, right? If something happens to me and I can't—"

"Claudia—"

"—and I can't open it for us, you just pull the inflation handle, you don't have to open the valise. Make sure you wait till you get it out the door first."

He managed a dry laugh. "That sounds like a good idea."

"Now get that jacket on. And then pull the seat belt tight. Don't worry, we're going to be all right."

"Of course we are." He said it like a man already dead, but he shrugged the mildewed orange jacket over his head and pulled the bands tight. Claudia did the same with hers.

"I'm really sorry I yelled at you like that," she said a few moments later. "I had no call to do that. You've been great to me, Mr. Torkelsson, you and your brother both."

"Oh, that's all right, I had it coming." He was very calm, very still. "Can I do something to help?"

"No, there's really not much to do. Can you see anything down there?"

"No, it's black as ink."

She checked the altimeter. "We're at sixteen hundred feet now. I'm going to put on the landing lights. If you can help me look for the waves, that'd be a help."

"Look for the waves?" he said blankly.

"Which way they're running. We want to come in parallel to them, between the crests, if we can. If we run smack into them, it'll be like running into a stone wall. Into a *row* of stone walls."

"I see. Yes, all right, I'll try."

Neither of them said what they both knew to be true: What did it matter whether they landed in one piece or ran head-on into a wave and got it over with all at once? They were in one of the most remote, little-traveled areas of the largest body of water in the world, it was pitch-black, and, most important, no one had any idea of where they were. They had taken off from Waimea after-hours, with no attendant around. No flight plan had been filed, the transponder had been turned off, no radio contact had been made. The chances of anyone accidentally spotting their little orange raft, if they ever made it out of the plane, were a million to one, probably less.

But the will to live, if even for a few hours longer, didn't depend on such considerations, and when she turned on the lights they both peered hard to determine how the waves were running.

It took a while for them to make sense of the water's surface. "I don't see any waves at all," Torkelsson said.

"There have to be waves."

"No, it's like a lake, there's nothing."

"There have to be waves," she said again, but she couldn't see any either, only a flat surface of green so pale it was almost white. She'd never come in over water at night, so she wasn't sure if the color was the result of her lights, or if it was a sign of relatively shallow water. *Shallow water . . . no waves,* she thought with a little jet of hope. *Could it be a lagoon? If it's a lagoon, that means land . . . an island—*

"Watch out!" Torkelsson shouted.

"*What?* I don't see—"

But in his agitation he had lashed out, and his arm hit her wrist, jerking the steering yoke to the left. The ailerons responded as they must: Up went the left one, down came the right one. The plane dipped precipitously to its left. The left wingtip touched the surface of the water. Like a stone skimmed over a lake, it touched, skipped, touched, skipped, touched . . . and finally broke the surface. The wing entered the water and caught.

The plane cart-wheeled, its forward momentum carrying it through the air for half a revolution, so that for one long, strange, dizzy second they were looking straight down into the floodlit water, tumbling tail-first. Claudia's ear was warm and wet with blood. She had hit her head on something but had never felt it. Helplessly suspended upside down in her harness, seemingly suspended in time and space, she saw the tow bar and a pair of sunglasses on a lanyard float past the windshield, caught in the glare of the landing lights.

Like in The Wizard of Oz, she thought dazedly, *when Dorothy was inside the tornado and things were whizzing all around her . . .*

No, no, it's only the baggage locker that's popped open, she told herself. It was her last coherent thought. When the left wing hit the water the fourth time, there was a terrible rending of metal, and the plane bounced once more, hung heavily in the air for another endless moment, and flopped with a terrific, bursting impact onto its belly. Claudia never heard Torkelsson's cut-off scream.

IN silence, the mortally wounded airplane lay on the surface, its cabin filling with water, its occupants slumped forward in their harnesses, unmoving.

It took a long time for it to sink in the warm, shallow lagoon, and when it did the strut of its nose wheel collapsed, so that the plane tipped gently forward onto its nose cone, only the tail still breaking the surface. The landing lights remained on for a while, outlining the plane's dark, broken silhouette and making a lovely, luminescent fairy ring of turquoise and white in the black, still waters. Then they blinked out.

TWO

June 8, 2004, Hulopo'e Beach Estates,
North Kohala Coast, Big Island of Hawaii

AT eighty-two, Dagmar Torkelsson was less inclined to melancholy than many people with half her years. She rarely dwelt on old regrets or might-have-beens, or on the losses, physical and emotional, that came with age. But on this particular afternoon, seated on the memorial bench that she herself had purchased for the community's cliff walk in the name of her long-dead brothers Torkel, Magnus, and Andreas, her thoughts were of the past; of Torkel and Magnus in particular.

The path, as usual, was deserted despite the twelve sumptuous homes in the walled, gated community. Few of the residents did much walking there, which was fine with Dagmar as long as a portion of their homeowner dues continued to go for upkeep. The existence of this lovely path had been the final selling point that had convinced her to purchase there, despite the obscene price (which she could certainly afford, but which offended her sensibilities all the

WHERE THERE'S A WILL   *13*

same). Hugging the rims of rocky, surf-splashed coves where green sea turtles could often be seen just below the surface of the water, it wound for a quarter-mile, mostly out of sight of the homes. In all the years she had lived there, she could count on the fingers of her two hands the days she had failed to stroll it, even when her arthritis required a cane or sometimes—hateful, clumsy thing—a walker.

She had had the bench placed at the cliff walk's highest, prettiest spot, a few feet off the path, at the tip of a little promontory that overlooked what she thought of as her own private cove twenty feet below. There she knew the resident sea turtles by sight and had given them names of old friends they reminded her of, regardless of the fact that she didn't know and didn't want to know how to tell the males from the females. Most days would find her seated here at four-fifteen, forty-five minutes before her dinner was delivered. For three quarters of an hour she would contentedly smoke her two pre-prandial cigarillos, sip her pre-prandial schnapps from the worked silver cap of the antique flask that had come with her from Sweden such a long time ago, and delicately toss canned sardines in tomato sauce to the turtles, using a linen napkin to wipe her fingers between tosses. She had decided that they preferred the tomato sauce variety to those that came in oil when she concluded that the strange grunts they sometimes uttered were expressions of appreciation. Dessert, as always, would be pieces of cinnamon bun left over from her breakfast.

Usually, her mind was pleasantly empty of all but her surroundings when she sat here; the ever-present warm breeze, the murmuring of the ocean, the rustling of the palm fronds, the salt air. When anything approaching a complete thought crossed her mind, it was likely to be of her own dinner to come. As a resident of Hulopo'e Beach

Estates she had a membership at the posh Mauna Kai Resort a few hundred yards up the coast; and while the tennis and golf privileges didn't do her much good, she took full advantage of the access to their maid services, their kitchens, and their catering. Her home was cleaned by Mauna Kai staff every other week, and her dinners came from their menu at least four times a week; six or seven, if you counted leftovers. The good-looking young waiter with the black, bedroom eyes would put the meal on her dining-terrace table, then politely come and get her, proffering his arm to be leaned on. It was all very nice.

Tonight it would be rack of lamb crusted with macadamia nuts, with tiramisu for dessert. Ordinarily, that would be enough to occupy whatever stray thoughts she happened to have, but not this afternoon. Her mind, for reasons she didn't know, was on the past, the distant past of the 1950s and 1960s. On how hard those early years on the ranch had been; on how the four of them had worked to make something of it. There had been few days on which her brothers had not come home at night stinking of sweat, cattle, and horses, so drawn and fatigued they could barely speak, and sometimes so tired they couldn't eat but would fall into bed in their clothes. And Dagmar herself had not only worked right out on the range with them when they needed her, but had fed them, and kept the house spotless, to say nothing of keeping up their often-sagging spirits.

Later, when they'd turned the corner and the Hoaloha Ranch was on its way to becoming a profitable enterprise, she hadn't had to work on the range anymore, but for almost five years she'd cooked three big meals a day for twenty-five hungry cowboys and ranch workers and had done it all by herself, including the shopping and clean-up. Once, she'd kept count of the number of dishes and implements she'd had to wash in a typical week. It had come to

1,050 cups and glasses, 1,323 dishes, 1,890 utensils, and 126 pots and pans. And that was before automatic dishwashers. It seemed unthinkable to her now.

In addition to all that, she'd managed the accounts and supervised the payroll, no easy tasks during the lean years, when staying one step ahead of their creditors had been honed to a fine art, and the cash flow was so negative that one week out of four, on average, there was no money to pay the men.

She and her brothers had juggled and planned and gone without in anticipation of the time when the grueling work would pay off and the ever-expanding ranch would be carrying its own weight and more or less running itself. The brothers would then be real managers—managers on horseback—not glorified laborers. They would all get out of the miserable shack in which they lived and build a big, rambling ranch house for themselves—already they knew they would call it the Big House, as in those Westerns—where Dagmar would supervise the kitchen and household help instead of *being* it.

That time had eventually come, although Andreas had not lived to see it, but with human nature being what it was, it had failed to bring perfect happiness. Though none of them would admit it, they had missed the exhilaration of building something from nothing. Maintaining a cattle empire was pale stuff compared to carving one out. Dagmar, plagued by arthritis in her worn-out joints by then, had begun to dream of the days when the ranch was behind her and she could move down the mountain to the warmer, sunnier coast as a woman of leisure. And to be perfectly honest, she couldn't wait for a house of her own, away from the two meddling, quarrelsome old men she had lived with almost her entire adult life. For peace.

And now she had that, too; she'd had it for almost ten

years. Yet here she sat in her gated enclave for the wealthy, in what was surely one of the most beautiful spots in the world, holding a forgotten sardine in her left hand and dreaming, with a faint, wry smile on her face, of the laughter, the irritations, the lively arguments, and the many little trials of life with her brothers. *Be careful what you wish for,* she thought.

Had it truly been ten years since the terrible night she'd lost them both? In one way, the killing, the fire, and her surviving brother's escape (if he did escape) seemed as vivid as if they had been a week ago; in another, it all seemed as if it had happened to another person, in another lifetime.

She was in the midst of these pointless, dismal thoughts when the sound of footsteps on the gravel path behind her brought her back to the present. Someone was rounding the curve that led to the cove. She threw the sardine, wiped her fingers, and quickly picked up the jet-black wig on the bench beside her. It had been taken off, as it usually was here, so that she could enjoy the breeze flowing through her scant gray hair. She had barely gotten it back on her head when the waiter from the Mauna Kai who usually brought her dinner came smiling into sight.

Could it be five o'clock already? Had she dozed without knowing it? The thought that she might turn into one of those drooling oldsters who couldn't stay awake in public was a source of terror to her. She would end it all before it came to that. But no, when she turned to greet her visitor, he held an envelope that he held politely out to her. "It's an e-mail for you, ma'am."

Inasmuch as she refused to have a computer in the house, Dagmar had an arrangement with the Mauna Kai (one of many expensive but life-easing arrangements with the Mauna Kai) in which they kept an e-mail account for her. They would bring her any messages received and would send off whatever she might dictate in response.

"Thank you, Steven," she said with a final, subtle adjustment of her wig from behind.

"I'm Faustino, Mrs. Torkelsson," he said.

"Yes, of course. Faustino," she said. "Now let me read this."

From: <u>Inge</u>
To: <u>Felix</u>; <u>Axel</u>; <u>Hedwig</u>; <u>Aunt Dagmar</u>
Sent: Monday, June 08, 2004 2:17 PM
Subject: Amazing Development

Hold on to your socks for this one!

I just got off the phone with an Officer Pacheco of the Waimea Police Department.

The Grumman has been found! After ten years! A couple of skin divers spotted it in a few feet of water in a lagoon on some uninhabited, Godforsaken island 400 miles from here, and Officer Pacheco wants to know what we want to do about it.

The thing is, they saw some human bones in the cockpit! Can you imagine?

I told Pacheco I'd get back to him in a couple of days. I don't think this is going to turn into a big deal, but I'm sure everyone will agree we'd better talk about it when we get together on Thursday—not at dinner, though, because John is coming with his friend at six. Suppose we meet here at four and we can talk it through. The last of my customers will be gone by then.

I should know more by the time I see you.

"Oh, dear," Dagmar murmured, with an illogical but deeply felt sense that she had made this happen, that this unwelcome message from her niece wouldn't have come if she hadn't been maundering on about Torkel and Magnus, and about that appalling night. What would this mean? God forbid that the whole affair was going to be ripped open and reexposed like an ill-healed scar. Did she have the strength to go through it again? She was an old woman now. It would kill her.

She reread the message, this time with growing irritation. How flippant they were, this new generation, how little respect, how little appreciation, they had for the old people, the ones who had thanklessly slaved their lives away to build something for them. Silently, she shook her head. *Hold on to your socks*—as if this were an amusing bit of trivia to be passed on. Oh, it wasn't that she didn't love them—they were all she had—but they were almost like strangers to her now, this gaggle of nephews and nieces; members of a different species. They talked too fast, laughed too much—

Faustino cleared his throat. "Would you like to send a reply, Mrs. Torkelsson?"

"No, thank you," she said. "But I believe I'd like to rest here a little longer than usual today. Will you bring my dinner at six instead of five? And please cancel the rack of lamb. I think all I want tonight is a large bowl of the chicken-and-rice soup. I realize it's not on tonight's menu, but Gabriel will make it up for me."

"Yes, ma'am. Thank you."

"Thank *you*, Steven," she said, absently reaching with two fingers for another sardine and holding it up by its tail. "Here, Greta."

FIFTEEN miles from where Dagmar sat communing with her turtles, in a sprawling ranch house in the cool, interior uplands of the island, her nephew Axel Torkelsson was having an argument with his wife Malani. A friendly argument, to be sure, but vexing all the same. As usual, it was about ranch expenditures.

Alone among the four Torkelsson nephews and nieces that constituted the current generation, Axel was carrying on the family's ranching tradition. He'd been bitten early by the cattle-ranching bug; at thirteen he'd declared to his Uncle Magnus that he would study rangeland management and ecology when he went to the University of Hawaii. He had, too, with Magnus's generous financial help, and he'd rarely regretted it.

Like the others, he had inherited a sizable piece of the 30,000-acre Hoaloha Cattle Ranch that his uncles and aunt had built, but while the rest—his sisters Inge and Hedwig and his brother Felix—had put theirs to other uses, Axel had kept his 11,000 acres as a ranch—the Little Hoaloha.

No one would mistake him for a sinewy, rough-riding cowboy, either by physique or by temperament, but he was devoted to the idea of building and maintaining a productive, profitable cattle ranch according to modern, ecologically sound principles of livestock management and production. The trouble was, you had to spend money to make money, and when it came to spending money, Malani, who kept the books, was a tough sell.

Today's dispute was about a new retinal scanning system for the herd, which he dearly wanted, and he was at his most bright-eyed and enthusiastic. "Honey, try to look at this reasonably. Retinal scan would give us a tremendously more accurate database for breeding and for life history, and for disease control. I mean, think about the mad cow scare on the mainland."

"Highly unlikely to be a problem here," Malani said absently. They were having their afternoon coffee in the ranch house living room, Axel with the *GlobalAdvantage Retinal-Scan Livestock Tracking System* brochure on his lap, Malani with the laptop computer on hers as she went through the day's e-mail, deleting one piece of spam after another. "Our cattle are range-fed. How could they get mad cow disease?"

"That was just an example. What about blackleg? What about pinkeye? If we ever had another outbreak of anything like that, God forbid, we'd know for certain exactly which animals had or hadn't come in contact with the diseased ones. And after the initial cost, it wouldn't be that much more than the barcoded tags and transponders we put on their ears now."

"*After* the initial cost, yes," she said dryly, clicking steadily away at the DELETE key. "Have you noticed that that always seems to be the catch?"

"Well, you can't very well make money if you don't—"

"Spend money," she said, reaching for her cup. "Oh, look, here's an actual message from a live person, someone we know, imagine that! It's a note from Inge. It's to all of you." She scanned it, sipping her coffee. "Oh, my," she said, looking up. "It looks like they've found your Uncle Magnus."

"They *what?*" He got up to come and peer over her shoulder at the message, leaning close and adjusting his glasses to see it better. "Holy moley," he said quietly. "Well, that would explain why we never heard from him. He never got where he was going. The plane went down."

"But how would they know it's his plane?"

"The registration number, I suppose. It's on the fuselage."

"Do you think it's really Magnus? The bones, I mean. It's kind of gruesome."

Axel shrugged. "I don't know who else it would be, assuming they've got the right plane."

"So what's next? What are you all going to do? Do you bring the bones back?"

With another shrug he turned away. "Now how would I know that? I'm guessing that's what the meeting is for."

"What are you getting mad at me about?"

"Ah, I'm not . . . I'm just . . ." He leaned down and kissed the top of her head. "I'm sorry, Malani. I guess it's just kind of a shock. The thing is, we just finished reliving that whole miserable business when they finally declared him legally dead, and now—"

"That was three years ago."

"It was?" He blew out his cheeks. "Yes, I guess it was, at that."

"Time does fly when you're having fun."

Axel tried but wasn't quite able to smile in return. "I sure thought that was the end of it, didn't you?" he said, shaking his head. "And now this. It seems like we just can't put it behind us."

Malani held out her mug for him to refill. "Look at the bright side," she said. "At least this means we now know for sure he's not going to show up someday and say, 'Hey, there, you people, I'm still alive, I'm not dead, and I want my property back.' I always wondered about that, you know—about what would happen with the will if he turned out to not be dead after all. Would we have to give up the ranch?"

"I know. I used to worry about that, too. He was a funny guy. With Magnus, you never knew." He sipped meditatively at his coffee, thoughts of retinal scanning gone from his mind. "God, I wonder how Hedwig is going to react to this."

"Why Hedwig in particular?"

"Well, you know Hedwig. She's going to think this is bad karma."

Malani laughed. "To Hedwig, what isn't?"

She went back to scanning the junk mail. "Here's one for you," she said. "Are you interested in having your johnson enlarged?"

That did bring a smile. "I don't know," he said. "You tell me."

Malani thought for a moment. "Couldn't hurt," she said.

FOR some people, their roles in life—the personas they henceforth occupy, not always full-heartedly—are thrust upon them as children, as often as not by some casual or inadvertent happening. For Axel, the groundwork was laid when he was eight: a combination of protruding, weak eyes, bookish interests, and an oddly grown-up vocabulary, oddly delivered. The Torkelsson adults began to refer to him affectionately as "the little man," and then, almost inevitably, as "the little professor." And with that, the wheels of his life had been set in their ruts. Axel was, and would always be, the deep thinker in the family, the impractical far-reaching visionary who couldn't see what was six inches in front of his eyes.

For his sister Hedwig, the crucial moment had come a few years later. Like Axel, she was a reader, voracious and wide-ranging in her choice of books, and one day, one of the stack she'd brought home from the library in Hilo had been *Astral Travel for Beginners: The Linga-Sharira Pathway to Experiencing Other Realms of Existence*. Her response to being teased about it at lunch a few days later had been to rise from the table, to dramatically quote the book's epigram: "There are more things in heaven and earth, Horatio, than are dreamt of in your philosophy," and to stalk majestically from the room. She had been thirteen.

From that moment on she was the family mystic, the Knower of Strange Things, a role she had embraced, first out of contrariness, and then, over the years, with a certain amount of conviction. Now, three decades later, she was the proprietor of one of the island's many holistic retreats, the Hui Ho'olana Wellness Center for Spiritual Healing and Body-Centered Empowerment.

The Center was situated on the land she had inherited from her Uncle Magnus, a narrow strip ill-suited for cattle-raising but blessed with several restful groves of eucalyptus and pine, a small, tranquil lake, and the house that she had grown up in with her widowed father and her three siblings. It was smaller than either Axel's or Inge's inheritances, but spiritual healing hardly required great tracts of open rangeland. What it did require was an environment conducive to inward contemplation. In other words, peace and quiet.

The trouble was, Hui Ho'olana bordered her sister Inge's property, which was neither peaceful nor quiet. Inge, too, had converted her inheritance into a money-making enterprise—the Kohala Trails Adventure Ranch, an upscale dude ranch that had become popular with junketing Far Eastern businessmen, due mostly to a lucrative arrangement with two Asian airlines. As a result, it was often filled with weekend cowboys from Indonesia or Thailand engaged in various kinds of loud and violent activities. Today, the Center's afternoon self-affirmation session had been a shambles on account of the noise from one of Kohala Trails' signature activities, ridiculous in the extreme: a quick-draw contest for which guests were issued cowboy hats, chaps, and holsters with pellet-shooting six-guns, with prizes going to the winners.

A steaming Hedwig had gone straight to her office to use the half-hour before cocktails (non-alcoholic) and hors d'oeuvres (vegan) to send a furious e-mail to Inge, complaining about the disruption. It was the second time this month, and she was damned tired of it. When she opened up her Outlook Express, however, she found the new message from Inge awaiting her. She read it with a steadily sinking heart. Her anger faded. Problems of noise and disruption sank to a distant second place.

"Whoa," she murmured. "This is *really* bad karma."

FELIX Adolphus Torkelsson was the only one of the current crop of Torkelsson siblings who had chosen not to live on the land his uncle Magnus had left him. His first semester at the University of Hawaii, during which he'd roomed with three footloose and free-thinking bachelor friends, had convinced him that the peace and simplicity of rural life weren't for him. When he'd finished his law degree he'd settled in Honolulu's modest Palolo Valley neighborhood while he repaid his loans, passed the bar (on his second try), and worked his way up through a couple of law firms. But soon after he'd been made partner at what was now Gergen, Dugan, Torkelsson, and Karsch ("Like the sound of a huge rank of giant toilets flushing at almost, but not quite, the same time," was the in-house joke), he'd bought his dream condominium on Kalakaua Avenue, a twenty-fourth-floor corner unit looking northeast over the grand hotels and white-sand beaches.

Felix was a robust man given to loud speech and expansive gestures. His reaction to reading the print-out of Inge's e-mail (he didn't like reading computer screens; all of his e-mail was automatically printed out) was to utter a not-so-muffled oath and to fling the sheet of paper ceilingward. Or rather skyward, inasmuch as he was sitting on the balcony of his condo. A man of quick reactions despite his size, he managed to jump to his feet and snatch it out of the air before it drifted over the edge and got away. Then he sat down again with the end-of-a-good-day's-work double martini he had mixed for himself and reread it, his open, cheerful face slowly darkening.

Inge was wrong about its being no big deal. It could turn into a very big deal indeed, with outcomes that none of them would care to see. The important thing was going to be to keep the police out of it. And that might not be so easy, inasmuch as they were already aware the plane had been found. But the more he thought about it (and the more of the martini he drank), the more it seemed to him that there might not be so much to worry about after all. Really, why should the police want to get involved again? So the plane had been found. So there were human remains in it. What did that prove? What unanswered questions did it raise?

No, if they handled this calmly and rationally and made sure they were all on the same wavelength, there would be no problem. He went to the railing, taking in his vast domain of sea, sand, and hotel, thoughtfully swirling the ice in his glass. Almost directly below him, adjacent to Kuhio Beach Park, was the Waikiki Division of the Honolulu Police Department, which shot another little jolt of worry through him. Not about HPD itself—they had nothing to do with it—but about John Lau, who had worked in that very building before he'd hired on with the FBI. The idea of having an FBI agent and ex-cop hanging around at this particular time, even an old friend of the family's like John, was a little nervous-making. And that friend he was bringing—Gideon Something? Oliver Something? Wasn't he some kind of forensic expert, too?

He shook his head slowly back and forth. They were going to have to watch their step, all right.

Oh boy.

THREE

"BILLIE? Hi, it's Norma. Guess where I am right this minute. I'm sitting on the plane in Honolulu. Yes, I am . . ."

What was this irresistible impulse, Gideon mused, sitting six or seven rows in front of the speaker, that compelled people to flip open their cell phones the second they got on a plane or train, and inform someone, somewhere, that they had just gotten on a plane or train? And what was it that then turned ordinary, perfectly-normal-voiced men and women into people who could be heard—who couldn't be ignored—from six or seven rows away?

Ah, well, these were mysteries best left for another day. Right now, he didn't intend to let anything bother him during the brief flight to the Big Island. He was relaxed, even a bit sleepy, he was looking forward to the next few days, and he was, frankly, a little hung over—enough to want to do nothing but vegetate for the next forty-five minutes, looking down on blue water and lush green islands, and maybe catching a doze or two.

At a large-boned, well-put-together 6'1" he was cramped in the window seat, but he was used to that, and in a flight this short it wasn't going to bother him. It'd be nice, though, if the aisle seat beside him remained empty. Now there was another mystery for you: Why did the seat next to you so often remain appealingly vacant until the last minute, so that you got your hopes up, only to have a sweating, panting 250-pounder come jogging down the aisle just as the door closed and the jet-way swung aside? He sighed. How the gods loved to toy with our emotions.

Gideon Paul Oliver, Professor of Physical Anthropology at the University of Washington's Port Angeles campus, was, in general, feeling pretty good. He was coming from the annual meeting of WAFA, the Western Association of Forensic Anthropologists, held this year at the Army's Central Identification Laboratory at Hickam Field in Honolulu. He'd caught up on things, presented a paper on blunt-force post-cranial trauma, contributed an oddball item or two to the guess-what-happened-to-*this* quiz (a much-pitted cervical vertebra that had been through the digestive system of a cougar; a scapula that had been perforated by a pneumatic riveter), and renewed some friendships. His only mistake, and it wasn't much of a mistake, had been the extra couple of beers at the annual pizza party last night.

He was on his way now, or would be when the 717 took off, to Kona Airport on the island of Hawaii, some 125 miles to the south. He'd been to Kona before, and to Hilo on the opposite coast as well, but he'd never spent any time in the northern uplands of the Big Island, other than to drive through them on his way from one coast to the other.

He'd also never spent any time on a working cattle ranch. Now he'd be doing both, thanks to John Lau.

John, a special agent at the FBI's Seattle office, wasn't quite Gideon's oldest friend, but he was the closest. A big, hearty, resilient man with whom Gideon had worked on several cases, he had once saved Gideon's life on a flowered hillside above Germany's Rheingau. Gideon had returned the favor a few years later in Normandy, on the treacherous tidal flats of Mont St. Michel. As if that weren't enough, the two men had simply clicked from the beginning, and now Gideon and his wife Julie, and John and his wife Marti, were a frequent foursome for dinner in the city, at a Mariner game at Safeco Field, or on a hike in the Olympics.

John was a native Hawaiian, born to a Tahitian-Chinese mother and a Hawaiian father, and though he had lived on the mainland for almost twenty years the lilt of the islands was still in his speech and in his laugh. Once every couple of years he and Marti went to stay with his relatives near Papeete and in Hilo, and when he realized that this year's family visit coincided with Gideon's trip to Honolulu for the anthropological meetings, he had suggested that Gideon stay on in the islands. He could hop a plane to the Big Island and spend a week or so in the clean, fresh air of the Little Hoaloha cattle ranch, a sprawling, eleven-thousand-acre spread owned by his old college friend Axel Torkelsson. It had been Axel himself who had extended the invitation, and he'd generously included Julie in it, which naturally cinched it once she'd heard about it. Julie, a supervising park ranger at Olympic National Park headquarters in Port Angeles, was an enthusiastic horsewoman, and the prospect of a vacation spent cantering over open rangeland on well-trained horses was too much for her to resist. Especially in Hawaii. She would be arriving in a couple of days for a week's stay before they all headed back the following Friday.

And that was something Gideon was very much looking forward to as well. Even after seven years of marriage, the last four days had seemed like a long, long time to be away from her.

As expected, the Law of Late-Arriving Seatmates was in full force. Five seconds before the door was pulled shut, a flushed, flustered-looking woman came trotting down the aisle, hauling a wheeled carry-on and juggling three plastic ABC Store plastic bags and a hefty purse. She wasn't sweating and she wasn't a 250-pounder, but you could see from the look of her that she was something worse: an affable, inquisitive chatterer. So he was not to have his forty-five minutes of peace after all. With an inward sigh and an outward smile he got up to help her get her carry-on into the overhead rack, and then to try to stuff the rest in after it.

"Just push 'em in," she said cheerfully. "It's just junk."

Once she sat down beside him and strapped herself in, she looked appraisingly at him for a few seconds, then apparently decided that the hard-backed book she'd brought with her would be more entertaining. She opened it to the bookmark, and was quickly, deeply absorbed. Gideon caught a glimpse of the title: *Making Compost in Fourteen Days*.

It made him laugh. He propped a pillow against the window, leaned his head on it, and was asleep, still chuckling, before the plane left the runway.

AMONG the few contributions that Hawaiian has made to the language of science are the words for two common types of volcanic lava: *pahoehoe* and *a'a*. On the Big Island of Hawaii, *pahoehoe* predominates, familiar to anyone who has ever watched a television documentary on the unending eruptions of Kilauea, the world's most active volcano, in the south of the island. The word means "like ropes," but it could just as well mean "like giant licorice twists"; great, black loops and coils of ropey lava cover Kilauea's flanks and extend all the way to the sea's edge in the southeast, not so very far below Hilo town. This *pahoehoe* form results when red-hot, flowing lava slows and stops gradually as it cools and becomes more viscous, so that its original, rounded, curving shapes are preserved in the newly formed rock. The effect of standing in a field of *pahoehoe* is grand and somber; one feels not quite secure in this vast, tarry, black world. It's all too easy to visualize the petrified black landscape as the boiling, subterranean, liquid rock it was not so long ago, and one is always looking over one's shoulder for the next eruption.

But in the northwest, above Kona, the effect is more desolate than grand, more drab than somber. Here, the lava is *a'a,* which is lava that flowed more quickly and cooled more suddenly, cracking and splitting into great fields of dull, brown basaltic "clinkers"—spiny, jagged chunks of honeycombed volcanic rock, mostly not much bigger than a fist. The Hawaiians say with a straight face that it is called *a'a* because that's the sound people make when they walk on it with bare feet. There is nothing pretty or inspiring about a field of *a'a,* and driving northward from Kona International Airport on the Queen Kaahumanu Highway, for the first fifteen miles at any rate, is pretty much like driving through fifteen miles of scorched rubble, its barrenness emphasized rather than relieved by the sparkling blue sea a couple of miles to the east and the fresh green slope of Mauna Kea in the west.

"Isn't this great?" John enthused from behind the wheel of the dusty, non-air-conditioned pickup truck he'd borrowed from the ranch. "I love this part of the island!"

"It's . . . different," Gideon said. He knew that his friend wasn't joking. John had been born and had grown up in Hilo, the rainiest city in the United States and one of the chillier places in Hawaii, and it had left him with an abiding love of hot, dry weather, the hotter and drier the better. Although not a complainer by nature, he frequently bemoaned the evil turn of fate that had gotten him assigned to Seattle, of all places. He was just waiting—so he said—for the Bureau to open a regional office in Yuma or Needles, before he applied for a transfer.

Gideon pointed toward the gently sloping mountains twenty miles ahead, where the landscape gradually turned to bright, crisp green with the change in elevation. "Is that where we're headed?" he asked hopefully.

"Yeah, the ranch is up there, on those slopes. We're probably looking at it right now. I know you can see the coast when you're on it, looking down. You'll love it, Doc. Fog every morning, lots of rain—mist, anyway—cold. You need a jacket two days out of three. Just your kind of place. Uck."

"Sounds great." Gideon had been raised in sun-drenched Los Angeles. Unlike John, he had come to love the pearly, cool days of the Pacific Northwest. And Honolulu had been not only hot but miserably muggy. Cool mist sounded wonderful.

"So when's Julie coming in, Doc?"

John had been calling him "Doc" from the first day he'd known him. When Gideon had suggested "Gideon" instead, John had shaken his head. "Sounds like I'm talking to someone in the Bible." He had offered "Gid" instead, but Gideon had promptly rejected that, and it had been "Doc" ever since. They were both long-comfortable with it by now.

"One-fifteen, the day after tomorrow. Is that going to be a problem?"

"Nah, it's only a forty-minute trip down from the ranch. No sweat. We can come down and meet her together. Or you can drive yourself if you want. The pickup's ours to use while we're here."

"Great. And what about Marti? Is she already up there?"

"No, she's not going to make it. She flew home yesterday, from Hilo. Staff emergency at the hospital. Two people down with the flu."

"Ah, that's too bad."

John hunched his shoulders. "Yeah, but aside from being bummed out about missing time with you and Julie, she's not too disappointed. The truth is, she doesn't get along with the Torkelssons too well."

"You're kidding me. I always thought Marti got along with everybody."

"It's nothing serious. She just gets a little tense when she's around these people. I mean, they eat beefsteak five times a week."

Gideon nodded his understanding. "Ah."

John's wife was a nutritionist at the Virginia Mason Medical Center in Seattle, where she enthusiastically invented saltless, fatless, sugarless, meatless recipes for her captive clientele. Happily for her marriage to John, who was an enthusiastic trencherman and an undiscriminating omnivore, she didn't enjoy the hands-on process of cooking, so they ate out most evenings.

"It's not that they *eat* the stuff, you understand," John said, "it's that they're so goddamn *healthy*. That's what bugs her. It's against her principles."

"I understand completely," Gideon said. "Uh, John, look. If you'd rather be home with Marti, if you're staying on for our sake, we could just—"

"Forget it," John said at once. "I'd rather be here. She invited her sister and her meathead of a husband to house-sit while we were gone, and they're staying on the rest of the week even though she's home early. You know me, I get along with most people—"

"That's true," Gideon said.

"But Meathead drives me up the wall. It's not just what he says, it's the way he says it. This little pinchy smile, like he knows so much more than you . . . It's . . . I don't know, it's a chemical thing. Anyway, forget about getting rid of me. I'm not going home till the coast is clear. Understood?"

"Understood."

They rode in easy silence for a while, with the windows rolled down. The highway ran, straight and level, parallel-ing the coast for twenty-five miles, and then turned inland to begin climbing the long, steady incline that was the southwestern flank of the Kohala mountain range. The nat-ural landscape was still brown and scrubby at best, but the temperature soon dropped by a few degrees; the air be-came crisper and less humid, and Gideon breathed more freely. On his side, John rolled up the window.

"John, tell me something about the ranch. How does your friend Axel come to be running a cattle ranch on the island of Hawaii?"

"Oh, ranching's been big business up there in the north forever. There've been cattle here since 1793. It all started way back, with Vancouver—"

"No, I know all about Vancouver and his gift of cattle to Kamehameha I, and how they turned wild, and how John Palmer Parker arrived and started up his ranch with a land grant from Kamehameha III in the 1830s, and all that. What I meant—"

John sighed. "Jesus, Doc, you can really be irritating

sometimes, you know that? I know you're a professor and all, so you can't help it, but it'd be nice if once in a while there was something you *didn't* know more about than anybody else. Could you try that sometime? Just as a change of pace?"

"Look, the fact is, I didn't know anything about it before, but once I knew I was coming up here, naturally I took a little time and read up on it. I read Vancouver's *Voyage of Discovery,* Dawes' history of the islands, Brennan's books on the early Parker ranch—"

"Naturally." John was shaking his head. "You're the only guy I know who treats a vacation like a Ph.D. research project. Pathetic."

"Well, it was interesting," Gideon said defensively. "And it wasn't as if I read every word. I was just skimming."

"Yeah, right."

"Anyway, I was really asking about your friend. Axel Torkelsson doesn't exactly sound like the name of a guy who runs a cattle ranch in Hawaii. How did that come about?"

"He inherited it from his uncle a few years ago. Magnus Torkelsson. There were nieces and nephews; they all got a piece of the old ranch from old Magnus."

Gideon laughed. "Okay, then, let me rephrase the question. How does a guy named Magnus Torkelsson come to be running a big cattle ranch in Hawaii?"

"Well, actually, that's a long story," John said. "But something new just came up on it—"

"Go ahead and tell me the long story. I'm at your mercy, and I don't have anything else to do."

In the early fifties, John told him, Magnus Torkelsson, along with his equally adventurous brothers Torkel and Andreas, had jumped ship off Kona, from a Swedish freighter that was picking up a shipment of beef cattle from the

Parker Ranch, which was then the only cattle ranch of any size in Hawaii. Being quick learners, knowing a good thing when they saw it, and taking an immediate liking to the rolling Kohala hills, which reminded them of the Smaland highlands of their childhood, they used the nest egg they'd been building up to buy two hundred cattle from the Parkers and eight hundred acres from nearby landowners. In their thirties at the time, they called their ranch Hoaloha— "Beloved Friend" in Hawaiian—and their combination of hard work, dedication, and penny-pinching good sense turned it into a money-making proposition after relatively few years. By the time they died, the Hoaloha encompassed over thirty thousand acres and ran a herd of fifteen thousand cattle, mostly Herefords, but also Holsteins, Durhams, Charolais, even a few Angus and Brahmas—

"Well, see, there's something you know more about than I do," Gideon said. "If you asked me ten seconds ago to name five breeds of cattle, I don't think I could have done it. I'm not sure I could do it now."

"Well, remember," John said, pleased, "I roomed with Axel at college and he used to talk about this stuff a lot. And I still see him every few years. And then I spent a couple of summer vacations working on the ranch."

"No, I didn't know that. So you must know quite a bit about ranching, then."

"Well, I wouldn't . . . that is, I'm not any kind of . . . well, yeah." And then, as he often did with little or no reason, he burst into laughter. John had a wonderfully infectious laugh that crinkled up the skin around his eyes, made his eyes themselves gleam, and rarely failed to make Gideon laugh along with him, as he did now.

"They brought over their sister Dagmar a couple of years after they got here," John went on, "and all four of them worked like dogs to make the ranch go. Andreas, the oldest one, he died before I met any of them, but I got to know old Torkel and Magnus and the rest of them pretty well. Real well, in fact."

They had climbed to two thousand feet—never a switchback, just one long, steady rise along the flank of the range—and while John nodded to himself, remembering, Gideon gratefully took in the prospect around them. The afternoon shadows had lengthened, adding texture and depth to the rolling countryside. Trees were still sparse, but the duns and ochres of the lowlands had given way to green, healthy pasturelands. The temperature had gotten more comfortable still, and there were veils of mist in some of the hollows and around some of the peaks—if you could call these lovely, rounded, hummocky rises "peaks." Over his right shoulder, he could look back down the slope and see the coastline all the way to Kona, as John had said. The whole scene was very beautiful. It surprised him that he'd zipped through it a few years ago, hardly noticing it.

John surfaced and went on. "The two brothers were kind of crotchety by then. You know, two old bachelors, living in the same house together with their old-maid sister, always carping at each other; not real easy to get along with, but they loved the ranch, they ran a tight ship—Jesus, did they—and somehow they kept it all together, until . . ."

He was still smiling, remembering days long past, but now he sobered. The smile faded. "Until Torkel got murdered—"

Gideon stared at him. "Murdered?"

"—and Magnus disappeared."

"He *disappeared?*"

"Took off into the night in the ranch plane, never to be heard from again."

"You mean they never found out what happened to him?"

"Not until just this week, as a matter of fact. Tuesday. A

couple of skin-divers found the plane. Axel was telling me about it. It crashed in the lagoon of some rinky-dink island in the Pacific. They think he never got where he was going, that it went down the night he left."

"Was there anything in it? Any remains, I mean?"

John nodded. "Yeah, some bones, apparently."

"Are the Torkelssons having them brought back?"

"I don't know. They're gonna talk about it today—they get together for dinner once a month or so to hassle out any problems—and figure out what they want to do. Why, you want to volunteer your services?"

"Sure, if they want someone to look the bones over, see if maybe there's something to confirm it really is Magnus. You know people appreciate that kind of closure."

"They do, yeah, but my impression is they just want to put it all behind them. My guess is that if they bring the remains back they'll just want to bury them. That'll be all the closure they need."

"Huh. Well, go on back to the story. What was it all about? Did Magnus kill his brother? Is that why he ran?"

"No, no, no. I wasn't around anymore by then, but from everything anybody knows, it was some kind of vengeance thing . . . you know, retribution, payback."

"For what?"

John shrugged. "Beats the hell out of me. All they know is *somebody* shot Torkel to death and burned down the main ranch building. They tried to get Magnus too, but he managed to get away, make it to the airport, and take off. That's it."

"And nobody knows who did it?"

"Nope. There were plenty of candidates, more than they knew what to do with. See, these old guys weren't that easy to get along with, and they drove a hard bargain besides. Shrewd, you know? There were a lot of people with grudges. Lemme see . . . oh, there was a neighboring ranch, part of a consortium, that wanted right-of-way access for a water line. When Torkel and Magnus said no way, the place went bust, wound up having to sell for next to nothing. And who do you think bought it? The Torkelssons, of course, who immediately laid in a water pipeline."

"That would have gone down hard," Gideon said.

"You're not kidding. And then there were some kind of famous cattle negotiations in Honolulu, where they supposedly aced out one of the big Kauai ranching syndicates. There were threats against them on record, there was even—"

"But nobody was ever convicted?"

"Nobody was ever *indicted*. The cops never even brought charges. There just wasn't any evidence, Doc. Nothing to tie anybody to it. Remember, they burned the place down. That doesn't make the job any easier."

Gideon leaned back in his seat and thought it over. "John," he said with a shake of his head, "I have to say . . ."

John glanced at him. "What?"

"Well, you have a case where one brother is murdered and the other one takes off. You have to wonder—"

"You have to wonder if Magnus didn't kill Torkel."

"Well, don't you?"

"Sure, and naturally that was where the cops looked first, but that angle petered out inside of a couple of days. For one thing, the autopsy on Torkel showed that they did him in classic gangland execution style. Two shooters, the whole bit. This wasn't just one ticked-off old geezer killing his geezer brother."

"You mean, hired killers."

"Exactly. A professional hit all the way, very smooth."

"But why couldn't Magnus have been the one who hired them?"

"No way. He was too cheap."

"Seriously."

"Seriously, what kind of sense does it make? If he wanted to have his brother killed, he'd have had it done when he wasn't around, when he had some kind of alibi, over in Honolulu or something, wouldn't he?"

"That's a point," Gideon said. "He sure wouldn't have done it this way, putting himself right in the middle of it."

"Another thing, too," John pointed out. "No motive. None at all. Also, if he arranged for a couple of hitmen to do it, why would *he* run? No, he's not the one who killed his brother."

"Okay, that I can buy, but if these killers were after him, why didn't he just go to the police for help? Why leave everything—his family, his ranch—and run for his life?"

"Well, all I can tell you is, that's what people do when hitmen are on their tail. And between you and me, it's a pretty good idea. Besides, the Waimea PD would be in way over their heads on something like this. They probably get, like, one homicide every ten years, and then it's just some out-of-his-skull meth-head."

"Then why not go to the state police in Honolulu? Or the FBI?"

"Look, people do funny things when they're scared; you know that. Anyway, that was the last time anybody ever saw him. Or heard anything about him, until this week."

They had reached the outskirts of Waimea now, a pretty little 1950s Western town with feed and grain stores, and stores that sold farm equipment, and rugged-looking men in Stetsons, and even a little white church with a wooden belfry. The only thing that told you you weren't in Kansas or South Dakota were the tropical red and blue tin roofs. That and the impossibly lush green hills in which the town nestled.

"Let's stop for a bite," John said. "You hungry?"

"Sure," said Gideon, whose salivary glands started working at the mention of food. "I guess I forgot about lunch."

"*Forgot* about lunch!" John said incredulously. "Jesus, you're worse than I thought."

They turned into Opelo Plaza, a neatly maintained corner strip mall on the main street, and pulled up before Aioli's, a simple, white frame building with blue awnings on either side of the screen door and a giant painted garlic clove above it.

"I admit, it looks kind of like a health food place—but it's good," John explained.

They ordered sandwiches at the counter—grilled chicken and avocado for Gideon, grilled mahi-mahi for John—and sat in rattan chairs at a bare table under slowly turning ceiling fans. Everything was spotless. The red glazed tile floor looked as if it had been cleaned thirty seconds ago. The clientele was about fifty-fifty native-Hawaiian and *Haole*.

While they ate, John went on with the story. Once the family had gotten over its shock at the loss of its patriarch-brothers, another kind of shock took over. They realized that the future of the wealthy ranch and its holdings was now on hold. Because the two men had reciprocal mutual-beneficiary wills, in which the brothers left virtually everything to each other, it was only when the last living brother died that the inheritance could pass on to the next generation. So, for the seven years it took for the Third Circuit Court to formally conclude that Magnus was really dead and gone, the ranch was managed under receivership and the bulk of the Hoaloha fortune remained in limbo, while the would-be inheritors chafed. All except Dagmar, who got an identical lion's share of the liquid assets under both wills, and who soon pulled up stakes and retired to the seclusion and beauty of Hulopo'e Beach Estates on the Kohala Coast.

But the seven years finally came to an end. Three years ago Magnus had been declared legally dead and his will had gone through probate and been executed. For all intents and purposes the great Hoaloha Ranch no longer existed. The thirty-thousand-acre property was cut up and divided between the brothers' nephews and nieces. Even after selling off part of their assets—cattle, art works—to pay the death taxes, each of them wound up with a good-sized chunk of land.

"Wait a minute," Gideon said. "These would have been Andreas's kids? The brother that died before? And your friend Axel was one of them?"

"Right. Axel and his brother and his two sisters. Axel's the only one who's running his property as a ranch."

"The *Little* Hoaloha."

"Yup, if you can call eleven thousand acres little. But the rest of them all had different ideas. You interested enough to know the details, or am I boring you?"

"No, you're not boring me. I'll let you know when you are."

"Well, there's Inge, Axel's sister. She turned hers into a yuppie dude ranch, and from what I hear it's doing okay. Then there's his sister, Hedwig. She . . . what?"

"You rolled your eyes when you said 'Hedwig.' I wondered what that meant."

"I did? Ah, Hedwig's all right, I guess, if you can stand . . . well, you'll see. Anyway, she runs hers as a wellness center."

"She's a doctor?"

"Um . . . no."

"A therapist?"

"Um . . . no, I wouldn't say that. She's into, like, karmic power massage, and, um, past-life regression, and—"

"Okay, I get the picture," Gideon said, charitably resisting the urge to roll his own eyes. "And then there's one more, right?"

"Felix. He's a lawyer. He lives in Honolulu."

"He didn't inherit a piece of the ranch?"

"Oh, yeah, he got the smallest piece . . . only a couple of hundred acres, with no buildings, no water, no decent grazing land, nothing like that—but it includes a quarter-mile of prime, white-sand oceanfront up above Kawaihae. It's probably worth more than all the rest put together, and he's selling it to some Swiss chain that develops these super-upscale communities. Felix's pretty sharp about that kind of thing—he's a land-use attorney—and he's gonna be one rich Torkelsson."

"Interesting family," Gideon said. "Unusual."

"And you're gonna meet every last one of them in a few hours."

"I am?"

"Yup. We're invited to dinner."

"That's nice of them, but—I don't know, didn't you say they'd be talking about what to do about Magnus's remains? I'd be a complete outsider at something like that. Maybe I could just—"

"Don't worry about it. They meet once a month anyway to hassle out any problems, and they get that stuff out of the way early. By the time we show up, they'll have their family matters settled and everybody'll be pretty well into the schnapps. You'll enjoy it, you'll see. Anything you ever heard about these 'dour' Swedes, forget it. And you wouldn't want to miss the dinner. Best steaks you ever had; from prime ranch cattle."

Leaving Aioli's, they headed back east and John turned the truck north on Highway 250, at the edge of town. They were soon back in open country and climbing again. Now occasional straggling lines of chestnut-brown cattle, heads lowered to the grass, could be seen.

"Herefords," John said. "You can always tell from the white faces. In case you wanted to know. If they were Jerseys they'd be brown all over."

"Thank you, I always wondered about that. So you said tonight's steaks would be from ranch cattle. Dinner's at the ranch, then? At Axel's?"

"No. That's where we're staying, but the family dinners are always at Inge's—at the dude ranch. She closes it to paying customers for the day. See, Inge and Hedwig are the only ones with professional cooks—because of their businesses—and naturally nobody wants to have it at Hedwig's, so it's always at Inge's. Felix flies in from Honolulu, Dagmar hires a limo to drive her up from the coast, and— here we are. This is Axel's and Malani's place. Home for the next week. Open the gate, would you?"

Gideon jumped out, pulled open the unlocked swinging gate in the barbed wire fence, and closed it once the truck was through. The only indication of where they were were the neatly stenciled words on the mailbox mounted on the gatepost: *Torkelsson. Mile 12.2, Kohala Mtn. Road.* Once he was back in, John followed a dirt track between the hills toward a rambling, much-weathered, white frame house a quarter-mile off, with porches all around and six or seven smaller outbuildings trailing away to the rear.

"It's one of the old section managers' houses," John said. "They built them in separate units back then: cook house, bath house, laundry house, bunk house—I spent a few nights in the old bunk house myself. Murder going out to the privy on a cold night."

Gideon frowned. "And we're staying . . . where?"

"Don't worry, we're in the main house. Indoor plumbing." He laughed. "Jeez, Doc, what a weenie you are. I always thought anthropologists slept out on rocks when they had to, and ate bugs and snakes. Till I met you."

"I happen to love eating bugs and snakes. I was thinking of Julie."

"Yeah, right." John pulled the car into the dusty parking area beside the porch and turned off the ignition. "Okay, let's go find 'em. Knowing Axel, he'll be right where I left him."

The interior of the house was just what the exterior suggested: roomy, worn, simply built of wooden planks in serious need of re-painting, simply furnished with wood-frame furniture, and filled with the dusty, unidentifiable smells of old, well-lived-in houses. The living room had a massive, soot-blackened lava-stone fireplace topped by a mantel jammed with antique brown and blue bottles, dusty glass fishing floats, oddly shaped pebbles, and other knick-knacks that must once have meant something to someone. The plank walls had yellowing pictures of Swedish and Hawaiian royalty on them—mostly unframed, cut from newspapers and books, and held up with tacks—along with fading family photographs and a couple of old school pennants: the University of Hawaii and the University of California–Davis. This was a room—a house—that had never been "decorated." It had grown—or, better, *evolved*—by accretion, by slow accumulation. All the same, it looked right for the house of a rancher; an honest, straightforward kind of place, utterly without pretensions.

John led the way into the white-painted kitchen, where they found Axel and his wife Malani at a scarred table in somber consultation over a dog-eared account book. Two half-filled mugs of coffee were beside them, the cream congealing at the surface. A difference of opinion hung in the air: Malani was in the process of shaking her head "no," while Axel, with his finger on one of the columns, was making an earnest point, but when they came in he jumped up.

"The romance of modern ranching," he said with an embarrassed grin. "Now you know the truth. It's all about number-crunching. I haven't been out on the range lassoing cattle for almost two hours now."

Indeed, for a cattleman, Axel Torkelsson looked as if he didn't get out much. He was somewhat puffily built to begin with, and a bookish stoop, a concave chest, and a pair of mild, watery, pale eyes behind black-rimmed, 1970s-style glasses did away with any intimation of the open range. Add to that a worried, slightly dazed expression that suggested he was always trying to remind himself not to forget something, and he seemed as if he would have been more at home with a green eyeshade and arm-garters than in a ten-gallon hat.

John made the introductions. Gideon was warmly received and told that he and Julie were to consider the house, and indeed, the ranch, as their own. When Gideon had thanked them and expressed some interest in, and even some knowledge of, the history of cattle-ranching in Hawaii, Axel's wrinkled brow smoothed. His pinched face seemed to fill out.

"Actually, ranching is a totally different affair from what it was ten or twenty years ago—back when John was our number-one hand."

"I wouldn't say that," John said.

Axel clapped John shyly on the shoulder and went on speaking to Gideon. "Of course, the *paniolos*—that's what we call the cowboys here; it comes from the word *español,* because the first ones came from Mexico, but you probably already knew that—anyway, they still use lassoes, and they brand and castrate and all the rest, but nowadays it's really about devising and maintaining a viable system of intensive range management because, if you think about it, a cattle ranch is first and foremost a grass farm. Today's cattle-rancher has to understand that if he's going to survive."

"I never thought about it before," Gideon said, "but I can see how that would be."

Encouraged, Axel plowed ahead, his weak eyes blinking enthusiastically away. "See, you can't just depend on the natural range grasses if you want to compete. You have to sow. But what do you sow? That's the big question. Right now, I have experimental plots going of Natal red top, brome, cocksfoot . . . well, you name it. And then besides that, intensive range management means a whole lot of things they never heard of in the old days: symbiotic seeding, selective brush control, and, above all, above everything else, a strategy of long-range water-resource development and conservation. And today's—"

John was laughing. "I knew you guys would get along. You both talk in lectures."

"I most certainly do not," said Axel.

"You most certainly do," Malani said, "but it's hard to tell with Gideon. You haven't given him the chance."

"Come on, honey, he *said* he was interested—"

"I *am* interested—"

"May I make a suggestion?" she said. "It's a beautiful day. Why don't you show our guest his room and let him freshen up, and then get some horses and take him out and show him around the ranch. Take Johnny, too. Wouldn't you like that, Gideon?"

Malani, a porcelain-doll-faced Hawaiian woman a few

FOUR

A *pu'u*, Gideon learned, was a volcanic cinder cone, a common, relatively minor vent in the long, sweeping sides of Mauna Kea, the colossal volcano that had created the northern half of the Big Island. Most dated back to the 1500s and before, so that by now they were grassy, treeless hillocks, smooth and symmetrical, anywhere from a hundred to five hundred feet high. It was these old *pu'us* that gave the Kohala uplands their characteristic hummocky, green-carpeted appearance.

While they trudged single-file up a narrow horse trail that wound around the hill, Axel, in the lead, prattled happily on about ranch operations without requiring much— without requiring any—feedback. The Little Hoaloha was a "cow/calf" operation, meaning that they raised calves but didn't "finish" or butcher them. At six hundred pounds they were shipped by container ship to Vancouver, Canada, where they grazed on local grain until they reached nine years older than her husband, had taught at the Kamehameha School on Oahu before she married Axel, and she still had something of the resolutely patient schoolmarm in her speech: a natural bossiness moderated by a precise, sugary, sing-song trill, as if she were explaining things to a not-particularly-swift class of fourth-graders, or maybe to a hard-of-hearing, not-quite-with-it group of oldsters. Heard occasionally, it was no doubt pleasant rather than otherwise, but Gideon wouldn't have wanted to live with it day in and day out.

"I'd love it, Malani," he said dutifully.

"So would I," Axel said, "but I'm due at Inge's at four-thirty. See," he said to Gideon, "they just found my uncle's bones in—"

"I told him all about it, Axel."

"Oh, fine. Anyway, the thing is, there isn't time to saddle up the horses and—"

"Then don't take the horses," Malani said. "At least you can walk up along the side of Pu'u Nui. You can see half the ranch from there. A beautiful view."

"But what about the accounts?" Axel asked her, looking longingly at the columns of figures.

"I can take care of the accounts, sweetie. Go. You can use some fresh air."

"Well, but—"

"Go," she said, hustling him away from the table with a fluttering of hands, as if she were scattering a flock of pigeons. "Go-go-go-go-go."

hundred pounds, whereupon they were trucked to feed lots in Calgary, fattened for a hundred days until they reached twelve hundred pounds, and then slaughtered.

Now, Axel proudly pointed out, if John and Gideon looked around, they would see not a sign of over-grazing, even though they ran eight thousand head of cattle on their eleven thousand acres; a heavy load on the land—had Gideon known it took almost seven pounds of grasses to put one pound of meat on a cow? The lushness of the landscape was the result of a fenced paddock arrangement that Axel himself had devised, in which the cattle were rotated to a new grazing section every three days . . .

John, who had heard all this before, was mostly looking out at the view, humming a little to himself. But Gideon, who hadn't, was also drawn to the constantly changing scene as they rounded the hill. They were at an elevation of four thousand feet. Around them were clumps of scrub oak, prickly pear, a few small trees, and some rocky outcroppings, but the overwhelming impression was of a wonderfully green, rolling grassland, dotted with groups of grazing cattle, that fell gradually but spectacularly away to the ocean in one direction, and flowed equally gradually and spectacularly up toward the distant, two-mile-high summit of Mauna Kea in the other. That, he realized, was why this stupendous landscape could be so peaceful, so calming. There were no vertical surfaces, no threatening precipices or jagged mountain walls. Just these welcoming, gently upsloping fields of green and brown, so gentle that it looked as if one could begin at the coast and easily, even pleasantly, stroll right to the top of the immense volcano, given the time.

From here he could see all the way to the gorgeous, gleaming hotel- and resort-lined Kohala Coast, thirty miles away, three-quarters of a mile below, and seemingly exist-

ing in some future century. Farther off and looking like
Bali H'ai itself, was the island of Maui, from this distance
a huge, mysterious, fog-wreathed mountain growing
straight out of the ocean.

". . . is piped by gravity-feed to on-ranch reservoirs,"
Axel was saying, "from where it goes via one-inch plastic
pipe to troughs that have been placed through mathemati-
cally computed—oh, gosh, where did the time go? We better
go back. Gideon, I know you must have some questions." He
waited inquiringly.

Gideon searched his mind. The last thing he'd really
heard was that the cattle were trucked to Calgary, but that
had been a while back. He looked desperately around for
inspiration. A quarter of a mile away, on a nearby hillside,
were a dozen or so peacefully grazing cows. They were
brown. They did not have white faces.

"I see," he said with more confidence than he felt, "that
you raise Jerseys here. Do you have Herefords as well?"

"That's a really good question," Axel said as they turned
around and headed back down, with Gideon now in the
lead. "We used to have Herefords on the old ranch—you
remember, Johnny."

"Sure do," John said.

"But in the last few years we've phased them out.
White-faced cattle don't bring as much on the market. Isn't
that interesting? Nobody knows why. You know what I
think? I think it's because they make people think of milk
cows, not beef cows."

"Yeah," John said. "I guess nobody wants to eat Elsie."

At the bottom of the hill they separated, with Axel going to the back of the house to bring around a truck for the
short drive to Inge's. John looked at Gideon and made an
odd face.

"What?" Gideon said.

John screwed his mouth up into a little knot and put on what he must have thought was a professorial tone of voice, throwing in a prissy English accent for good measure and tipping his head back as if he were looking through a monocle. "I see thet yaw raise Jehseys heah. Do yaw heve Heffahds as well?" he said.

And then dissolved in laughter. "I love it."

Gideon laughed, too. "I think I got away with it."

"THIS place, Maravovo Atoll, where they found the plane," Inge began when she'd finally got everyone settled, "is part of something called the Republic of Kiribati—"

"Actually, it's pronounced *kiribass*," Axel said. "Not *kiribati*. It used to be the Gilberts, you see, but when they changed the name, they had no way to spell—"

Felix exploded with a shout. "Axel, for God's sake! I mean, Jesus Christ!"

"Sorry," Axel said, blinking, clearly wondering what Felix was so upset about.

Inge covered her mouth. It was hard not to laugh. It was so like Axel, so like Felix. What a pair.

"This island, or atoll, or whatever it is," she continued, "is totally uninhabited. No one ever went there until two months ago, when Odysseus Cruise Lines started offering a ten-day Hawaiian Islands cruise out of Honolulu and included a two-day round trip to the place for a beach picnic. See, they have to do that because Odysseus is Greek-owned, and non-American ships aren't allowed to travel between American ports without including at least one foreign call on their itinerary, and Maravovo Atoll was the closest—"

"For God's sake, Inge," Auntie Dagmar snapped, "we don't need a lecture on United States maritime law. You're getting as bad as Axel. Get to the point."

"What did I do now?" Axel bleated.

"Dammit, Auntie," Inge said, "all I'm trying to do . . . all right, okay, yes, sorry." When Dagmar was in one of her cranky moods there wasn't much point in trying to reason with her. Besides, it was natural enough for everybody to be a little edgy.

A week ago, she explained, a group of snorkelers from the cruise ship had paddled in an inflatable boat to a relatively distant part of the atoll's lagoon, where they had seen the old Grumman sunk in five or six feet of water, its tail protruding. They had dived down to it, looked through a missing window, and seen some bones inside. The doors had been jammed or rusted shut, and since they didn't have underwater flashlights or breathing equipment, and everything was a jumble inside, they hadn't been able to see much else.

"Jesus," Hedwig breathed. "As if we needed this."

The snorkelers, Inge went on, had gotten the plane's registration number from the fuselage and reported it to the ship's captain, and eventually the number was traced back to the plane's Hoaloha Ranch ownership. The Waimea police department was notified, and they were the ones who had called Inge with the news.

"N7943U," Axel said from memory.

Inge checked her notes. "That's it."

"What do they want us to do?" Dagmar asked.

"The police?" said Inge. "They don't want us to do anything. They just called to tell us. But the Kiribati—pardon me, Axel, Kiribass—officials want to know if we want the remains back. Personally, I think the best thing to do would be to just leave them where they are. The less attention we stir up, the better. And it's not as if it's *him* out there, it's just a few bones that don't really mean anything any more."

"I agree," Axel promptly put in.

"Amen," said Hedwig. "Don't meddle with Fortune's wheel. The plane went down there for a reason, whether we understand it or not. Let it be."

"Fortune's wheel!" Dagmar was shocked. "And what do you mean, 'a few bones that don't mean anything any more'? Sometimes I don't know what's the matter with you people. To leave him out there like that, on that little . . . no, no, I want him back here on his own land." She stared imperiously around her, challenging them to disagree, and muttering: " 'A few bones that don't mean anything.' "

Inge hesitated. "What do you think?" she asked Felix, who was silently swirling the ice in his glass.

Felix took a moment before answering. "In my opinion, we should have him brought home," he bellowed—his normal speaking voice ranged anywhere from bellow to roar. "Not only because of what Dagmar says, but because it would look strange—suspicious, even—if we don't."

"But who's going to know either way?" Axel asked.

"The police, bird-brain," Inge said fondly. "I'm supposed to call them back, remember? Felix is right."

"Oh, yeah," Axel said, then nodded. "Okay, I'm with Felix, then. We better bring him back and bury him here, what's left of him. A quiet, private, family burial."

Dagmar nodded regally to signify approval, although she'd glowered at the "what's left of him."

"So how do we go about getting the remains back?" Hedwig asked. "Does anybody know?"

"I wouldn't think there's much to it," Felix said. "We'll probably have to get some kind of formal approval from the Kiribati government, wherever it is—"

"The capital is Tarawa," said Axel.

"—but any reputable ocean salvage firm will know the

ropes. When I get back to Honolulu I'll check around for one. We can split the cost between us."

"*I'll* pay," Dagmar said. When the others opened their mouths to protest, they were silenced with a fierce tilt of her chin.

"She who must be obeyed," said Felix, salaaming in her direction.

"Idiot."

"Okay, that's the way it'll be, then," Inge said. She glanced at the antique Swedish clock over the mantel. "Now. John and Gideon will be here at six. That gives us almost an hour to make sure we're all reading from the same script, in case the papers get hold of this, or if the police have more questions."

"Speaking of John and his friend," Hedwig said, "I don't see any reason for them to know anything about this."

"Too late," Axel said. "I already told John and he told Gideon."

Hedwig looked disbelievingly at him. "That was dumb."

"Well, I figured it was bound to come out anyway, and if I didn't mention it, it would look as if we were hiding something."

"We *are* hiding something."

"Yes, but we don't want to *look* as if we are," Axel pointed out.

"Point taken," Hedwig said, submitting gracefully to this superior logic. "Okay, let it all hang out."

"Not all," amended Felix.

FIVE

THE wood-branch lettering above the entrance in the split-rail fence said "Kohala Trails Adventure Ranch," and just inside, where a couple of dirt roads intersected, there was a post with two handpainted signs: a "Stop" sign—or rather, a "Whoa" sign—and one below it that said "Howdy, Podnuh. Horseback Riding Adventure, Thisaway. Ranch House, Thataway."

They turned Thataway, toward a white frame house that looked like a bigger, better-kept version of Axel's and Malani's. "John," Gideon said, "when we were driving up from the airport, you said that 'naturally' nobody wanted to have the dinners at Hedwig's. Why is that? Why 'naturally'?"

"Well, for one thing, the Wellness Center menu is strictly vegetarian, and just a little weird besides. But mainly because it wouldn't be the same if Auntie Dagmar wasn't there, and Auntie Dagmar won't go to Hedwig's."

"Uh . . . Auntie Dagmar?" He had been drifting a little during the short drive from Axel's place, lulled by the gentle rises and falls of the road, the fragrant air, and the long, long views down to the slowly darkening sea.

"Dagmar," John said. "Torkel's and Magnus's sister. Remember? She's eighty-something now."

"Oh. Right."

"Pay attention, now."

"Sorry, I'm doing my best. So, is there a family feud? Between Auntie Dagmar and Hedwig?"

"Nah, nothing like that. It's just that Auntie Dagmar doesn't go anyplace where they won't let her drink her schnapps and smoke her cheroots, and smoking and booze are *verboten* at the Hui Ho'olana. Just like meat. They mess up the karma."

Gideon sat up a little straighter and peered at John. "John, you wouldn't be pulling my leg just a little, would you?"

John laughed. "See for yourself, buddy."

AT forty or so, Inge Torkelsson, the proprietor of the Kohala Trails Adventure Ranch, was a rangy, wind-seared woman, as sinewy and tough as a stick of beef jerky, with a small, active head, short, graying blonde hair, lean hips, and little in the way of breasts. In her jeans and checked cowboy shirt, and with her swaggery, slightly straddle-legged walk, anyone seeing her from behind would have taken her for a man; a cowboy. Given a few yards' distance, most would have thought so from the front as well.

Taking Gideon by the arm with a grip like a barroom bouncer's, she heartily dragged him around the handsomely rustic living room—deer-antler chandeliers, woven floor mats, heavy, polished, matching koa wood furniture, paintings of Hawaiian queens and Swedish kings (unlike those in Axel's house, these were framed originals, neatly hung; the whole place was like a sanitized, coordinated, updated version of Axel's house)—to introduce him to the others. There were six of them all together: the five blood-related Torkelssons—siblings Axel, Felix, Hedwig, and Inge, plus Auntie Dagmar—and Inge's Hawaiian husband, Keoni, who had arrived only seconds before John and Gideon. Obviously, they had been told about Gideon, because several of them made some small witticisms about bones or skeletons, which he took in the amiable spirit in which they'd been intended.

Inasmuch as Hedwig was the last person he was introduced to before Inge was called to the telephone, Gideon was left pretty much in her clutches. Hedwig, knowing he was an anthropologist, had expressed open-mouthed astonishment at learning that he was unfamiliar with the differences between Celtic and Druidic shamanism ("I'm not quite up to the minute on that," he had admitted) and was doing her best to repair this sad hole in his scholarship, gesturing where necessary with a glass of frothy pink liquid that looked to Gideon like Pepto-Bismol over ice. A large, flowing woman with cropped blonde hair, and wearing a large, flowing, purple-flowered muu-muu, Hedwig had a tendency to overwhelm. Partly, this was because she had a disconcerting way of standing too close when conversing, in addition to which she favored an incredibly potent jasmine scent. As a result, they had done a sort of tango across the floor, with Gideon slowly backing up, and Hedwig relentlessly tracking, until he ran out of room, bumping his hip against a table holding appetizers and drinks.

"Well, this has really been fascinating, Hedwig," he said brightly, leaping in at one of the infrequent pauses. "I guess I'll get myself a drink now—"

"Gideon—oh, my God!" she exclaimed delightedly. "You have an aura!"

"Pardon?"

"An aura!" Hedwig repeated, leaning even closer to sniff at him, to peer at his ears, his shoulders, the top of his head, drowning him in jasmine. "And not your every-day, low-level bodily kind, either." More sniffs. "It's won-derful! A high-frequency UV thing, a real astral-plane consciousness-level entity. It's *very* visible. I could help you learn to see it in no time. There's a . . . let me see . . . a tall, white-bearded man with one blue eye and one gray eye who looks after you. Hasn't anyone ever told you? Surely you've *felt* him?"

Gideon was practically bent backward over the table. "Well, actually, Hedwig, I can't say that—"

"My friends call me Kuho-ono-enuka-ilimoku, Gideon. It's my past-life vision name."

"Uh . . . past-life vision name?" he said and bit his tongue, but he was saved by the appearance of Auntie Dag-mar, a diminutive, erect, elderly woman with a well-tended but slightly askew black wig and piercing, intelligent gray eyes in a lean, Swedish face. In one hand was an unlit black cigarillo; in the other a cordial glass of amber-colored liquor. Her clothes looked expensive: a plum-colored pant-suit, silk blouse, and turquoise earrings in the form of tor-toises. Around her neck was a carelessly knotted blue Hermes silk scarf with small white stars. (Gideon knew it was a Hermes because she had put it on inside out and the label showed, which merely added to her queenly air, as if she were above the need to dress in front of a mirror.)

"And what exactly is wrong with 'Hedwig'?" she de-manded. "It was good enough for your grandmother." Gideon heard the gliding, lilting vowel-sounds of Swedish in her speech. "It was the name of royalty."

"So you've told me, Auntie Dagmar," Hedwig said with her too-bright smile. "Three or four hundred times. But the fact is, I don't like it because it sounds like 'earwig.'"

"That's ridiculous, and you know you just say it to annoy me."

"Besides which, it's too hard to pronounce. It's very tiring when everyone asks if the "w" is pronounced *wuh* or *vuh.*"

"Oh, I see. But 'Kuku-ono-mono-eenyweeny,' that's easy to pronounce."

Hedwig threw Gideon a "see what I have to put up with?" look and changed the subject, grimacing at Dagmar's glass and cigar. "You have to be more careful at your age, Auntie Dagmar," she said lightly. "I keep telling you. You're getting on now. You're not the woman you were."

"No, and I never was." She turned to Gideon. "Young man, can you light this damn thing for me? There are matches on the table over there."

"Of course," Gideon said.

Hedwig shook her head. "Darling Auntie, I hope you don't expect me to stand here and watch you kill yourself right in front of me."

"You mean you're going to pester someone else? Excellent!" said Dagmar. "Thank the Lord for small mercies. Goodbye and good luck to you."

As Gideon held the match to her cigarillo, she spoke around it. "In my opinion, a woman of forty-five—a sedentary, morbidly obese woman with some *very* peculiar ideas, if you'll forgive my saying so—has no business telling an active, perfectly healthy person of eighty-one how to live her life, would you agree?"

"Yes, I would, Miss Torkelsson," Gideon said truthfully.

"Oh, for God's sake, call me Auntie Dagmar. Are we related?"

"No, ma'am."

"That's all right, you call me Auntie Dagmar anyway." Exhaling a lungful of blue smoke, she patted him absently on the shoulder. "Will you excuse me? I just thought of something else to irritate my niece about."

Across the room, Felix Torkelsson banged a spoon against a glass for attention. "Six-thirty, everybody!"

Felix, the lawyer-brother who had flown in from Honolulu for the occasion, was a ruddy, outgoing teddy bear of a man with twinkling eyes, round cheeks, and a short, neatly clipped pepper-and-salt beard. Given a few more years, he would be everyone's choice to play Santa Claus, if he wasn't already. His normal speaking voice was a penetrating drawl with a wry, nasal touch of W. C. Fields in it, and when he raised it a few notches, no one inside of a hundred yards could escape hearing it. Nevertheless, he repeated himself with another honk. "Six-thirty, fellow Torkelssons and friends. Lift your glasses. Time for . . . The Toast!"

"Malani's not here yet," Axel called.

"Too bad," said Felix, "but we must always remember what Magnus said." He scowled ferociously, ran his tongue in and out between his teeth, and spoke with a deep, melodious Swedish accent. "In this house we enjoy our cocktails at six-thirty—*one* cocktail—and dine promptly at seven. This does not mean seven-oh-one."

There was obviously a funny story connected with this because they all laughed appreciatively, and it started them on a round of Magnus-quotations.

"You are never going to get much of anything done unless you go ahead and do it before you are ready," Inge contributed with the same slow Swedish lilt.

"No farmer ever plowed a field by turning it over in his mind," Hedwig said.

More happy laughter. Felix raised his glass. "To Uncle Magnus and Uncle Torkel, may they forever be riding their faithful old Palominos over pastures rich and green!"

"To Uncle Magnus! To Uncle Torkel!" they echoed, including Gideon, who was now on his second Scotch-and-soda.

Everyone turned expectantly to Auntie Dagmar, who lifted her glass of aquavit and, pink-cheeked, delivered a long toast in Swedish.

This pleased everybody, and they fell into fond stories about the two brothers. Even John had one: about how he was a few minutes late the very first day he reported to work at the ranch, and Magnus, who had ridden in on a sweating horse to meet him and then had to wait for him, had told him to go find another job, firing him on the spot and riding back off onto the range. It had been Torkel who had intervened and given him another chance.

"He was always the soft-headed one, Torkel," Dagmar agreed. "The romantic in the family."

"I think you mean soft-*hearted,*" Felix said, shouting with laughter.

Dagmar's icy gray eyes impaled him. "That is what I said."

Malani made her entrance in the amused silence that followed this. "So what's the latest on Magnus?" she asked into the vacuum.

"The good news is, he's dead for sure!" said Keoni Nakoa, Inge's husband. "That's why everybody looks so cheerful. The inheritances are safe!"

This prompted snorts of umbrage and disgust, which didn't seem to bother him. Keoni was clearly nobody's favorite. A big, handsome Hawaiian, but now running to fat, he looked something like John—the same thick black hair, big frame, and flat, Asiatic cheek bones—but he was smoother, slicker, without John's rough edges, and with something of the lounge lizard about him; a kind of Hawaiian Dean Martin. Dressed totally in black—T-shirt, jeans, boots—he carried himself with a somewhat heavily-laid-on air of insouciance, as if he couldn't help but be amused by the shenanigans of this droll gang of *Haoles* he'd so improbably gotten himself entangled with.

His initial greeting to Gideon, delivered with a heavy, affected Hawaiian inflection, had been, "What's happenin', brudda? If you lookin' for skeletons in da closet, you come to da right place."

According to John, Keoni had been an accountant for the Keck Observatory on Mauna Kea when he married into the Torkelssons. Now, no longer needing to work for a living, he managed the books for the dude ranch and ran occasional errands around the place, and he had too much time on his hands. There were rumors of affairs with female clients. His marriage to Inge was believed to be on shaky ground.

"I meant," Malani said to the others, "are you going to have the remains brought back?"

"Yes, child," Dagmar said. "It would be a sin to leave him out there like that, so far away." She spoke without visible emotion, almost harshly. "Besides, bringing him home would be . . . it would . . ." She searched for the words she wanted. "It would end the story. *Fini,*" she said, and made a little motion with her hands, the way an orchestra conductor might conclude a quiet chamber piece. "So."

Gideon nodded to himself. It was something he had seen often in families with a long-missing, presumed-dead member. The deep, deep need to heal over the wound for good, to finally put the past behind. The need for closure.

"He should be laid to rest on the ranch," Dagmar continued, "if you and Axel will let us use a site on the Little Hoaloha."

"Of course," Axel and Malani said together.

"Shouldn't take up too much space," Keoni observed. "Just a few old bones." Talk about a tin ear, Gideon thought.

Felix turned pointedly away from Keoni and spoke to Gideon: "This is your field. How much *would* be left after eight years?"

"Oh, please, let's not get all grisly," Hedwig said.

"No, I'm interested."

"I am, too," Inge said.

"If the plane has been in the lagoon for eight years," Gideon said a little uncomfortably, "there won't be anything like a skeleton left—an articulated skeleton. And with a window knocked out, the chances are there won't be much in the way of bones at all. Only whatever the fish and crabs couldn't haul away." A skull was the most likely possibility, since few sea creatures could get their jaws or claws around a skull. But even that was doubtful after eight years. Marine environments were not kind to organic remains.

Dagmar looked at him with prim distaste. "Thank you for explaining that, young man."

"What salvage company are you using?" Malani asked Felix.

"I don't know yet, honey. I'll ask around when I get back home. There are several of them in Honolulu."

"That's hardly necessary. There's a marine salvage company right here on the island, in Kona—Ocean Quest," Malani told him. "They're clients of mine." For the last few years, John had told Gideon earlier, she had been running a website-design consulting business from home.

"Thanks, Malani, but I think we want something just a little more professional than one of your Kona-coast outfits with two kids and a dinghy," Felix said with a tolerant smile. "Now, then—"

"Oh, now, Felix, they're hardly two kids and a dinghy," Malani warbled at him in full grade-school-teacher mode. "Ocean Quest has eight divers, they have their very own Cessna 310, and they have two salvage tugs under contract. Their specialty is rapid-response deployment. In the last fiscal year alone they did contract work for the State of Hawaii, for Blue Star Shipping, for the government of the Tuamotos, and for the Army Corps of Engineers. They handle all regional small towing and salvage work for two different marine insurance companies—"

"What is the woman doing, reading or something?" Felix said, laughing. He threw up his hands. "Okay, okay, you win. I don't know what I was thinking of to doubt you. Madame, we leave it in your ever-capable hands."

"I'll call them now," Malani said, rising.

"At seven o'clock at night?" Hedwig asked.

"These are not the most formal people in the world. They won't mind."

"The salad's on the table," Inge said as Malani left. "We might as well start before the flies find it."

Over a simple but wonderfully fresh lettuce-and-tomato salad, the conversation turned to everyday topics.

"Axel," Inge said, "one of your calves got onto my property again this morning. You're going to have to do something about that fencing."

"Sorry about that, Inge. Did it scare any of your Indonesians?"

"Worse than that," Inge told him. This was a young bull that had somehow found its way to the dude ranch petting farm, had managed to get in, and had tried to mount one of the female calves, traumatizing not only the calf but a school group from Hilo who witnessed the whole thing.

"Oh, for heaven's sake," Hedwig said, "it's as good a way as any for them to learn about sex."

"This wasn't sex, it was rape."

"Inge," Axel said in the midst of general laughter, "he isn't capable of rape. He's been castrated."

"Well, he sure didn't seem to know it. Maybe you should tell them when you castrate them."

"Do you suppose we might change the subject?" Dagmar interjected with a shake of her head. "I'm trying to eat my dinner. Felix, when exactly can we expect to see your land turned into Happy Harbor Estates?"

"Now, Auntie, you know they haven't decided on what the name's going to be," Felix said patiently. "And I promise you, it'll be very nice when it's finished. They're preserving the landscape as much as possible. They have a great deal of respect for the land."

"Tell us another one," Dagmar said.

"It's not a joke, you'll see. And as to when, they're hoping to start in the fall, but the Environmental Quality Control Board is still haggling over the impact statement."

"Hey," Keoni said. "How many *Haoles* does it take to screw in a light bulb?"

"I have no idea," Felix said with an air of stolid resignation. "How many *Haoles* does it take to screw in a light bulb?"

"Six. One to call the electrician, and five to write the environmental impact report."

John laughed, Gideon smiled, and the Torkelssons glowered.

"You like that?" Keoni said. "Okay, how does a *Haole* show his racial tolerance?"

Before anyone could reply, Malani came in, taking the

seat that had been kept for her next to Axel, across from Gideon and John. "All right, it's tentatively arranged. They gave me a price, and if I get back to them within the hour, they can do it tomorrow."

"Tomorrow!" Felix exclaimed. "I see what you mean about rapid response."

"Yes, well, you see, since the plane is only in a few feet of water, and since all we want are the remains, and not the plane itself, they say it won't take a great deal of work or much in the way of equipment. And if they leave first thing in the morning, they ought to finish up and be back by the end of the day."

"Wait a minute, now," said Axel. "How in the heck are they going to land a Cessna 310 on Maravovo, let alone take off again? Is there a nice, big, two-thousand-foot landing strip on this deserted atoll? That's what it would take. Fifteen hundred feet at the absolute minimum." As the only person with flying experience in the room, Axel's word carried weight. He had learned to fly fifteen years or so ago, briefly serving as the ranch pilot before discovering that, as much as he enjoyed the navigational calculations, he didn't much like flying itself. "I think maybe Felix is right, sweetheart; we'd better find an outfit in Honolulu."

But *this* Cessna, Malani triumphantly explained, didn't require any landing strip at all. It had been converted to a float plane. It could land in the lagoon.

"Really? I didn't know there was anybody on the Big Island who could do that kind of work."

"They did it themselves," Malani explained. "They also serve as their own pilots, which saves considerably on the cost."

"Oh, brudda," Keoni said, "I'm just glad nobody's asking *me* to fly in it."

Undeterred, Malani went on, meticulously referring to

the neat, columnar notes—she wrote in tiny uppercase let-
ters—that she had made on a note pad. "The Cessna's
cruising speed is about two hundred miles an hour, so to be
on the safe side they're allowing a total of five hours for the
eight-hundred-mile round trip, plus an hour for landings
and takeoffs, and five hours for the work itself. Eleven
hours altogether."

At this point, the grilled steaks, brought in by a perspiring, aproned cook, drew everyone's attention. There were
no inquiries as to rare, medium, or well-done; the perfectly
charred, two-inch-thick tenderloins were simply plopped
onto the plates (all except Hedwig's) with a simple accom-
paniment of spinach and baked potato that was served in
bowls, family style. No steak sauce, ketchup, or mustard;
the only condiments on the table were salt and pepper.
Gideon was surprised to see that the steaks were all
medium-well-done, a barely pink-tinged brown at the center, and said as much to Axel.

"Oh, yeah," Axel said. "You won't find too many ranchers who like their steaks rare." He wrinkled his nose.
"Smells too much like cow."

"You don't suppose," said Hedwig, digging into the
plate of couscous, kohlrabi, and gingered squash that the
cook had plopped in front of her with undisguised con-
tempt, "that might be because it *is* cow? And am I the only
one able to see that the very fact that you try to hide it
from yourselves proves my point? You prefer to avoid
dealing with your own innate self-knowledge of the ethi-
cal consequences, to say nothing of the karmic consequences, of eating our brothers and cousins; things with
faces, things with mothers. I know I've probably said it
before—"

" *'Probably'*?" Dagmar said loudly. "Don't make me
laugh."

"—but it's impossible to reach any kind of higher consciousness—"

"Oh, put a cork in it, Hedwig," Felix shouted amiably, his jaws grinding audibly away on flesh and fat.

"Cannibals," sighed Hedwig. "Surrounded on all sides by ravening carnivores."

"You can thank ravening carnivores for everything you have," Dagmar said, chewing.

"Actually, I'd have thought Marti would get along pretty well with Hedwig," Gideon whispered to John.

"Actually, she does."

Over coffee and a dessert of baked apples and cream, Malani gave them the rest of the details: Ocean Quest's plane was loaded with equipment and ready to go, but it was currently hangared at the Honolulu airport, where it had just gotten a new paint job. In the morning they would put two of their salvage divers, who would double as the Cessna pilot and co-pilot, on the first Aloha inter-island flight from Kona to Honolulu, where they would pick up the Cessna and take off for Maravovo, hoping to touch down in the lagoon by nine or ten A.M. They would expect to finish up by two in the afternoon at the latest and be back in Honolulu with the remains in time for one of the commercial evening flights to Kona. The estimated fee would be $16,000. "They think that's a maximum. It'll probably be less."

Keoni pretended to choke on a chunk of baked apple. "Sixteen thousand dollars for one day's work? And I thought Felix was the expert on screwing his clients."

"Damn it, Keoni," Felix said, "if that's supposed to be humorous—"

"The largest single cost is the plane," Malani cut in. "Nine hundred dollars an hour flight time and three hundred dollars an hour wait time. Add that to the divers' hourly rate of five hundred dollars, the air fare to and from Honolulu—"

"Still—" Keoni said.

"I don't want to argue about it," Dagmar said. "I'm sure they're not overcharging us. You go ahead and tell them to do it, my dear."

"Don't forget about getting permission from the Kiribati government," John said.

"They say they'll take care of all that," Malani said. "They've dealt with the Kiribatis before."

"They'll need to file a flight plan," Axel said. "They'll have to—"

"They know all about that; they'll get started as soon as I call back." She paused, chewing on her lip for a moment. "Oh, there is one other thing. They've never recovered human bones before, and they're nervous about how they're supposed to handle them, and even how to recognize them. So you can imagine how excited they got when I told them that we had the world-famous Skeleton Detective himself staying with us"—she turned a brilliant smile on Gideon and actually batted her eyelashes—"and he just might be willing to . . ." With a teacherly motion of her hand she encouraged him to finish the sentence for her.

"Go with them?" Gideon said. "I'd . . . be happy to help out any way I can." He'd been on the narrow edge of exclaiming "I'd love to!", which would hardly have been appropriate in the circumstances, but the fact was that he'd been hoping they'd ask him ever since John had told him about the find.

What he had told Axel about being interested in cattle-ranching was true enough, but when it came to real, gut-level interest, cows didn't hold a candle to bones. For Gideon, as for every other forensic anthropologist he knew, the skeleton was a source of inexhaustible fascination, and to sit down with the bony remains of some anonymous, long-dead human being was to accept a challenge: What could be told from them about the person's life, the person's death? About who and what the person had been, had looked like? The skeletal system, the part of us that was left after everything else had rotted away, retained, for the knowing eye, an exhaustive and indelible record of the habits, diet, health, injuries, and activities of an individual's life.

What could be determined, of course, depended on how much skeletal material was left, which bones they happened to be, what their condition was, and a host of other things. But there was always something to be learned, some connection to be made with a human being no longer living, a being whose future was gone, but whose past could still be brought back, at least a little. The forensic anthropologist, one of Gideon's teachers had liked to say, was the last one to speak for the dead.

"Oh, I'm sure Gideon has other things to do than—" Hedwig began.

"No, I'd like to," he quickly interrupted.

"Well, that's just great, Gideon," Felix said. "Thank you. We'll pay your usual fee, of course. That goes without—"

"*I'll* pay his usual fee," Dagmar said.

Gideon waved them off. "No, no, no. Thank you, but it's a pleasure to repay you all for your hospitality." He hesitated. "There is something you need to know, though." He wasn't eager to throw a monkey wrench into the closure machinery, but in good conscience he couldn't let it pass. "At this point, unless I missed something, you don't really have any way of knowing for sure whose bones are in that plane. You're assuming it crashed the night he left and that it's been there ever since, but for all anybody knows it might have gone down months or years later. The plane's ownership might have changed hands."

"Uh-uh," Inge said. "According to the police, the plane was never registered to anyone else. Hoaloha Ranch is still the last recorded owner."

"Yeah, but that doesn't mean a lot," said John. "Trust me, planes can change hands without paperwork. Doc's right, it's most probably him, but it *could* be anybody."

That made for a few wrinkled brows, until John spoke again. "Doc, couldn't you tell from the bones whether it was him or not?"

"Well, I wouldn't go as far as that," Gideon said, addressing everyone. "But depending on what there is, I could probably narrow it down some. With a little luck, I might be able to determine the sex, age, race, and maybe the approximate height. That'd help." With a little luck—and the right bones—he could very likely come up with a lot more than that, but he didn't like to promise more than he could deliver.

"But you have to remember, exclusion is a lot easier than positive identification," he went on. "That is, say the bones are those of an elderly white male of such and such a height—"

"My brother was not 'elderly,' " Dagmar said crossly. "He was an extremely vigorous man, not yet out of his seventies."

"—a white male in his seventies of such and such a height," he amended, "then we'd know that they *could* be Magnus's, and we could reasonably conclude they probably are, given that it's the ranch airplane and no one's seen it or him since he flew off in it. But if we were to find the bones of a female, say, then we'd know with a hundred percent certainty that it *couldn't* be him."

"Well, of course not," Dagmar said. "*I* could have told you that."

Axel had found an atlas somewhere and brought it, open, to the table. It took him a while to locate Maravovo Atoll. "This place is absolutely in the middle of nowhere. Where the heck were they trying to get to?"

" 'They'?" Gideon said. "He wasn't alone?"

"No, there was a pilot," said Inge. "Magnus didn't know how to fly."

"Lydia What's-Her-Name," Dagmar said.

"No," Inge said, frowning. "It wasn't 'Lydia' . . ."

"Could they have been trying to get to Tarabao Island?" Malani asked. She had gotten up to lean over her husband so she could see the map. "Or Beckman Atoll? Maravovo is between them."

Axel studied the map and fingered his chin. "Maybe, but it's an awfully long way from either one."

"They were a long way from anything," said Malani. "Wherever they were headed, they must have gotten good and lost."

"Well, frankly, I can't say I'm bowled over," Hedwig said. "Lydia wasn't really much of a pilot."

"Wasn't much of anything," Dagmar grumbled. "Should never have hired her."

"Claudia, that was her name," said Inge. "Claudia Albert. Oh, she wasn't really a bad person, Auntie Dagmar. She'd had it hard growing up—"

"And how do you think I had it?" Dagmar said heatedly. "Or Magnus, or Torkel, or your father? But we didn't turn to drugs, we didn't get in trouble with the police, we just *worked* for a better life, not like that big lummox of a Claudia-Lydia. And we got it, we got a better life for ourselves, and now you have it. We didn't have to run off to the psychologist because we had some imaginary eating disorder . . . anorexia—"

"Actually, it was bulimia, and it's not really imaginary,"

Hedwig said, "although there is a psycho-spiritual compo-nent. No that I ever thought mainstream psychologists would do her any good. Remember, I offered her a place free of charge in the Self-Evolvement Wellness Seminar, but she—"

"It wasn't free," Dagmar pointed out. "Torkel was going to pay for it." She relit her dead cigarillo, making a show of it.

"Well, yes, technically," Hedwig mumbled, "but only to cover the cost of food and refresh—"

"Gideon, let me ask you something," Inge said. "Or maybe this is a question for you, John. Isn't it possible that there might be some identifiable personal belongings still in the plane, even after all this time? A watch, a ring, maybe even a driver's license or something? Wouldn't that settle the question of who it is?"

"I would think so," said Gideon. "Paper wouldn't last, but plastic might. Metal would."

"Doc, how about I go along with you, if that's okay?" John said. "Maybe I could help."

"Sure," Gideon said, pleased. "I'd appreciate the com-pany."

"Listen, you two," said Felix, "you'll be bushed by the time you get back to Honolulu from there. I don't think you should have to get on another plane to come here. Let me put you both up for the night in Waikiki. Someplace nice. You can have a good dinner, get a good night's sleep, catch a plane back to Kona the next day."

"I appreciate that, Felix," Gideon said, "but it's not nec-essary, we can—"

"Hey, speak for yourself, Doc," John cut in. "It'd be nice—"

Felix talked—shouted—right on through them. "My condo doesn't have a guest room, unfortunately, but I can book you a room at the Royal Hawaiian. It's just a few blocks from where I live. You like the Royal Hawaiian, don't you? Of course you do, who wouldn't?"

"Yes, sure," Gideon said, "but my wife is coming here to the Big Island the next day—"

"Not till one-fifteen," John said. We'll be back in Kona ourselves before that, and we can meet her plane. Better yet, we can catch her at the airport in Honolulu and fly the last leg in with her."

"Well—" Gideon began.

"Oh, let him do it for you, for God's sake," Auntie Dagmar said. "He can afford it."

Felix whacked the table with a paw-like hand. "It's settled then. I'll take care of everything. I'll look forward to dinner with the two of you in Waikiki tomorrow night."

"Fabulous," said John.

"Thanks, Felix," Gideon said, having run out of arguments. "It's nice of you."

"And now," commanded Felix, "I think we ought to let these two fellows get some rest. They'll have to be up early tomorrow. First flight is five-fifteen."

"Five-fifteen!" whispered John, horrified. He was not an early riser.

"That's right," Inge said. "Sad but true. If you two want to get through security and make the plane, you'd better be on your way to the airport by four A.M. At the latest."

"Four . . . A.M.!" John could barely get the words out, but he stuck gamely, stalwartly, to his guns.

His chin came up.

He'd said he would go, and he would go.

SIX

SEEN from an altitude of fifteen hundred feet, Maravovo Atoll lay at one end of a curving archipelago of tiny islands, the first land they'd seen since leaving Hawaii. Maravovo itself was the largest, or at least the longest, of them—an elongated, C-shaped island, its spine thickly covered with vegetation, and perhaps a mile from end to end and no more than a hundred yards wide at its broadest point. The inside rim of the "C" was a narrow sliver of white sand bordering a lagoon of the brightest, greenest aquamarine imaginable, strikingly different from the deep blue of the sea that surrounded it. The only signs that man had ever set foot on the atoll were a floating pier and a couple of small, new-looking structures on one horn of the "C," at the mouth of the lagoon, built by the cruise line for their picnicking day-trippers.

On the ocean side of the low coral reef that formed the outer border of the lagoon two brown-skinned, loincloth-clad men paddling an outrigger canoe waved as the plane passed over them.

"I thought the island was uninhabited," Gideon said.

"It is," said Lyle Shertz, one of the two salvage divers, who was in the co-pilot's seat. "But according to the CIA Factbook, there are some people living on a couple of nearby islands, and they come here to fish along the reef. Hey, what do you know, there's the Grumman. Up ahead, about one o'clock, right in close to shore. Boy, that didn't take long!"

"Well, you were right; we're sure not gonna need the sonar," the pilot, Harvey Shertz, said to him. "That'd be pretty hard to miss."

The two men were brothers; identical twins in their thirties, with husky, well-padded frames. Although they dressed similarly—tank tops, baggy khaki shorts, and flip-flops—they had resorted to different techniques for disguising their receding hairlines. Lyle's head was shaved, although he was overdue for the razor, so that his rippled, globular skull was coated with black stubble. Harvey wore his equally black hair long enough to comb it forward over his forehead, where he cut it straight across. From Gideon's point of view, it gave them a worrisome resemblance to two-thirds of the Three Stooges.

Sitting in the seats behind them, John and Gideon peered around them and through the front windows. "But it's plain as day," John said. "Even if the tail wasn't sticking up out of the water. How could it take ten years for anybody to find it?"

Harvey answered. "It took ten years because we're a hundred and fifty miles from any commercial airline route and four hundred miles from the nearest land. No one flies over it. No one sails to it; not on purpose, anyway."

"What about those natives down there? They must have seen it," Lyle said.

"Sure they did, dumb ass," his brother answered. "So what were they supposed to do, call 911? Even if they had cell phones, which they don't, there aren't any communication satellites down here to tap into. Oops, sorry about that," he said as the floats hit the water more heavily than they might have and the four men were jounced in their seats. "I haven't landed this baby very much."

"I'm the regular pilot," Lyle volunteered.

"Now they tell us," John said.

Two more long, slow, glancing skips, much softer, and the Cessna settled onto the surface of the lagoon, turned, gunned its engines, taxied to within a few yards of the wrecked plane, and let out its "lunch hook," a small anchor that immediately snagged in the sandy floor of the lagoon. With the water as clear as glass and the cabin roof of the downed plane only a few feet below them, it was perfectly visible: a smaller craft than Gideon had anticipated, white with dark blue trim, lying right-side up but tipped forward onto its nose cone and listing to the left, the collapsed strut of its nose wheel twisted to the side and both ends of the propeller blade bent straight back. A few unidentifiable chunks of metal and plastic lay scattered on the bottom nearby.

Gideon had been expecting a rusting hulk thickly encrusted with sea life, but in fact, other than a heavy layer of dull green algae on those windows that were intact, the encrustations were minimal and the oxidation was pretty much limited to the damaged areas, to seams in the metal, and to the regions around the rivets. (The corrupters of metal, it occurred to him, operated on the same principle as the putrefiers of flesh: go for the weak spots first; the weak spots and the natural openings.) The fuselage number,

N7943U, painted on the horizontal blue stripe, seemed as bright as the day it had been put there. The tail, which was in the open air, seemed to have weathered a bit more than the submerged part.

From the Cessna it was impossible to see inside, even with the Grumman's right window broken out—a patch of almond-colored seat trimmed with blue plastic, a glimpse of the rightmost rudder pedal, nothing more.

Lyle and Harvey tethered a small wooden raft to the Cessna and set it on the water loaded with a few pieces of equipment: an oxyacetylene torch and an open toolbox with some simple implements in it—a cold chisel, a hammer, a hand axe, a couple of pry bars, a few pairs of pliers, and some unfamiliar-looking wrenches. Then, not bothering with wet suits, they strapped on their scuba gear and weight belts. "This is gonna be easy," Harvey said.

"As pie," Lyle happily agreed. "No pumps, no compressors, no nothing. We're gonna be home for dinner. Okay, we'll take a look-see now," he told Gideon. "Don't go 'way."

They hooked on weight belts, slipped their masks over their faces, got their flippers on, climbed clumsily out onto the Cessna's wing, and slipped backwards into the water, not taking any of the tools with them. As they approached the Grumman, a school of tiny fish darted out of it, flashed silver as they wheeled, and disappeared. A crab or something like it flopped out of the broken window and scuttled its way into the sand under the fuselage. After a few seconds Harvey popped back up, water streaming from his shining hair.

"What did you—" Gideon began.

"Can't talk now," Harvey said cheerfully. He grabbed the torch, cleared his mask, said "Glub-glub," and pushed himself back down. This time they stayed under for a few minutes, first using the torch to cut through the canopy, after which Lyle squeezed inside.

After a few seconds an orange and blue flickering showed through the algae on the front window.

"They're working on something with the torch," John said.

"Let's hope it's not the skeleton."

A minute later, they were at the surface again, with Lyle hanging on to the raft with one hand while grasping in the other a white, angular object about the thickness of a human long bone, and shaped like a distorted, square-cornered "U." Barnacle colonies clung to it here and there, tightly closed against this unexpected depredation.

"Well, here's your skeleton," he said, holding it up for inspection. "And there's another one just like it, if you want it."

"What is it?" Gideon asked, feeling let down. He had known from long experience that most of the "human" bones found and reported by laymen turned out to be from bears, or rabbits, or deer, or dogs, or sharks, or just about any animal other than humans, but still he'd been hoping. But whatever this was, it had never been part of the structural framework of any living thing.

"It's the yoke—the steering wheel—from the co-pilot's side. You want it?"

When Gideon shook his head, Lyle said, "Happy, happy barnacles, this is your lucky day. Go in peace, my friends." He dropped the yoke and watched it drift slowly down, gently turning over, until it came to rest on the floor of the lagoon.

"Hey, prof, don't look so blue," Harvey said. "We could find something yet. We hardly looked in there. Things are all messed up. It'll take us a while to go through the inside. You guys want to stretch your legs on the island while we work?"

That sounded like a good idea to both of them. At six-two, an inch taller than Gideon, John had been even more cramped during the flight. And inasmuch as the space behind the passenger seats had been crammed with salvage gear, neatly stowed and secured, but taking up every available inch (even the third row of seats had been removed to make room for it), they had been unable to move around the plane.

Ten minutes later they were seated, canvas tennis hats on their heads, sunglasses on their noses, and smeared all over with sunscreen, in a yellow, eight-foot inflatable dinghy that Harvey had pulled from a rack, inflated with an electric pump, and set in the water. Beside them on the seat-slats were a couple of liter-bottles of water and a bag with four thin ham-and-tomato sandwiches from the Cessna's cooler. John, on the center-slat, had the oars.

Gideon gave the brothers a few brief instructions—they were to extract anything at all that they thought might be bone, they were to handle all such objects with great care, doing nothing more to them than rinsing them in fresh water, and they were to be on the lookout for any personal belongings—clothing, jewelry, credit cards, etc.—that might be useful in confirming the identity of the occupants. And if they found anything, he would appreciate the use of a ruler and a tape measure, and any kind of measuring calipers they might happen to have. Oh, and a magnifying glass—

"Yeahyeahyeah," Harvey said, adjusting his mask and regulator preparatory to going back down. "Have a good time, don't talk to any strangers. See you later."

WALKING on Maravovo was easier said than done. The seemingly inviting beach of smooth white sand was appallingly hot—even John wilted—and the thousands, the many thousands, of grayish land crabs stirring underfoot and scuttling for their holes made walking unpleasant.

The "interior" of the island—the outside of the "C"—was even worse; crammed with palm trees and pandanus, breezeless, stifling, and practically impenetrable. Creeping lantana and morning glory vines grabbed like snakes at their ankles, and gnarly, above-ground roots tripped them up at almost every step. Before they'd gone a hundred yards they were pouring with sweat, and clouds of gnats and biting black flies were hungrily gathering on them, retreating only a few feet when they batted at them, and then even more aggressively buzzing back.

"Talk about carnivores," Gideon said, swatting away.

Retreating to the beach again—at least there was a sea breeze and no flies—they took off their shirts and shoes, left them in the dinghy, and waded up to their knees in the calm, crabless, blessedly cool water of the lagoon, occasionally sipping from the water bottles, toward where the cruise line had set up its compound about a quarter-of-a-mile ahead. At one point they set the bottles and sandwiches on the shoreline and took a swim, regretting that they hadn't taken the brothers up on their offer of snorkeling masks and fins. Even without them, paddling around in the five-foot-deep water was like swimming in a giant tropical-fish aquarium, but after fifteen minutes the salt had begun to sting their eyes and they got out, rubbing their eyes but much refreshed.

The compound consisted of two structures other than the pier: a large, unlocked metal storage building (uninhabited islands made locks irrelevant, as John pointed out) with barbecue equipment, boxes of plastic eating utensils, beach chairs, and picnic tables stacked inside; and a small, canopied, thatch-roofed pavilion with a plastic-topped table in the center, a raised wooden floor, open sides, and a sign bolted to one of its four roof-support posts:

SHANDARA MASSAGE. TREAT YOURSELF TO A LOMI-LOMI ON-THE-BEACH SPECIAL. BODY EXFOLIATION, SEAWEED AND KUKUI NUT FACE THERAPY, TROPICAL AROMA SCALP TREATMENT, SEA SALT FOOT SCRUB, ALL FOR $75. LIKI-LIKI VERSION, $35. CHARGE TO YOUR CRUISE ACCOUNT.

They chose the massage hut in which to have their sandwiches, inasmuch as it was the only place that was both protected from the sun and open to the breeze. As they were finishing their first ones—the tomatoes had made the white bread soggy, but they weren't complaining—they heard the Cessna's engines start up and saw the plane begin to taxi slowly toward the dinghy they had left on the beach. By waving and calling, they managed to get the plane's attention, and a minute later the Cessna was bumping gently up against the floating pier. The brothers were both looking down at them and grinning.

They had found something.

"YES, it's human," Gideon said, looking at the bone that Lyle had just placed in his hand. "A mandible."

"A jawbone," John explained.

Lyle was delighted. "Oh, that's why it has teeth!"

"Of course that's why it has teeth, putzhead," Harvey said. "Didn't I tell you that?" If anything, their resemblance to Moe and Curly was becoming more pronounced, and Gideon half-expected Harvey to deliver a two-finger poke into Lyle's eyes or kick him in the ankle, but all he did was shake his head.

"Where was it?" Gideon asked.

"Under the console, in front of the pilot's seat. It was snagged around one of the hydraulic brake lines."

"Ah, that's probably why it didn't get carried off." He took it from Lyle, gently turning it from side to side. "So this is it, then? This one bone?"

"So far. We're gonna head back now and see what else we can find, but we wanted you to see this first. Everything is shifted and kind of crumpled up. We'll need to use the torch some more, and we'll see what we see. I wouldn't get my hopes up if I was you, though."

Except for a few dead limpet shells on the inside of the left ramus—the part that rises, behind the teeth, to form the hinge that attaches the jaw to the cranium—the mandible was as whole, as clean, and almost as white, as a specimen from a biological supply house. A right lateral incisor and one of the right premolars were missing, but they had worked their way out after death; the deep, crisp-edged sockets, with no signs of the bone-resorption that would have gone along with eventual healing, made that clear. The other fourteen teeth were still in place and only a little loose, the natural result of the loss of the soft tissue surrounding them. Both first molars and one of the remaining premolars had cheap amalgam fillings in them. The bone itself had a slightly spongy feel—a "give" to it—but so would anything else that had been soaking in a warm lagoon for ten years. It would be solid enough, once dry.

With the Shertz brothers having forgotten to bring him any of the tools he'd asked for, the table wasn't going to do Gideon any good, so along with John, he sat down at the shady edge of the wooden platform-floor, with his bare feet in the cool, damp sand. He flicked the limpets from the bone with a fingernail and slowly turned it in his hands, running his fingers over the bumps, ridges, grooves, and hollows. After a while he gently set it upright on his knee so it was "facing" him and studied it for another minute. A single drop of sweat rolled from his forehead, down his nose, and onto the leg of his shorts.

"Well, I can tell you who it isn't," he said at last. "It isn't old Magnus."

"No, it's female," John said promptly.

"Right. And the age, too. This came from a young— wait a minute, how'd you know it's female?"

John had once taken a three-day forensics course for law-enforcement personnel, at which Gideon had been the lecturer for the anthropology segment, and while he had been a willing student, it quickly became apparent that osteology was never going to be his strong suit. Thus, his quick, almost instant, determination of sex came as a surprise. The mandible in Gideon's hand would have been a good one with which to challenge his graduate students' abilities at sexing. The overall size and ruggedness suggested a male jaw, he said half-aloud. On the other hand, the sharpness of the anterior edges of the rami and the delicacy of the condyles were more typical of females. The symphyseal height and the gonial angle could probably have gone either way, although, without measuring instruments, it was impossible to say for certain . . .

As Gideon droned on, detail after detail, John nodded sagely, perspiration dripping from his chin. "True, my good fellow, very true, indeed."

"So how'd you come up with female?"

By now John was laughing out loud. For once Gideon responded with a frown. "What? What am I missing?"

"How I came up with female," John said, "was that I figured the odds were pretty damn high that the plane really did go down that night, and if it did, there were two people aboard—Magnus and the pilot, Claudia—and since I knew it wasn't him, it had to be Claudia. And Claudia was a female. That's how."

"But how'd you know it wasn't Magnus?"

"I knew because you just *said* it wasn't, two minutes ago," John said, breaking out laughing again, and this time Gideon went along. When he sobered, he went back to turning the mandible in his hands and running his fingers over it again.

John, whose interest in forensic anthropology did not extend to sitting around watching Gideon stare at a bone and mumble to himself, stretched, stood up, and announced that he was going off to take another swim.

"Okay, right," said Gideon, absorbed in the examination.

However he'd arrived at it, John was correct about the mandible being Claudia Albert's. According to the Torkelssons, she had been a big, sturdily built woman (a lummox, Dagmar had called her) of twenty-five, troubled with bulimia. And the jawbone perched on his knee had almost certainly belonged to a big, sturdily built woman of twenty-five or so, afflicted with an eating disorder, most likely bulimia. Given the context and the circumstances, there wasn't much room for doubt as to who she was.

Despite some of the ambiguous criteria, determining the sex had been the easy part. (Determining the sex was *always* the easy part, given that you started with a fifty percent chance of getting it right if you simply flipped a coin.) But beyond that, the classic curvature of the chin (in anthrospeak, the convexity of the mental protuberance), as opposed to the two-cornered squareness (the bilobatedness) of the male chin, was so archetypically female that it overrode everything else, even the ruggedness and size. It was female; he was certain.

But the ruggedness and size were useful in their own right, in that they were what had told him that the mandible's owner had probably been large and strongly built. When a mandible, or any other bone, was robust and heavily ridged and roughened by muscle attachments, it meant that the muscles that had been attached to it were strong and well-developed. And if the mandibular muscles were well-developed, it was reasonable to assume that the cranial and neck muscles were well-developed, and if that was the case, then it was only reasonable to suppose that the trunk and limb muscles were well-developed, etc., etc. The good old Law of Morphological Consistency.

So it was possible, even from a single bone—the mandible—to make some assessment of overall size and physical condition. Of course, the Law of Morphological Consistency wasn't exactly a law, it sometimes happened that a person might have a strongly developed jaw and neck coupled with a weak thorax, or thick arms coupled with spindly legs, and when such things occurred, anthropological assessments went awry. But they didn't happen very often, and unless something turned up to contradict it, Gideon would stick with his reading. He'd rather have had a few more bones to look at, but in this kind of work, fragmentary remains were the rule.

Ageing skeletal material was trickier than sexing it (to begin with, you had a lot more than two possibilities), but in this case it was made easier by the presence of the two partially erupted third molars—the deservedly much-maligned wisdom teeth. Inasmuch as third molars, the most variable of the human teeth as to time of eruption, generally came in (when they came in at all) somewhere between the ages of eighteen and twenty-five, and these particular ones had not quite broken all the way through, it followed that the person had probably been somewhere between those ages when she died. (Forensic anthropology, he thought, not for the first time, involved an awful lot of "probablys.")

The eating disorder? That had been easy, the work of a single glance. The edges of the incisors were thinned and "scalloped," almost as if they'd been gently filed. And the lingual surfaces—the sides toward the tongue—were deeply eroded and discolored, almost through the enamel. On the two central incisors, it looked as if the dentin might be showing through in spots. When you saw incisors like these, especially on a young person, the most likely cause, and the first thing that came to mind, was bulimia: the habitual, repeated vomiting that went along with it brought up stomach acid that ate the enamel away.

Ergo, he was looking at the mandible of a large-boned female. In her early- to mid-twenties. With an eating disorder.

Claudia Albert. And the fact—well, the high probability—that it was Claudia Albert added weight to the idea that Magnus Torkelsson had been aboard, too, even if nothing of him were to turn up.

All these observations had been made without benefit of measuring instruments, regression equations, or statistical tables, but he had been at this long enough to feel reasonably comfortable about his conclusions without them. The numbers and tables came in handy when you were trying to convince a jury or a skeptical defense lawyer that you knew what you were talking about, but Gideon, like most of his colleagues, trusted more to his instincts—that is, his educated and well-honed instincts—than anything that came out of a computer. Anyway, in this case, there were no lawyers or juries to worry about.

Drowsy with the heat, his back against a post, his head drooping, he sat musing over the mandible for a while. If she had lived, those third molars would have given her a lot of trouble. They were both impacted—tipped toward the second molars in front of them—so that when they had fully erupted they would have been pressing hard against them, putting a strain on the fabric of the entire mouth. Most likely, they would have had to come out.

Wisdom teeth, he reflected; one of those little mistakes that the evolutionary process makes, or rather one of those little lapses. What most people never seemed to get clear about the way evolution worked was that Mother Nature didn't give much thought to the big picture. She fussed and tinkered with the details that caught her interest, and let the rest take care of themselves. Once the hominid brain-case began to expand and the snout to retreat a million and a half or so years ago, the new, shorter face had less and less room for its mouthful of big, grinding, crushing teeth. They began to be squeezed uncomfortably together, not that that bothered Mother Nature. She just kept on squeezing, and the third molars, being the last to erupt, were always being faced with a shortage of space by the time they got there, so that they started coming up sideways or back-to-front, or any which way they could.

The way she usually took care of annoying little problems like that was to let us solve them for ourselves. That is, if impacted, diseased wisdom teeth and unhealthy, crowded mouths got to be enough of a problem, people would die from them earlier than the general population did, and as a result their representation in the gene pool would diminish, and eventually, given enough time, the trait would die out and be no more. In other words, Mother Nature left it to us to work the bugs out of her program. ("Sort of like we do for Bill Gates," a student had aptly remarked the previous quarter.)

In the case of third molars, we were obviously still going through the process—they seemed to be becoming rarer with time—but modern dentistry, well-intentioned as it might be, had complicated things . . .

He became aware that the Cessna's engines had been chattering for a while, and, looking up, he saw that the plane was slowly motoring over the lagoon toward them again. Had he been dozing? Apparently so; John had returned from the lagoon without his noticing and was just finishing his second sandwich and crumpling up the plastic wrap.

"Welcome back," John said. "Have a good snooze?"

"I was thinking," Gideon said. "Turning things over in my mind."

"Yeah, right. I always snore when I turn things over in my mind, too. Listen, I got a question. This girl, this pilot, she had bulimia, right?"

"Right, bulimia nervosa."

"Which is where you make yourself throw up after you eat."

"Mm-hm." He yawned, scratched his back against the post, and straightened up.

"But she was supposed to be this big, strapping kid. Aren't bulimics underweight?"

"Interestingly enough, no. They're never very much underweight, and usually above average weight, actually. You see, they don't do it all the time. They go on periodic binges where they overeat, then make themselves vomit. You're thinking of anorexics, who starve themselves or make themselves throw up or take laxatives or whatever, but they do it day in, day out."

John cocked an eyebrow. "They're *never* underweight?"

"No."

"Never?"

"No."

"It's *impossible* to have a bulimic who's skinny?"

"That's right, because technically you can't be a bulimic and an anorexic at the same time, so if a bulimic is morbidly underweight, she's automatically classified as having anorexia, not bulimia."

John, who had thought he was closing in for a rare Socratic kill, was clearly disappointed. "That's . . . but that's . . ."

"That is a salutary example of one of the tools of modern science," Gideon said. "We experts use it all the time. It's known as disposing of nonconforming data by means of semantic recategorization."

"Science," John said, shaking his head. "It's wunnerful."

"Hey, we're done!" one of the brothers yelled from the plane as it neared the pier. "Got some good stuff for you."

Gideon got up, stretched, swished some water around his dry mouth, and went with John to meet them. This time they tied up and Lyle quickly climbed down holding a small mesh basket. "Possible personal effects," he said.

In the basket were the bent, lens-less frame of a pair of wire-rimmed glasses; a few coins—two quarters, a dime, a penny; a lidded coffee mug with a hula dancer on it; an enameled metal tourist souvenir, probably a trivet or a wall ornament, in the shape of the Big Island, complete with its two white-capped volcanic peaks in relief; a black plastic comb; and the rubber heel of a boot or shoe.

The Big Island souvenir was snarled in a crumpled tangle of gray duct tape, which Gideon picked at and managed to unstick.

"Amazing," he said. "This stuff really does last forever."

"That and Twinkies," said John.

Some of the metal objects had a layer of green patina on them, but otherwise everything was in fairly good condition, and the ornament, the mug, and the glasses could well turn out to be helpful in identification. No bones, however, and Gideon had a hard time hiding his disappointment.

"Well, this is good," he said. "Somebody might remember some of this. See anything you recognize, John?"

John fingered the glasses. "These, maybe," he said doubtfully. "I don't know."

"We can do better than that, prof," Harvey said, jumping down onto the pier. "Lookee here, what we found jammed down under the right rudder pedal on the co-pilot's side." In his hand was a sodden, water-blackened cowboy boot, swollen and distorted, and missing its heel, but with the intricate stitching still in place. "You'll love this."

"A boot?"

"No, no, boot-shmoot, take a peek inside." He tipped it so that Gideon could look into the top.

And there, nestled deep within, was the skeleton of a right foot, or at least all that could be seen of it: the talus and the calcaneus, the two uppermost bones of the human ankle and foot. There was little doubt that the rest of the foot was there, too. The bulky talus and calcaneus, their anatomical relations to each other only minimally disturbed, blocked the opening, and with the leather whole and the sole of the boot still attached, there was no place for the other bones to go.

"Hey, how about that?" he said, his enthusiasm reviving. The twenty-six bones of the foot and ankle were far from the most useful parts of the skeleton when it came to ageing, sexing, and so on (given his druthers he'd naturally have chosen a skull or pelvis or even a femur), but he had long ago found that there was always—always—something to be learned, whatever turned up. And a complete foot was not to be sneered at.

The boot, oozing water, was placed, sole down, on the massage table. With a pair of metal shears from the plane, Gideon sliced it open from the top down, first at the back, then down the front, and then—very carefully—over the instep, while John held it upright for him. When he had finished, he peeled the halves of leather apart, snipping a little more at the sole where it was necessary to get the halves completely spread. The few falling-apart shreds of sock still present were picked off and put aside.

"Wow," breathed Lyle.

"Whoa," said Harvey. "Fantastic."

The skeletal foot, *ossa pedis,* lay upon the bed of clean, moist, white sand that covered the sole like an illustration in an anatomy text. Only a few of the phalanges—the toes—had been disarranged. The four men silently admired it for a few seconds, until Harvey abruptly sang out: "Lunch time, we got chicken fingers, we got barbecue chips, Twinkies, uh, we got Ding Dongs, uh, uh . . ."

"You got Ho Hos?" John asked hopefully.

"Of course, Ho Hos. Uh, Zingers, uh—"

"You guys go ahead," Gideon said. "I want to look this over a little more. I still have a sandwich left. I could use a Coke or something, if there is one."

The Shertz brothers, with chicken fingers on their minds and their interest in bones exhausted, retired to the Cessna for their meal.

"John, give me a hand with the table, will you?" Gideon said. By now the sun had started down and the massage table was no longer fully shielded by the thatched roof. "I don't want the bones baking in that hot sun. They've been in the water too long; they'll split if they dry too fast."

"Thanks," he said after they moved the heavy table a couple of feet. "Go get yourself something to eat if you want, John. I'm fine here."

"Nah, I'm fine, too, Doc."

Gideon stood looking down at the foot again. His sunglasses, smeared with perspiration and sunscreen, were laid on the table. He'd already made his first determination: The foot and the mandible were from two different people. You didn't see feet like this in twenty-five-year-olds. The signs of arthritis in the joints, especially the metatarsals, the incipient osteoporosis, and the trivial and not-so-trivial deformities that sadly but predictably plague the ageing shoed (or booted) human foot suggested a minimum age in the fifties and probably older. The grainy look and feel of the bone went along with this; nothing like the young, baby-bottom smoothness of the mandible. As to sex . . .

"Well, you know," John said brightly, "maybe I'll just go see what the situation is with those Ho Hos, after all."

"Hm? Okay, sure," Gideon mumbled abstractedly.

"I'll bring you that Coke when I come back."

"Uhm."

As to sex, he wouldn't want to make a guess at this point; not with just a foot to go on. The bones were neither too big and robust to be female, nor too gracile to be male. There was a method, not a hundred percent reliable but better than guessing, for determining sex from combined measurements of the talus and calcaneus, but it took discriminant function analysis to do it, a statistical technique requiring a table of coefficients carried out to the fifth decimal place. And that he didn't have. Besides which, the only measuring instruments the Shertzes had come up with were a metal tape measure and a yardstick, neither of which could come close to handling the tricky measurements involved on these asymmetrical, uniquely shaped bones.

There was also a way to estimate height from the length of the metatarsals, the long bones of the foot, but that, too, would have to wait, and for the same reasons.

For the moment, he was absorbed in looking closely at

the calcaneus, which he now held in his left hand, turning it this way and that to examine the rough, curving, asymmetrical surfaces. Yes, this was a row of tiny exostoses—little spicules of bone—just forward of the calcaneal tuberosity, on the underside. And another little ridge that didn't belong there, running longitudinally just in front of it, and a third bumpy, inch-long crest of bone on the upper side, where the bone was narrowest, behind the posterior articular surface. These irregularities were calluses, the strong, bony reinforcements the body laid down to heal fractures and strengthen repairs.

So this heel bone had been broken at least three times, maybe more (bone calluses could disappear completely, given long enough). All appeared to have been "stress" or "fatigue" fractures: not the result of sudden compression or blunt-force trauma, but of the building-up of repeated, relatively low-grade stress over time. Gideon examined the rest of the bones, looking for similar injuries. Nothing. So here was a man that had fractured his heel bone three times, but had never, as far as he could tell, broken any of the other bones in his foot.

Now that was interesting. The usual fatigue- or stress-related foot injuries—from walking, running, jogging—were found in the metatarsals and the toes; not in the calcaneus. Heel spurs, yes; you got those in spades, but not fractures, not usually. When you did see stress fractures of the calcaneus, however, they tended to be found in people who jumped or otherwise dropped from heights, with recreational parachutists and hang-gliding enthusiasts topping the list of orthopedic surgeons' favorites. In those cases, however, associated injuries of the other bones of the foot could be expected; you didn't just break your heel bone, you snapped a couple of metatarsals or crunched a cuneiform as well.

But recurring stress fractures of the calcaneus with *no* accompanying damage? Repeated forceful impact of the heel, but not the rest of the foot, against an unyielding surface? He had come upon the phenomenon in monographs before, but never in the flesh (so to speak). It was called "rider's heel," and it came from the way cowboys typically dismounted a horse, swinging their right leg—never the left—up and over the saddle and coming down hard on their foot, their right foot, smack on the narrow, raised heel of their boot. Again and again and again. Ouch. And the older the bone got, the thinner the cortex, the less dense the trabeculae, the more susceptible it would be to breaking.

Putting everything together, that seemed to mean—

"Lyle and Harvey—they need to know how long you're gonna be." Gideon, deep in his ruminations, hadn't noticed John's return.

"Not long." He turned toward the plane and called: "If you can let me have a carton"—with his hands he indicated something shoe-box-sized—"and some paper for packing material, we can be on our way in ten minutes."

"Roger, prof," Harvey yelled back.

Gideon turned back to John, gesturing at the bones with a sweep of his hand. "It's Magnus, all right, John."

"Yeah?" John said, looking at the bones with renewed interest. "You *know* that?"

"Ninety percent sure," Gideon said with a shrug. "Well, make it eighty-five." He went over his reasoning, using the small, folding magnifying glass the brothers had provided, to show John the calluses, which John dutifully, respectfully, fingered.

"Of course," Gideon said, "for all I know, there might be other things that would account for a repeatedly stress-fractured right calcaneus without signs of injury to the metatarsals or anything else—but I sure as hell can't think of any likely ones."

"Hold on a minute, Doc. If you don't have his left, uh, calcaneus, how do you know that wasn't broken, too? And if it was, then this dismounting theory wouldn't work, would it?"

"No, it wouldn't. And, of course it would have been nice to have the left foot, too, but there isn't very much I can do about that, is there?"

"Hey, don't go all defensive on me, Doc. I'm just asking a question."

"Who's getting defensive?" Gideon said.

But of course he was. He'd just completed what seemed to him a neat bit of reasoning, and he could have used a little amazement, or at least approbation, and not a string of skeptical questions. "Come on, John, you're a cop. How often do you get every single piece of evidence you'd like to have? You play the hand you're dealt, and this particular hand plays out to one conclusion: Magnus Torkelsson."

It wasn't just the foot, he pointed out. Everything added up, and there was nothing to lead off in any other direction. An airplane from the Hoaloha Ranch, lost since the very night Magnus flew off in it and disappeared; a woman that nicely fit the description of his pilot;—he ticked the items off on his fingers—and a male of advanced age who, as it happened, had spent a lot of time in the saddle. How many other people—missing people—would that combination fit?

John held up his hands. "Hey, if you say it's him, that's good enough for me. Magnus it is. What do I know?"

A smile twitched at the corners of his mouth, and then the skin around his eyes crinkled up, and then they both were laughing.

"I'm sorry I got defensive there, John."

"No problem, Doc."

There was only one thing that nagged at him a little, he admitted, and that was the fact that he'd known too much about the case to start with. Forensic anthropology was like anything else: You tended to find what you were looking for. It wasn't supposed to work that way. When he consulted for the police or the FBI, he made a point, when possible, of *not* knowing anything about the suspected identity of the remains he was to examine: not the sex, not the age, not the race, nothing. But here he'd been aware of how old Magnus was, of his sex, of the fact that he rode a horse, of the age and sex of the pilot, even of her bulimia. And what do you know, his analysis of a *very* few bones had confirmed every single expectation. That was slightly worrisome: Had he over-reached for what he'd believed, *a priori,* to be the facts?

"Nah," said John airily. "You're never wrong about that kind of thing. Well, not that often."

"I appreciate the vote of confidence, if that's what that was. Anyway, I have an ace up my sleeve. When I was checking the bones for fractures, I saw that a couple of toe bones were missing after all, and when I took a closer . . . well, take a look at the middle phalanges of the second and third toes."

"The, uh, middle . . . ?"

"These two," Gideon said. "The distal phalanges—the outermost parts, the segments that had the toenails—are the missing ones, and these two are the ones that adjoined them."

"They are?" John said, bending closer. "They don't look like the others, do they? They're barely half as long. And they're thinner, and they, like, come to a point, almost . . ."

"The toes have been amputated, John. The distal phalanges and a segment of the middle phalanges have been
removed. And when that happens the bone that's left—the
proximal portion of the middle phalanges, in this case—is
likely to develop osteoporotic atrophy over time and become resorbed——absorbed back into itself—starting at the
end where the amputation occurred. That's why they look
that way."

"So this happened a long time ago?"

"Oh, yes. Years and years. Decades, probably."

"And when you say 'amputation,' you mean by a doctor? An operation? Not some kind of accident?"

"No way to tell, not anymore. There's been too much
remodeling. The site of the original separation is long
gone."

John was looking a little confused. "So . . . why is this
an ace up your sleeve? What does it tell you?"

"It doesn't tell me anything, but it ought to tell the
Torkelssons something. It's a 'factor of individuation,' as
we so grandly call it. If it turns out that Magnus Torkelsson
had two toes missing—which it will, I think—that'll settle
it for good. Case closed, all doubts resolved."

Harvey had brought the materials he asked for, and
Gideon began wrapping the individual bones loosely in
newspaper. "You wouldn't happen to know, would you,
John?"

"If he was missing any toes?" He shook his head. "I
wouldn't know. He didn't have a limp; nothing I noticed,
anyway."

"Well, we'll be seeing Felix tonight in Waikiki," Gideon
said, fitting the cover on the carton with the satisfying sense
of having accomplished what he'd come for. "He'll know."

SEVEN

"WHOO," said John, having completed his first long swallow of the frosted Mai Tai that had been placed before him. "I'm in heaven."

So was Gideon. After the stagnant heat of Maravovo Atoll, the ocean breezes of Waikiki Beach, perfumed with gardenia and frangipani, flowed over them like balm. They had arrived at the Honolulu airport two hours earlier and had taken a taxi to the Royal Hawaiian Hotel—the posh, venerable "Pink Palace"—where the desk clerk had apologized for not having two ocean-view rooms available, but Gideon, if not John, was happy to be looking out over the green canopy of the giant banyan tree and the quiet, shaded gardens, rather than the jammed beach with its pungent smells of sunscreen and its multitudes of bare, glistening, not-so-beautiful bodies slow-cooking on their roll-up straw mats.

There had been a message from Felix waiting for them:

He had been delayed at a meeting on Kauai and would not be back until five. And he had to be on a red-eye flight to San Francisco later in the evening, but with any luck he would meet them for a drink at six-thirty at the House Without a Key, the open-air restaurant-bar at the Haleku-lani Hotel. They had showered and changed, then walked the two blocks down Kalakaua Avenue from the Royal Hawaiian to the Halekulani, both of them slightly dazed by an enjoyable sense of disjunction, of disconnect. Only a lit-tle while ago they had been on a tiny speck of land in the Pacific, one of the most remote and isolated places in the world, with nothing but black flies and land crabs for com-pany (but plenty of those). Now, later that same day, here they were on one of the most cosmopolitan boulevards to be found anywhere, fording streams of avid shoppers, tourists, and locals, seemingly of every race and sub-race on the planet. There were flip-flop-shod surfers toting boards on their heads or under their arms, perspiring, grim-faced joggers, dignified Japanese elders walking with their hands behind their backs and taking in the sights, tight clumps of nervous-looking Eastern Europeans, prim Asian ladies handing out brochures for shows and bus tours, and piratical, dissipated men with parrots and macaws on their shoulders ("What do you say, Jack, take a picture with one for ten bucks, with all four for twenty bucks?").

The terrace at the House Without a Key, by contrast, was an oasis of taste and tranquility. When they arrived, the evening's Hawaiian music was just getting underway. They had listened contentedly to the soft, agreeable melodies and the surf for a while, then ordered drinks—John's Mai Tai and a Fire Rock Pale Ale from Kona for Gideon.

"Pretty romantic place," Gideon said, taking in the

scene. The musicians—a guitarist, a slack-key guitarist, a Hawaiian falsetto singer with an achingly sweet voice—and a smiling hula dancer performed on a low bandstand beneath an ancient kiawe tree, with the purple sea and the setting sun at their backs. The drinkers and diners sat at tables under a tropical sky of deepening blue-green tinged with rose. Off to the left, the unmistakable profile of Diamond Head loomed, slowly losing its folds and hollowed contours to shadow.

"It sure is," John replied. "So what am I doing here with you?"

They settled back to watch the hula dancer, an elegant, fawnlike creature in a long flowered dress, perform a few more graceful numbers, but a part of Gideon's mind kept turning back to Magnus Torkelsson.

"John, I've been thinking—"

"Uh-oh."

"There are some things about this whole case that are starting to bother me."

John's arms flew out to either side. "What, now it's *not* Magnus? Why do you always do this, Doc? You know what my boss says? Every time we call you in on something, no matter how simple it looks to be, by the time you get finished—"

"No, no, it's Magnus, I'm not changing my mind on that."

"What, then?"

"Well, something doesn't quite compute. Something's missing."

"What's missing?"

"How do they know for sure what happened to him?"

"They don't, for sure. Isn't that why we went out there?"

"No, I mean how do they know that he flew off in the first place? How do they know that's what happened to him? Is it just that the plane was missing, and Magnus was missing, and the pilot was missing, so they assumed . . ."

"Oh, I see what you mean. I don't know the answer to that, Doc. In fact I don't know a whole lot about any of it; they don't like to talk about it, for which you can't exactly blame them. But I guess Magnus must have told someone before he left—I don't know—Dagmar, probably. He probably called his sister."

"No, if he'd done that they'd have known where he was going. But they didn't. Remember? At dinner last night? They were trying to figure out where he was headed."

"So? Maybe he felt safer if no one knew where he was going to be. Maybe he thought it was safer for *them*."

Gideon shook his head. "Could be, but something still seems off to me. Maybe it's just that the whole thing—I mean the murder, the disappearance, the will, the finding of the plane—it all seems too tidy, too wrapped up. No loose ends. Don't you get that feeling?"

John thought it over, had another long swallow, and shrugged. "Nope. No loose ends is good, Doc. What do you want loose ends for?"

"Well, you're the expert," Gideon said, leaning back, almost but not quite convinced. "Julie thinks I'm developing a suspicious turn of mind. Maybe she's right."

"She is right. You gotta stop hanging around dead people. I could use another Mai Tai. You want another beer?"

BY the time Felix strode onto the terrace, the sun had dropped below the horizon, Diamond Head was a gray-black silhouette, and the lights were blinking on in the hillside houses. Jets coming into the airport a few miles away gleamed white, still lit by the vanished sun.

"Sorry I'm so late, boys! Sorry I have so little time!" His voice, marginally muted so as not to interfere with the music, was as hearty and honking as ever, but there was a hassled look around his eyes as he dropped his flight bag on the terrace, heaved a great sigh, and flopped into a chair. His linen sport coat was rumpled and limp, his trousers wrinkled. Closing his eyes, he took a moment to collect himself. "What a life," he said under his breath—or as close to under his breath as he ever got—and then to John and Gideon: "Your rooms okay? No problems?"

They assured him, with thanks, that their rooms couldn't have been nicer, and Gideon asked him what he wanted to drink. Also, they were thinking of getting something to eat. Did he want to order anything?

"I wish!" he said wearily. "But nothing for me, thanks, I don't really have time to eat." Wistfully, he eyed John's Mai Tai. "And, unfortunately, I have a truckload of work to do on the flight, so I better keep a clear head. So," he said, turning to Gideon. "How did it go? What's the story?"

"Well—" Gideon began.

"Ah, what the hell, it's been a long day." Felix twisted in his chair and waved their waiter over. "Good evening, Sanford. May I trouble you for a martini, straight up? Gin, two olives. And while you're at it, why don't you bring us some *pupus?* One order of your coconut shrimp, an order of chips and guacamole, and, oh, um, an order of vegetable spring rolls, just to keep us healthy. Better make it snappy, I don't have much time."

"Yes, sir, Mr. Torkelsson," said Sanford. "I'll be right back."

"On second thought," Felix shouted after him, "make the martini a double! Thank you, my friend!"

Watching him is like watching a character in a play, Gideon thought. Everything he does is larger than life, a performance played to the last row in the balcony. He'd be a knockout in a courtroom.

"I thought you wanted a clear head," John said.

Felix shrugged. "Oh, it'll be clear enough. It's only legal work," he said with one of his belly laughs, loud enough so that a woman at the next table scolded him. "Will you kindly keep it down there? We're trying to listen to the music."

"Sorry, sorry, sorry," Felix responded, immediately lowering his voice. "It won't happen again. So," he prompted once more—and even his attempt at a whisper brought an irritated look from the next table. "What's the verdict? Have we caught up with dear old Uncle Magnus at last?"

"It looks like it," Gideon said and told him what they'd found: the mandible of a strongly built young woman in her mid twenties whose dentition showed that she'd apparently suffered from bulimia—

"Ha. Claudia," whisper-shouted Felix.

—and a boot in which there were the foot bones of a man in his fifties or older, which had suffered stress fractures of a kind that suggested its owner had been a horseman.

"And Magnus," Felix said with a nod. His martini had come and he downed a little of it, gratefully closing his eyes. "A boot with a foot in it," he said and gave a little shiver. "That's kind of . . . did you bring it back? Do you have it with you?"

"The salvage team took it back. They thought there'd be less hassle if they did it, because Security and Customs are used to them bringing in all kinds of weird things. They also have a few other things they found—a pair of glasses, a comb, I forget what else."

"A heel—probably from the same boot—a kitschy souvenir shaped like the Big Island, and a mug with a hula dancer on it," John said promptly. "We figured somebody might recognize them."

"Good idea," Felix said.

"Does any of it sound familiar to you?"

Felix rolled the martini around his mouth while he considered. "Not really. The cup with the dancer on it, maybe. I'm not sure. There must be ten million of those around."

"Well, some or all of it may have been the pilot's. But the boys are dropping everything off at Axel's when they get back," Gideon said. "All part of the service. Maybe somebody else will see something they remember."

When the appetizers arrived they helped themselves, with Gideon and Felix digging into the spring rolls and coconut-crusted shrimp, and John happily confining himself to the guacamole and thick, Maui-style potato chips.

"Gideon," Felix said, "it sounds like you've already identified him from the bones. Why do you need the other things—the cup and all?"

"I wouldn't say we need them. Partly, we had them sent back because they could be his last effects, and there might be some sentimental value to someone in them."

"In a boot heel?"

"You'd be surprised. But the main thing is that on something like this, people are likely to have lingering doubts. Sometimes they don't surface till years later. So the more confirmation we have, the better. Which brings me to the question I want to ask you: Did your uncle have anything the matter with his right foot?"

Felix looked puzzled. "Well, you just said he'd fractured—"

"No, aside from that. Anything else?"

Felix looked more puzzled. "Not that I know of. Like what?"

"Like missing a couple of toes," John said.

Felix's reaction went beyond theatricality. His mouth clenched, his eyes bulged, and with a resounding snort a thin double-spray of gin and vermouth exploded from his nostrils, further displeasing the party at the next table, who instantly began gathering up their drinks. In the space of five seconds, Felix's face registered surprise, confusion, consternation, doubt, and uncertainty, more or less in that order, all while coughing. Startled, John and Gideon glanced at each other, wondering what it was they'd set off.

"Felix, are you okay?" John asked, but Felix, choking away, lowered his head and waved him silent.

A final splutter, a mopping of lips and beard, a dab at his tearing eyes, and he was ready to attempt speech again, emitting a strangled "Toes?"

"That's right," Gideon said. "The foot had two missing toes."

"Yes, but are you sure—" Another brief episode of choking, during which Felix held up his hand again and downed a slug of his martini, this time managing to keep it in him. "How do you know they didn't disappear after he died? I mean, for gosh sakes, practically everything else got carried off by the fishes, didn't it? Couldn't they have—"

"No, these were amputated long before. You can tell."

"My God," Felix breathed. He shook his head slowly back and forth, then, surprisingly, giggled. "Oh, lordy."

He was raising his glass again when John, not the most patient of men, finally exploded. "*What,* already? What? WHAT?"

Felix ran his tongue around his lips. "Magnus wasn't missing any toes."

Now it was Gideon's turn. *"What?"*

"Torkel was the one with the mangled foot. He got it

caught in a threshing machine back when I was a little kid. In the sixties."

"*Torkel?*" cried John. "His *brother* Torkel?"

"Yes, of course his brother Torkel," Felix said. "How many Torkels do you think there are around here?"

"Slow down a minute, you've really lost me now," Gideon said. "I thought Torkel was the one who was shot and killed—before Magnus even took off in the plane."

Felix nodded gravely. "That's right. Shot, killed . . . and buried on the ranch eight years ago."

The three men looked at each other. John put down his glass. "Or not," he said.

EIGHT

THEY continued staring at each other, the churning of their minds almost audible. In the background the surf hissed and the gentle strains of the Hawaiian Wedding Song hung in the air. And then came the fusillade of questions, the three of them talking at once. If the skeletonized corpse in the Grumman was Torkel's, whose bullet-riddled body had lain buried in his grave on the Big Island for the last ten years? Magnus's? If so, what had really happened the night of the murder? If not, where was Magnus? Either way, how could everyone—family, friends, police—have mistaken someone else's body for Torkel's? And what had been the point of the deception, if deception there had been?

Felix had the answers to some, but not all, of the questions. "You have to understand, the body was burnt beyond recognition—"

"The body was burnt?" Gideon said, surprised.

"Beyond recognition," Felix said, "and then some."

"You knew that, Doc," John said. "I told you on the drive up to the ranch."

"No, you didn't. You told me Torkel was shot, and the headquarters building was burned down—"

"Right, that's what I said."

"But you never explicitly . . . okay, never mind. If the body was burnt beyond recognition," he asked Felix, "what made everybody so sure it was Torkel in the first place? Why couldn't it have been Magnus? Neither one of them was around anymore."

"Well, no, but he called Dagmar. He called her from the airport before he took off."

"Ha," said John, with a self-satisfied glance at Gideon. Then he frowned. "Wait a minute, *who* called Dagmar?"

"Magnus . . ." Felix blinked. "That is, Torkel. It must have been Torkel. But he *said* he was Magnus."

"And Dagmar couldn't tell the difference between their voices?" Gideon asked.

John heard the overlay of skepticism. "You don't buy that, Doc?"

"Well, I'm not sure. If I got on the phone to you and tried to sound like Felix, could I fool you?"

"Of course not, but that's because *nobody* sounds like Felix."

"Nobody sounds like anybody else, to the people close to them. The distinctive characteristics of a particular voice might be indefinable, but they're immediately recognizable."

"What about mimics?" Felix asked. "They can be amazing."

Gideon shrugged. "Was Torkel a mimic?"

"Well . . . who knows? But you have to remember, the two of them sounded a whole lot alike to start with."

"That's true," John agreed. "They did."

"Okay," said Gideon. "Forget it. I was just thinking out loud. Go ahead, Felix. What'd he tell her?"

Felix frowned. "If I remember right, Magnus just said—I mean Torkel, dammit—Torkel just told her that . . . that *Torkel* had been killed and he had to leave for a while because he was in danger himself."

" 'He' supposedly being Magnus," Gideon said.

Felix nodded. "And 'his brother' supposedly being Torkel. Hoo."

"What else did he say?" John asked.

"I don't really remember, John, it was ten years ago. I was just trying to give you the general idea. He probably said . . . hell, I don't know what he probably said. Whatever it was, Dagmar took him at his word. Why wouldn't she? She was excited, confused, she suddenly gets this panicked phone call in the middle of the night . . ."

While the sentence drifted away unfinished, the three of them sat quietly, listening to the rhythmic murmur of the surf and hearing occasional bits of conversation—people talking about normal, everyday things: whether there was weekend laundry service at their hotel, tomorrow's shopping schedule, the pros and cons of going to the Don Ho show at the Beachcomber. "So how's the wire rope business these days?" floated by them as distinctly as if the speaker were at their table, along with the stifled yawn that followed it. The musicians had either taken their break or else wisely quit until they were no longer competing with Felix.

"Okay," Gideon said, having pushed his glass around in circles for a minute or so. "That explains why Dagmar thought it was Magnus on the line. But it doesn't explain why the police bought the idea that the burned body was Torkel's."

"Sure it does, Doc," John said. "You got two brothers. One of them gets burned to a crisp—oh, sorry, Felix. The other one takes off so the same thing doesn't happen to him. The cops know—they *think* they know—which one took off. So whatever pile of ashes is left after the fire— damn, sorry about that, Felix—has to be the other one."

Gideon was unconvinced. "Look, when a body is burned up in a fire, it doesn't completely turn to ashes or cinders. There's always something left. Even when it's professionally cremated at high temperature, they have to pulverize what's left to turn it into ash, and even then a forensic specialist—"

"Gideon, you're assuming they brought in experts, consultants," Felix said. "They didn't. This is not Seattle we're talking about." He smiled. "As far as I know, there aren't any skeleton detectives anywhere near Waimea."

Gideon blew out his cheeks. "Body burned beyond recognition, supposed perps never even identified, let alone convicted, brother disappeared . . . boy, I tell you, I'm starting to see a few holes in this thing."

"Come on, Doc," John said, "there's no such thing as a homicide case without some holes in it, you know that. It's never cut-and-dried. The cops can never put every single piece together. You go with the preponderance of the evidence. Isn't that what you were telling me on the atoll?"

"This is different," Gideon said. "In this case they didn't even know who got killed. What else did they get wrong?"

"Now hold your horses just one minute," Felix said heatedly. "You're not suggesting Torkel killed Magnus, are you? Because that would be—"

"No, of course not," Gideon said, surprised by the question.

"Damn it, Gideon, Torkel wouldn't have known how to fire a gun. They didn't even *own* a gun. Not a handgun, anyway."

"Well, no, that's not completely true," John said. "There was a gun in the house. At least there used to be."

"There was?" Felix seemed honestly surprised.

"It was Andreas's, from the Second World War. Torkel got it out for me once when he was showing me around the place. A classic; one of the early Walther PPKs, made back in the forties. Probably worth a fair amount of money."

"But that was an *antique*. You couldn't shoot that thing."

"Didn't say you could," John said.

"Look, I just get the impression that you two are trying to make it sound like my uncle was some kind of monster, like he killed his own brother—"

As people at nearby tables looked around, John raised his palms in a shushing gesture. "Take it easy, Felix."

"Felix, nobody's implying that," Gideon said. But now he was wondering just what kind of nerve he'd hit.

"Okay, okay," Felix said tightly. "Sorry."

"After all," Gideon said, "at this point we don't even know for sure that Magnus is dead, do we?"

Felix's tension held for another moment, then slackened. Another belly laugh, but a quiet one, rumbled out of him. "Well, if he's not, who'd we bury in that grave?"

At which point they realized they had come full circle, back to the question they'd started with. "Damn, I better go," Felix said, jumping up. "I can't miss my plane. Sorry I got a little excited there. Look, you two. The others know more about this than I do. You'll be talking to them tomorrow, when you get back to the ranch. See what they have to say."

"You won't be there?" John asked.

"No way. I won't be back until Sunday night." He glanced at his watch. "But I think I'll give Inge a call from the airport, if that's okay with you; let her know what you've found, kind of break it to her gently. She can tell the others. I mean, this is going to be kind of a shock. I think it might be better if it came from one of the family. Is that all right with you, Gideon, or did you want to be the one . . . ?"

"No, go ahead. I'd just as soon they got it from you. I can fill them in on whatever details they want."

"Good. And thanks for the good work, both of you. Go ahead and splurge on dinner. Get the crab-crusted mahi-mahi; can't be beat. I've already taken care of the check."

When Felix had gone, Gideon sat there, slowly shaking his head. "Unbelievable. What have you gotten me into here?"

John grinned at him. "Hey, correct me if I'm wrong, but aren't you the guy who wanted a few loose ends?"

GIDEON had stayed at the Royal Hawaiian before, with Julie on their third anniversary. Their favorite part of the day had been sunrise, when they would go down and pick up a cup of wonderfully fragrant Kona coffee—not a blend, but the pure, pungent stuff—at the hotel's coffee bar the moment it opened at six A.M. and carry it a few steps to the pristine beach. There were no crowds yet, no smells of lotions and oil and mustard, no grizzled, wizened, once-and-always beach boys hawking rides in outrigger-canoes. Their only company was a few strollers, usually of "a certain age," carrying their shoes and quietly meandering hand in hand along the surf line, and one or two treasure-hunters, heads down, utterly absorbed, prowling the beach with their metal-detectors in hopes of buried gold. And of course the ragged, ever-present line of surfers (did they ever come in, even at night?) bobbing hopefully a few hundred yards out, endlessly waiting for the big one.

The weather had been cool, even a little chilly, at that time of day, the sand pure and sweet-smelling—the big hotels swept and raked their beachfronts clean every night—and the act of sitting quietly on the firm, fresh, damp surface with cardboard cups of steaming coffee while the first rays of the sun lit up, first the upper stories of the big hotels, then Diamond Head, and finally the blue Pacific, seemed to cleanse the mind of its clutter and get it ready to take on another day.

That was what Gideon had in mind for the morning after the meeting with Felix (he was stared at in amazement when he suggested, not with any real expectation, that John join him), but when he awoke at five-thirty there was a steady drizzle wafting down, so instead he had his coffee in the open-air coffee bar itself, dopey with sleep, in a pink chair beside a pink wall covered with black-and-white photographs of laughing Golden Age luminaries who had once stayed there: tiny Shirley Temple greeting admirers with her usual bubbly aplomb in front of a surfboard with "Aloha, Captain Shirley" on it; Esther Williams; William Powell; Carol Lombard; an uncomfortable-looking Bing Crosby getting soaked in an outrigger; Spencer Tracy signing autographs on the beach; an aged Duke Kahanomoku showing an attentive young Joe DiMaggio how to use a paddle.

The coffee, strong and hot, got his wits going, and although they immediately turned to the Torkelsson mess, he wasn't able to make any more sense of it than they'd been able to do over dinner the night before. The most reasonable explanation seemed to be that Torkel had taken on Magnus's identity as part of his effort to stay alive. If the killers and the rest of the world were under the impression that it was Torkel they had killed and Magnus who had escaped, it would be the non-existent Magnus they would be hunting.

Reasonable, yes, but subjected to a little thoughtful scrutiny during their walk back to the Royal Hawaiian—

they had returned along the beach, nearly deserted now and softly illuminated by the tiki lanterns of the beachfront hotels—the scenario had begun to come apart at the seams, or at least to spring a few leaks.

How likely was it, Gideon had asked, that the killers wouldn't be aware of which of the brothers they'd shot? And if they were, what good would it do Torkel to run around pretending to be Magnus? Even if they weren't, why would they be *hunting* whichever brother had escaped? Surely, murdering one of them, chasing the other one off the island, and burning down the ranch headquarters had made their point for them. After all, as John knew better than he did, organizations bent on retribution—especially organizations that chose to hire hitmen—didn't go around expending time and effort to assassinate people if it didn't serve a utilitarian, usually monetary, end.

John had had some answers ready for him. What the killers thought or didn't think, knew or didn't know, was beside the point. The only thing that counted was what had been in Torkel's mind, and Torkel very likely had been scared witless, understandably so, and had done the first and most obvious thing that came to mind: make them think he was dead, and run for it. Possibly, after a few days he would have thought things through and come to a different conclusion, but he hadn't had a few days. From all they could tell, it appeared that his plane had gone down that same night, only a few hours after leaving the Big Island.

Gideon had had one more critical question: Why would he have lied to Dagmar, his own sister, claiming to be Magnus?

For that one, John had no ready answers. But both men knew that a complex case with no unanswered questions was a rare bird indeed. They all had inconsistencies, implausibilities that couldn't be explained. That didn't mean you couldn't resolve the case. You went, as they kept telling each other, with the preponderance of the evidence, and all the evidence here told the same story: Torkel had fled Hawaii, and he had done it pretending to be his brother. His motive was less demonstrable, but ninety percent certain nonetheless: to escape what he believed to be his own imminent murder.

Ninety percent certain to John, in any case. Gideon would have put it at seventy. Those loose ends again.

When the rain had shredded away into trailing wisps and moved out to sea, and the first hint of bronze appeared on the upper slopes of Diamond Head, Gideon took a second cup of coffee out to the beach to think things through a little more. But as it had in the past, the combination of sparkling salt air, sea breeze, and irresistible, world-renewing freshness wiped his mind happily clean of murder, deception, and other nastinesses, turning it toward happier thoughts of Julie, who was now well on her way, only a few hours from Honolulu.

It wasn't until he sat down for an early lunch/late breakfast with John at Cheeseburger in Paradise—"The best restaurant in Waikiki, bar none," according to John—that they got to talking about the Torkelssons again.

"John, let me ask you something. You said that the murder was a classic professional-type hit, correct?"

John rolled his eyes. "You're not gonna leave this alone, are you?"

"Well, what does that mean exactly—a classic gangland execution? A couple of shots to the back of the head, close-range?"

But the focus of John's attention was elsewhere. His eyes glowed at the sight of his "Five-Napkin Special," a monumental hamburger thickly lathered with two kinds of melted cheese and engulfed in glutinous Thousand Island dressing, which was reverentially placed before him by a waitress in a fake grass skirt worn over denim shorts. Beside the hamburger and its accompanying mound of french fries, Gideon's order of three scrambled eggs, bacon, hash browns, and the ever-present spear of fresh pineapple looked like the day's diet plate.

Gideon let him get a few bites down and repeated the question.

"Sure, that's one way," John said, "but in this case he was shot in the chest. I don't know about the range." He bit into the burger.

"So what's so classic about that?"

"First of all, there were two shooters involved." John mopped his chin with the first of the stack of paper napkins that had come with his meal. "You don't get that in your everyday run-of-the-mill amateur homicide."

"That's another thing. How do they know how many shooters there were?"

"They know because there were bullets from two different guns in him."

"Ah." Gideon ate scrambled eggs and toast for a while. "So why couldn't it have been one guy with two guns?"

"One guy with . . . is that supposed to be a serious suggestion? This killer carries two different caliber handguns, like Wyatt Earp or somebody, and shoots him once with each one?"

"It's *possible.*"

"Yeah, it's also *possible* that I'm going to leave the rest of this hamburger over."

"But not likely."

"No."

"Well, okay, two hitmen. Anything else?"

"Yeah, the place was burned to the ground with everything in it—machinery, heavy equipment, supplies. That goes along with the retribution scenario, too."

"So the police knew for sure it was arson?"

John nodded until he got a mouthful of food down and could speak again. "Yeah, I'm pretty sure they did. There was kerosene or gasoline or something splashed all over the place." John put down the hamburger and wiped his grease-smeared fingers. The neat stack of clean napkins was becoming rapidly smaller, the pile of crumpled ones growing. "Doc, what's up with you, why all the questions? If you got another one of your theories about what 'really' happened, I don't think I want to hear it."

"Just asking," Gideon said thoughtfully. And for once it was true. More or less.

THEY met Julie's flight from Seattle at Honolulu International, something she hadn't expected, and her transparently delighted expression on seeing Gideon went to his heart like a shaft of sunlight. *How lucky I am*—the thought rolled through him, and not for the first time—*how lucky I am that this terrific woman should be so happy to see ME.*

Julie was Gideon's second wife. His first, Nora, had been killed in an automobile accident nine years before, plunging him into a year of stonelike apathy. He had loved Nora with all his heart—although it was starting to seem like a long time ago now—and had thought himself incapable of ever feeling anything like it again. It was something he hadn't even wanted. And then, when his guard was down, or rather non-existent, out of nowhere had come this pretty, black-haired park ranger, Julie Tendler, brimming with wit and sparkle and intelligence. She had brought him back to life; he had actually fallen in love again, deeply and totally. They had been married now for seven years (astonishing thought!), and when it occurred to him occasionally how accidental their coming together had been, how very easily they might have missed each other and never met, how improbable that they should both have been unattached at that moment, he would have knocked on the nearest wood, were he not a professor of anthropology and above such things.

"But what are you doing in Honolulu?" she asked when she'd gotten over her surprise and they'd finished embracing. "I thought you two were going to meet me in Kona."

"That's a long story," said John.

They started their explanation on the bus to the interisland terminal, but it wasn't until they were ten minutes into the flight to Kona that they finished, with John having done most of the talking. When he was done, she sat there nodding her head and smiling in a manner that suggested some long-held theory had just been confirmed yet again.

"Amazing. This must be a record, Gideon. Not even two full days into a Hawaiian vacation and you're already knee-deep in bone fragments and mistaken identities. Usually, you wait a little longer. I have no idea how you do it."

"You want to know what I think?" John said from across the aisle. "I think he brings it on himself."

"Hey, they *asked* me, remember?" Gideon said. "What was I supposed to say?"

"My guess is," John went on, "that it's his aura. Julie, did you know he had an aura? On the astral plane?"

"It wouldn't surprise me," Julie said.

When the flight attendant brought the drink cart around, John and Gideon got coffee, Julie a bottle of water.

"John, do you happen to know what was in Torkel's will?" she said, breaking the seal and unscrewing the cap. "That is, how he divided the ranch, or if he divided it at all?"

"Torkel? No idea," said John. "These guys were kind of like two peas in a pod, so it was probably the same as Magnus's . . ." He paused, frowning. "But I'm just guessing, I don't really know. Why?"

"Well, if the person in the plane was really Torkel and not Magnus—am I getting the names straight?—and the one who was shot and buried back on Hawaii was really Magnus . . . whew . . . then that means that Magnus must have died first and Torkel must have died last."

"That'd be true," said Gideon, who saw where she was heading.

"All right, then. With these reciprocal wills that John was talking about, wouldn't that mean that Torkel's will was the one that really should have gone into effect? Since he was the last one alive?"

"Yeah, you're right," John said slowly. "Technically, Magnus would have left everything to Torkel—for what it looks like turned out to be only a few hours, till Torkel went down in the plane. And when *that* happened—"

"Torkel's will would have become the operational one," Julie said. "So does that mean that Magnus's will is going to be invalidated now?"

"Beats me," said John. "Good question."

"Beats me, too," said Gideon. "But the thing is, there's no proof that the one in the grave is Magnus."

"Who else could it be?" asked Julie.

"I have no idea. It probably *is* Magnus, but I doubt if 'probably' is going to be enough to get the question of wills reopened. Not after all this time."

"What if *you* looked at the body? Couldn't you tell?"

"You mean examine it? Get it exhumed?"

She nodded.

"Well, maybe, but who knows what condition it's in? It

was burned, remember, and it's been eight years. That's a long time."

"It's been eight years since Torkel died, too, and you identified him. From one foot."

"Yes, but . . ." Gideon grimaced. "I hate exhumations. They open up old wounds, bring a lot of pain to the family. Besides, nobody's asked me."

"Oh, they'll ask you," John said brightly, and to Julie: "It's his aura."

NINE

"IT seems to me," Malani said, "that we could settle the question for good by having Gideon look at the autopsy report. He was able to tell that the body in the plane was Torkel's; he might well be able to confirm that the body found at the fire was Magnus's." She smiled sweetly at him. "Isn't that right, Gideon?"

"I don't think Gideon came to Hawaii to spend his time looking at bodies," Hedwig said before he could answer. "He's gone more than enough out of his way to help us already. Let the man relax." She turned to him with the self-complacent expression of a potentate about to bestow a precious gift. "Gideon, I have some space tomorrow afternoon. How would you like an oiled lotus-leaf body wrap?" She threw a similarly magnanimous look at Julie. "You and your beautiful bride both?"

"Both of us in the same lotus leaf? Wouldn't that be a little uncomfortable?" he said in a weak attempt at a joke.

Hedwig laughed, but it was obvious that it had gone right by her. She pressed on. "And if you wanted to stay overnight, we could do Lapa'au colon cleanses for the two of you. They're sensational, you've never felt anything like it. What do you say?"

He managed not to flinch, but only barely. From the corner of his eye he could see Julie, with a terror-stricken expression on her face, silently signaling him *NO!*

"Thank you very much, but—"

"No, don't thank me. It's just my way of thanking *you* for what you've done for us."

"Without charge, no doubt," Inge said dryly.

Hedwig speared her with a look. "Funny."

Inasmuch as Inge's facilities were overflowing with a group of happy would-be cowboys from an Indonesian businessmen's association, they were meeting on the wide, covered back porch of Axel's and Malani's house. From where they sat, they overlooked peeling, red-painted stables and a split-rail-enclosed corral in which three or four wiry paniolos, in from the range for the day, were leisurely unsaddling and grooming their horses.

Beyond them, moist, green hills rolled one after another to the horizon, with occasional small clumps of cattle—roaming black dots—visible here and there on the slopes. Other than Felix, who was still on the mainland, they were all there to hear Gideon's report from Maravovo, mostly sitting in a semi-circle in old wicker armchairs, some white and some green, none of which had seen a fresh coat of paint in a decade: Dagmar, Hedwig, Keoni and Inge—sitting on the porch railing, swinging one booted foot—and Axel and Malani. Julie, who had been invited by both Malani and Axel to come, and who was curious, but who was a little reluctant about being one outsider too many, had moved her chair a few feet back from the others, so as to be out of the general flow of conversation.

As he'd said he would, Felix had telephoned Inge the night before with the bizarre news about Torkel; Inge had informed the others, and for the last twenty minutes they had been tossing around the same questions that Gideon and John had already been through, and they had arrived at the same answers and non-answers. There was little new information to emerge, beyond confirmation that Dagmar had indeed received a telephone call, purportedly from Magnus, in which he'd said that "Torkel" had been killed, and that he had to leave for a while and was flying out in the Grumman, but would be back in touch soon. Which was pretty much what Felix had told them the previous evening.

As to what exactly had been said during the telephone call, Dagmar was the only one who would have had direct knowledge, but the information about Torkel and/or the re-opening of these old wounds had very obviously taken a toll on her. Gideon had assumed that if anyone was going to contest the notion that it had actually been Torkel, not Magnus, on the telephone that night, it would have been Dagmar herself, but she accepted it with no more than a seemingly unconcerned shrug. Yes, it was possible. It was all so long ago that she barely remembered. And what exactly had he said? Another weary shrug—it was too long ago. It was all in the police report somewhere. What difference did it make now?

Gideon had never seen anyone age more in two days. She was like a ghost of herself, passive, uncertain, and deeply, deeply depressed. Her cigarillo had gone out after a couple of minutes and had never been relit. The feistiness, the agile wit, even the barbed petulance, were completely gone.

The foot bones from the plane were now in a covered shoe box beside Gideon's chair. Only Keoni and Inge had shown any interest in seeing them. The others had shaken their heads and turned away.

"That's really a nice offer, Hedwig," Gideon said now, "but actually I'd be happy to see what I could do about confirming Magnus's identity. Only . . ." He hesitated.

"Only what?" Malani asked.

"I don't know how much I could come up with from the autopsy report. A pathologist looks for different things than I do. It'd be better—if you really want to go ahead with this—if we had the remains exhumed."

"But he was all burned up," Inge said. She had come straight from a Paniolo Chuck Wagon Cookout with her Indonesians and was still in full Old West regalia: big red bandana around her neck, scarred, creaking leather chaps, and snakeskin boots with clinking spurs.

"I realize that," said Gideon, "but there's bound to be some skeletal material left. There might be something helpful."

"No, you're not following. There is no skeletal material. There's nothing."

"But . . . I thought he was buried."

"So did I," John said, equally surprised.

"Well, he *is* buried," Inge said, "but there's nothing but a little box of ashes. He was cremated."

"Cremated, after he was burned?" John exclaimed.

"They wanted to make sure he was really, *really* dead," Keoni explained.

Inge glared at him. "It was in his will."

Keoni shrugged. "A likely story."

The old Dagmar suddenly emerged. "Damn your smart mouth," she snapped. "Why don't you be quiet until you have something worth saying?"

Keoni, obviously used to this kind of treatment, grinned and raised his hands in surrender. "Yes, oh great queen."

Dagmar turned disgustedly away from him and slipped back into her depression.

"Okay, then," Gideon said, "the autopsy report would be the only route to go." He looked around at them. "But are you sure you want me to do this?"

Hedwig, Inge, and Axel looked uncertain. Keoni shrugged again. Malani said yes, but then caught their hesitation. "Well, I *think* so. We do, don't we? Auntie, what do you think?"

"What do I think?" Dagmar said to the porch roof. "I agree with Malani. Let it all come out. But what does it matter what I think? I'm an old lady, my day is done." They waited for more, and after a deep sigh she went on. "What I think is, I'm tired to death of the whole thing. You people do what you want, I don't care. I shouldn't have bothered to come at all, I should have just . . . oh, the hell with it. Do what you want, I don't care." Finally realizing her cigarillo was out, she fumbled for a match, but Axel was up in a flash to light it for her.

Returning to his chair, he waited politely until he was sure she'd finished speaking, then he put his glass of guava juice and soda down on the worn planks beside his chair and leaned forward, looking at the floor, with his elbows on his knees and his hands clasped. "I can't help wondering how much we really want to get into this again. That was a terrible time, and, yes, it would be good to understand everything, but it's in the past. Everything is all settled now. Do we really want to stir it up again? Say they shot the wrong man . . . that is, if it's Magnus that was shot . . . well, what difference does it make now? They're both dead, there's nothing we or anybody else can do about it anymore."

Hedwig and Inge were nodding their heads. "That's so,"

Inge said. "The more I think about it, the more I think maybe it'd be better to just let them rest in peace. Drop the whole thing."

"Whoa, now, folks, let's just wait a minute," John said gently. "You don't really have any choice. Things are going to get stirred up whether you want them to or not. I know this isn't any of my business, but this is a homicide we're talking about. You can't let the cops go on thinking one man was murdered when it was really someone else."

"That's true," Gideon said. "Even though I went out to Maravovo at your request, I have an obligation to tell the police what I found—given what it was I found."

"Are you saying we're going to have to bring the police into this again?" Axel asked plaintively. "More interviews, more depositions, all over again? We're still doing late-spring round-ups, for Christ's sake."

"Oh, Jesus," Inge said with a sigh, "now I *am* sorry we started the whole thing."

"We can take care of telling the police about it for you," John said. "They'll need to hear it from Doc anyway. Who handled the case? They didn't run it out of Waimea, did they?"

"No," Hedwig said, "some detective from Kona took it over. He was from the Investigation Division or something. Not a very nice man. Very unsimpatico."

"That'd be the CIS, the Criminal Investigation Section," John said. "We'll go talk to them. I know a guy there."

"Thank you," Inge said. "We appreciate that."

"But they're almost certainly going to want to follow up with you," Gideon told them. "This raises a lot of questions. I'm sure you can see that. I wouldn't be surprised if they reopened the case."

"Probably, but maybe not," John said. "They just might

want to bury the whole thing and forget about it, seeing as how they screwed up the first time. Cops are different from scientists, Doc. Sometimes the search for truth takes a back seat to covering their rear ends."

Gideon thought about that. "Not so different, maybe."

"Oh, bother," Hedwig muttered. "What are we supposed to tell them? It was ten years ago. Who remembers anymore?"

"I still don't see what difference it makes," Axel grumbled.

"Axel, honestly," said Malani with a shake of her head. "Of course it makes a difference. I don't understand you people. Don't you *want* to know what really happened?"

"Well, of course we want to know, Malani," Inge said. "It's just . . . it seems so . . . I don't know, morbid."

"To put it mildly," Axel said.

Dagmar brusquely spoke up. "Will they want to talk to me?"

"I'd sure think so," John told her. "I'd be surprised if they didn't."

A frail hand went to her forehead. She looked physically sick, Gideon thought. "I've lived too long," she said vacantly. "I'm too old to go through it again."

In the corral below them, a horse, freed from its saddle, had flopped to the ground and was scratching its back in the dirt, rolling, snuffling, raising clouds of dust. They watched one of the paniolos get it to its feet with no more than a couple of gentle *clucks* and a get-up motion with his arm. He was the oldest of the cowboys, a mahogany-colored Hawaiian who wore a flowered Hawaiian shirt and a ten-gallon hat with a dust-caked garland of flowers around the band. The other paniolos, younger, were in tank-tops and baseball caps, most of them worn backwards.

"The old guy," John said to Axel, "that's Willie Akau,

isn't it? He was foreman of my section back when I worked on the ranch."

"That's Willie," Axel said. "He's our ranch foreman now, sixty-nine years old and still going strong. And the kid rubbing down the big gray? That's his grandson. I'm trying to keep it in the family, just like Torkel and Magnus did. Only we're not big enough. There aren't enough jobs for all of them. We only have five of them here."

"I have two of our old-time paniolos at the dude ranch, too," Inge said. "But we had to let the rest go. Sad."

"I hired one to help out at Hui Ho'olana," Hedwig put in. "Hogan Lekelesa, but it didn't work out. For some reason, he just couldn't fit in."

"Listen, folks," John said, as the conversation continued to stray. "There's one other thing you probably want to be thinking about, because it might raise some trouble for you."

"The wills," said Keoni. "Hoo boy."

"That's right. I'm no expert, and neither is Doc here, but we were thinking this might mean that since Torkel died after Magnus—we think—that Magnus's will isn't valid, never *was* valid—"

"And *Torkel's* will goes into effect instead?" Hedwig exclaimed. "After all this time? Would they really do that?"

"Sheesh," Axel said, slumping in his chair. "What a mess."

"We don't know," John said. "But if you want my advice, you better talk to a lawyer."

"Felix is a lawyer," said Inge. "What did he say?"

"It never came up. We didn't think of it until we were on the way here."

Gideon, more out of curiosity than anything else, was trying to figure out a way of asking what was in Torkel's will without seeming to pry, when John, with his customary directness, saved him the trouble.

"So what did Torkel's will say? Does anybody know?"

At which there was a lot of throat-clearing and foot-shuffling until Inge reluctantly spoke up. "Well, sure, because his will had to go through probate before Magnus's could become effective. But we knew long before that," she said with a shake of her head.

At a somber party on his seventieth birthday, it seemed, a melancholy Torkel, suffering from intimations of mortality, had announced that he had recently changed his will, and he felt it his duty to inform them of the new provisions, so that they wouldn't be caught by surprise when the sad time came. Formerly, his will had been almost a carbon copy of Magnus's, but after much earnest thought he had arrived at the conclusion that it was best for people to earn their own way in life; that large inheritances were morally corrupting. Thus, he no longer had it in mind to leave the ranch to his descendants, either in pieces, as Magnus had done, or as a whole. According to his new will, the nieces and nephews would each have gotten token, lump-sum bequests of approximately $10,000. But the great mass of the estate—the Hoaloha Ranch and its remaining assets—would have been placed in the hands of a charitable trust, the profits going to a home for indigent Swedish merchant seamen in Stockholm, with the exception that his sister Dagmar be generously provided for (even more generously than under Magnus's will) for the rest of her life.

In other words, Gideon thought, if Magnus's will were to be invalidated now, and Torkel's will executed in its place, Hedwig, Inge, Axel, and Felix would lose everything. No wonder they were looking a little hangdog.

"Well, now, wait a minute," Inge said, "it may not be an issue at all. Gideon, let's say you look at the autopsy photographs or whatever, and you're not able to say for *sure* whether it is or isn't Magnus."

"Which is highly probable," Gideon said.

"So in that case, it wouldn't be *proven* that Magnus died before Torkel—or after him, or anything. Wouldn't that mean that Magnus's will would stand as it is? There'd be no concrete basis for going over to Torkel's will."

"Beats me," Gideon said. "That's way out of my line."

"Well, I tell you," Keoni said knowledgeably, "I've had a little experience with wills, and the way I think it's going to play out is that it'll all depend on whether the Seamen's Home wants to take us to court over it. They might not."

"They'd have to hear about it first," Inge said grimly, then laughed to show she was joking. "But the thing is, we're getting ahead of ourselves here. Felix gets back home tomorrow, doesn't he? We'll see what he says. In the meantime, let's see what Gideon turns up or doesn't turn up when he looks at the report."

Everyone appeared to agree with this.

Gideon looked at his watch. "It's four-fifteen. A little late to start with the police today. Let's wait till tomorrow."

That seemed to end the discussion. People were getting to their feet when Gideon exclaimed: "Oh, I almost forgot. The Ocean Quest people were going to drop off another box here. Did they ever do that? I mean, besides the foot bones."

"Yes, they did," Axel said. "We were out when they came, but they left them with Kilia—our housekeeper. It's on the kitchen counter. What is all that junk, anyway?"

When Gideon explained that it contained what might well be Torkel's last effects and the family showed interest, Malani went to get it. A minute later she was back. "No, it's not there," she said to Axel. "I wonder if she put it away somewhere when she cleaned up this morning."

"Probably—you know Kilia and her clean countertops. We can ask her when she comes in tomorrow."

As they broke up, John approached Keoni. "So Keoni . . . how does a *Haole* show his racial tolerance?"

Keoni grinned at him. "Hee, hee. By dating a Canadian."

GIDEON, Julie, and John had a quiet dinner—steak again—at the ranch house with Axel and Malani, during which, by mutual but unvoiced consent, no one talked about Torkel, Magnus, or the wills. They did, however, briefly discuss Dagmar.

"Is she all right?" John asked. "She looked like absolute hell."

"She sure did," Axel agreed. "Well, we've been raking up some pretty painful memories, but she'll be all right. You know what a tough old bird she is."

"She also went in for her annual lube and oil change this afternoon," Malani said, then laughed at the puzzled expressions on her guest's faces. "That's what she calls her annual physical at Kona Hospital. She stays overnight, and she's always worried before she goes in . . . you wouldn't think she was a hypochondriac, would you, but she is. But she always comes out with flying colors. She'll make it to a hundred, you'll see."

"Knock on wood," Axel said and demonstrated on the table top.

The rest of the dinner conversation was devoted to Axel's ranting about a letter to *West Hawaii Today* in which a local environmental group had complained about pollution of the land due to cattle manure.

"You should never, never confuse human waste with animal waste," he fumed. "Cattle manure is not your everyday, ordinary crap, and cow droppings are not cat droppings. Cattle manure is nothing more nor less than a dilute multi-nutrient fertilizer filled with micro- and macro-nutrients that *improve* the soil—nitrogen, phosphorous, potassium. Not only that, it has physical advantages. It improves carbon exchange capacity, it increases water filtration, it does all kinds of beneficial things. Now, of course, I admit that the smell can sometimes be a little—"

"What charming subjects we talk about at dinner," Malani mused.

Julie laughed. "At my house it's skeletons and exit wounds."

"It is?" She thought about it. "Well, all things considered, I think I'd rather eat at your house."

That was the high point of the meal, and breakfast the next morning was much the same, with no talk of what was really on everyone's minds. But afterward, when Malani and Axel left to attend to ranch affairs, John, Gideon, and Julie went out onto the porch. Breakfast had been a heavy affair of sourdough pancakes, thick-sliced bacon, potatoes, fresh pineapple and mangos, and pot after pot of thick coffee, and it felt good to stand out in the fresh morning air, looking out over the morning-mist-cloaked hills, feeling the dew on their faces and listening to the hollow, distant lowing of cattle they couldn't see.

"You know," Julie said, "I was just thinking that now there does seem to be another one of those loose ends you two were talking about."

"What's that?" Gideon asked.

"No body."

"Nobody?"

"No . . . body," Julie said. "No Magnus. Presuming it *is* Magnus, he's just a pile of ashes in a little box."

"You know, that's true," John said reflectively. "No body, no trial, no perps, a misidentified victim . . . I have to admit, that's a lot of loose ends." He looked at his watch. "Well, time to see if we can tie a few of them up. Doc, ready to go talk to the Waimea PD?"

Gideon hesitated. "I guess."

John frowned. "What's the problem?"

"The problem is, I'm going to barge in on some detective's turf, totally unasked, a complete stranger, a self-proclaimed 'expert' he's never heard of, and tell him he botched a case he handled eight years ago, not even getting right who got killed. I've been there before, John, and I can imagine his reaction. I know how I'd feel."

"Hey, don't worry about it. In the FBI, we come up against that kind of situation all the time. There are techniques for defusing it. See, the trick is you have to make them see you as helping them, not horning in. Besides, I used to work for Honolulu PD, remember? I know these people, I know how they think. Trust me. Just follow my lead, we'll get along great."

"John, you have my implicit trust," Gideon said, "but if it was the Kona CIS that handled it, why are we going to the Waimea PD?"

"Because they would have been the first on the scene, and the ones who opened the case. And they're the local police force. It's a matter of professional courtesy. See what I mean? There's a right way to do this."

THE Waimea Police Department was closed.

"Closed!" John yelled through the glass front doors at the stern and preoccupied-looking woman on the other side. In response to their thumping on the glass she had grudgingly emerged into the unlit vestibule from somewhere in back to bark at them: she couldn't let them in; the office was closed. In one corner of her mouth a cigarette jiggled up and down as she spoke.

"How the hell can you be closed?" John shouted. "What, there's no crime in Waimea on Sunday?"

Her eyes narrowed. She took the cigarette out of her mouth. Her lips, thin to begin with, disappeared altogether. "Do you have an emergency, sir?"

"No, we don't h—"

"Are you in immediate need of the assistance of a police officer?"

"No, dammit, but we need to talk to—"

"Office hours are Monday through Friday, eight to five."

"Look, lady," John yelled even louder, holding his identification up to the glass. "I'm trying to be polite here. My name is Special Agent John Lau of the Federal Bureau of Investigation, and I damn well want to talk—"

"Monday through Friday, eight to five." She stuck the cigarette back in her mouth and went back out of sight around a corner. John was left steaming, holding his card case up to the deserted vestibule. "Do you believe this?"

Gideon had been prudently silent throughout. "Well, now, John," he began as they walked back over the neatly trimmed lawns of the Civic Center toward the parking lot, "that was certainly an instructive example of—"

John cut him off, jabbing the air with a warning finger. "Don't . . . say . . . anything."

"ARE you planning to tell me where we're going?" Gideon asked after they'd been driving a while. "At some point?"

"Where we should have gone in the first place," John muttered, eyes fixed on the highway ahead. "The Kona CIS." He set his jaw. "And they better be open."

TEN

THE West Hawaii Criminal Investigation Section was on a side road off the coast highway, in the flat lowland country between Kona and the airport. Its neighborhood was, to put it mildly, unprepossessing. The idea, it seemed, had been to gather up most of the necessary but unlovely community services and deposit them in one out-of-the-way place, where they would be least likely to offend the eyes, ears, and noses of the sensitive: the garbage dump with its huge, surreal pile of wrecked cars waiting to be compacted, the Humane Society holding pens . . . and the West Hawaii CIS, which doubled as the Kona police station. A trailer and heavy-equipment repair yard and two huge, steaming piles of "organic waste" rounded out the complex, adding their own distinctive touches.

But the police building itself was reassuring: a modern, white, one-story structure, clean and well-maintained, on its own little island of concrete walkways and decorative plantings.

And it was open.

Even better, the detective they were sent to when John said they wanted to talk about the Torkelsson case turned out to be an old acquaintance. Detective Sergeant Ted Fukida had been a new sergeant in the Honolulu Police Department when John was a young cop there, and he remembered him.

"How could I forget you, Lau?" Fukida said, extending his hand. He was a waspish man in his fifties who looked as if he was fighting a low-grade toothache. "You're the guy who couldn't fill out an expense form right if his life depended on it. So how're you getting along with the Feebies?"

"Still can't fill out the forms right," John said. "Other than that, okay."

"Good-good. So what can I do for you? Please, tell me this is not official Feeb business."

He was a study in restlessness: flip, talky, and fidgety. At the moment, he was cracking gum between his teeth, bobbing back and forward in his swivel chair, and jiggling a toe against the plastic carpet protector underneath him.

"No, actually, it's old CIS business," John told him.

Fukida, they quickly learned, had not been the original case-handler. When the detective who had run the investigation had retired not long after the active phase was over, the case had been given to Fukida to oversee; more or less a pro forma gesture, inasmuch as unresolved homicide cases, while they might well go dormant, were never formally closed. There had been little to oversee, but the workmanlike Fukida had familiarized himself with the case file, which meant that it wasn't necessary to spend a lot of time bringing him up to snuff. More important, from

Gideon's point of view, since it hadn't been Fukida's case during the investigative phase, he had nothing to be self-protective about.

Which didn't mean that he was going to sit there and accept everything he was told; certainly not on the strength of Gideon's supposed reputation. (When John had somewhat effusively introduced Gideon as the world-famous Skeleton Detective, his response had been a laconic, gum-cracking, "Yeah, I think I might have heard of him.") Indeed, when Gideon began by stating—maybe a bit too baldly—that the skeleton in the Grumman was not that of Magnus Torkelsson but of his supposedly murdered brother Torkel, Fukida had interrupted before Gideon had gotten out his first complete sentence.

"What? You're out of your mind. What is this supposed to be, a joke? We had an autopsy, we took depositions, we had a—how the hell did you come up with a royally screwed-up story like that?"

"There was a royal screw-up, all right," John told him levelly, "but you guys made it."

Fukida's head rolled back and then round and round on his neck. Gideon caught a waft of spearmint.

"All I can say is, you two better have a good reason for wasting my time."

"It's all yours, Doc," John said. "Just wait, Teddy, you'll love this, this is great."

Thanks a lot, John, Gideon thought.

"Mmf," Fukida said, his eyes closed, continuing to stretch his neck muscles.

Gideon was generally good at telling when a cop was going to be open-minded about what forensic anthropology could do and when he was going to dig in his heels and resist, and Fukida didn't strike him as a promising student. Happily, however, the sergeant proved him wrong, although he was anything but an easy sell. With the foot bones laid out in their anatomical relationship on his desk blotter, he had put Gideon through a detailed show-and-tell drill, interrupting with questions and argument, until he had more or less satisfied himself that the old talus fractures were really there and they meant what Gideon said they did. By the time they were through with it, he seemed a happier, more engaged man, his toothache perhaps gone.

"Okay, I'll buy it," he said, handing the talus back to Gideon, who wrapped it in a Kleenex from Fukida's desk and put it in the box. "I like that. And I like the age stuff. It's interesting. But you want to know what I don't get? I don't get why this has got to be Torkel. Why isn't it Magnus? They both rode horses, right? They were both the same age, right? As far as I can see, it could be either one of them, or am I missing something?"

"Yeah, you're missing something," John said. "Maybe if you'd shut up for one minute, Doc here could get to it. You sure haven't changed, Teddy."

Gideon expected Fukida to flare up at that, but he laughed instead; a not-unfriendly noise somewhere between a snuffle and a one-note giggle. "Okay, 'Doc,' get to it. I'll try and be quiet. But that's not a promise."

"It's the toes," Gideon said. "The toes are the clincher." He pointed to the foot. "The two that go here are missing. The distal phalanges of the second and third toes. They were amputated decades ago, the result of an accident that Torkel had forty years ago. Magnus didn't have any missing toes."

Fukida stared at the remaining bones. He was frowning and working his lips; he seemed surprisingly disturbed; the gears spinning in his mind seemed just short of audible. In the silence, the low hum of conversations drifted from the other cubicles. "You're sure you never saw his face?" a detective asked kindly. "You wouldn't recognize him if you saw him again?"

"Okay, how do we know the toes just didn't get lost after he died, like just about every other damn bone in his body?" Fukida finally demanded. "What makes you so sure they were amputated?"

"Because—" Gideon began.

"Because," John cut in, "when the distal phalanges and a segment of the middle phalanges are removed, the bone that's left, that is, the, uh, proximal segments of the, of the middle phalanges, undergoes, um, osteoporotic atrophy and becomes resorbed." He gestured at the bones. "I mean," he said blandly, "it's obvious, really."

"Yes, it seems that way to me, too," Gideon said, suppressing his smile.

"I'll be damned." Fukida wasn't looking at the bones, he was rocking lightly back and forth in his tilting chair, looking through a window behind them at the compost piles and snapping a rubber band that was around his wrist. The look on his face was part befuddlement, part amusement. "And so that's how you identified him as Torkel? That's the whole bit?"

"That was the main thing, yes," Gideon said. "There were some other things, but . . . why? What's the matter? Is there something funny about it?"

"Oh, yeah. Hilarious." He stopped rocking, gave the rubber band one more vigorous snap, and looked directly at Gideon. "The corpse in the burned building, that's how they identified *him* as Torkel. Otherwise, he was unrecognizable."

"I don't understand."

"*He* was missing two toes, too. The same two frigging toes, I'm pretty sure."

"But Magnus didn't . . . but Torkel was the one . . ."

"Right you are, champ," said Fukida. "And what does

that tell us, I asks myself? It tells us, I replies, that we got ourselves one too many Torkels."

"And not enough Magnuses," said John after a moment. He rolled his head back, working his neck muscles the way Fukida had. "I could sure use a cup of coffee."

IN the snack room, over cardboard cups of watery vending-machine coffee ("Can you believe it?" Fukida said sourly. "Here we are in the middle of the goddamn Kona Coast, and this is the crap they expect us to drink."), they talked about what was to be done and agreed that the place to begin would be to do what Gideon had come for: to look at the case's medical records to see what he could make of them.

"Okay, but between us," Fukida told them, "the guy who did the autopsy, old Doc Meikeljohn, he'd been having a serious affair with the bottle for a while, so by that time he was maybe, let's say, a couple of tacos short of a combination plate, you know? What I'm saying is, those two missing toes might have been in his head. I mean, considering the fire and all, the body was in pretty bad shape. Could have just been sloppy work. Or maybe the toes got burned off."

"But those exact two toes?" John said. "The same ones Torkel was missing? How likely is that?"

"Not very," Fukida admitted. "But then, the autopsy wasn't performed for a couple of days. By that time they had the old lady's deposition and everybody, including Meikeljohn, knew . . . well, they thought they knew . . . that it was Torkel. For all I know, he also knew Torkel was missing a couple of toes—he probably did. So, I mean, when you consider the condition of the body, and the fact that Meikeljohn wasn't the sharpest knife in the drawer—"

"He jumped to the wrong conclusion," John finished for him. "He expected amputated toes, and so that's what he found. Yeah, Doc says that happens to him all the time."

"John, when did I ever say—" Gideon began, then laughed. "Never mind."

"Wouldn't surprise me, Johnny," Fukida said. "But if you want to know what I think, I think we got ourselves a whole 'nother scenario."

"Which is?" John asked.

"That Torkel Torkelsson—the real Torkel—cut those two toes off his dead brother before he took off so that everybody would think *he* was the dead one, and the shooters would forget all about him."

"Yes, we were thinking along the same lines," said Gideon.

"One thing, though," John said. "How do we know for sure that the guy you autopsied is really his brother Magnus? Okay, it's not Torkel—Torkel was in the plane, we agree on that—but this guy here could be just about anybody, couldn't it? I mean, he was unrecognizable, right?"

"Real doubtful, sport," Fukida said. "Who else could it be? That was the last night anybody ever saw old Magnus alive. He sure hasn't been around since, and we don't have anybody else who's missing from then. No, I think we can be sure it's Magnus, all right."

"Yeah, like until twenty minutes ago you were sure it was Torkel."

Fukida scowled. "Wise guy. That was because—"

"Let's not get ahead of ourselves," Gideon interjected. "That's what I'm here to try and clear up. If there are any clear photos of the foot, and there's not too much damage from the fire, I might be able to tell for sure that the toes were lost after he died. That'd give us a starting point.

And who knows, maybe I might come up with something else."

"Okay, chief," Fukida agreed with a shrug. "Do your shtick. What do you need?"

"Any pictures you have. The crime scene photos, the pre-autopsy photos, and the photographs from the autopsy itself, if there are any."

"No problem," Fukida said.

"And I probably should look at the autopsy report itself, even if you think it's suspect. The coroner might have noticed something helpful."

"I wouldn't count on it." He stood up and poured most of his coffee into the sink. "Look, I have to run into Kona for a while, but I'll set you guys up in a quiet room and have Sarah bring it all over to you."

"How about sending the whole case file while you're at it?" John said. "I wouldn't mind looking through it."

"You're talking about a lot of paper."

John shrugged. "It'll give me something to do."

"Okay, but I can't let you guys take anything away with you, you understand that. It all has to stay here."

"No problem," John said.

Fifteen minutes later, with Gideon and John deposited in a pleasant conference room with comfortable faux-leather chairs, a dark, gleaming table, and windows whose views artfully managed to avoid the compost heaps and wrecked cars, instead looking over the lava fields, past the Boeing 717s floating down to the nearby airport, and onto the massive, cloud-wreathed hump that was Maui, an affable, carrot-topped clerk lugged in a rolling cart bulging with hanging folders and set it next to the table, between their chairs. A thick, yellow nine-by-twelve clasp envelope was plopped on the table as well.

"There you are, boys. The case file's in the folders. The envelope has the crime scene photos. If you need anything else, pick up that phone and dial forty-four. I'm Sarah Andersen."

"Is the autopsy report in with the case file?" Gideon asked.

"No, it wouldn't be in there. His Majesty didn't tell me you wanted it. Be back in a sec."

In the envelope was a stack of black-and-white eight-by-ten photos and a neatly printed log numbering and describing them; a hundred and sixty-five in all, as usual starting with the exterior of the building and working inward, gradually going from long- and intermediate-range shots to close-ups. Gideon was at the hundred and thirtieth before he got to the first relatively close full-length image of the body, which had been found lying half on its side, half on its face.

It made him close his eyes.

ELEVEN

BONES were one thing: smooth, clean, ivory-colored, usually suggesting little that brought one up against agony or violent death. A nick here, a tidy, round hole there, a few harmless-looking cracks. Even when there was more extensive breakage bone seemed to have more in common with broken pottery than with bloody, broken heads and spilled brains. His most timid, queasy students had no trouble glueing together a shattered skull or a crushed pelvis. But horribly maimed bodies like this one ... *crispy critters,* his colleagues called the burned ones, and while Gideon had no quarrel with the use of black humor to distance oneself from horror, for him it didn't work. Neither did anything else.

"Here's a picture of him," he said, sliding it over to John, who had been browsing through the case file.

John put down an open folder. "Jesus, is that after or before they cremated him?"

On the other hand, he had to admit that sometimes black

humor did help, and he was grateful for the opportunity to smile. "Before. But you're right, he was pretty well charred, especially the upper body. Externally, he's pretty well carbonized from the chest up. Not quite as bad below."

"Is there one of him face-up? They must have flipped him over."

Gideon paged through a few more photos. "Yes, here."

Both men leaned closer to look at it. "Ugh. You can see why they wouldn't have known who it was from the face," Gideon said.

"Face, what face? His head looks like a . . . like a lump of coal, like a . . . I mean, where are the eyes, where's the nose?"

Gideon nodded. "Notice the damage is so much more pronounced around the head and shoulders. Interesting."

"I can tell you why that is," John said. "I just read the arson investigator's report. There's no question at all about it being arson, by the way. They found traces of two different accelerants—paint thinner and diesel fuel oil—and at least five different origin points in the building, one of which was *him*."

"Him? You mean they set him on fire?"

"Yeah, pretty much. His face was resting right on a roll of straw matting that'd been soaked in diesel oil."

Gideon looked at the photographs. "Yes, I guess maybe you can see a few burned chunks of matting—of something, anyway—on the floor there."

There were six pictures of the body in all, and Gideon fanned them out so they could both look at them. From the chest up, it was barely identifiable as a human form, more like a black, barely started sculpture than the remains of flesh and bone and muscle. Below the chest, the form was recognizably human, but made of charred, piebald skin, split in places like a sausage left too long on the grill. The clothing had been completely burned away except for the residue of a wide belt at the waist—or perhaps it was just the impression the burning belt had left on the burning skin— and the coalesced remnants of cowboy boots on the feet.

"John, I can't tell anything from this. There's just nothing distinctive, nothing to say if it's Magnus or it isn't Magnus. It's human, that's about it. And obviously, the toes aren't visible. I just hope there's something more in the autopsy report."

"Well, I can tell you who Torkel wanted everyone to *think* it was: himself—Torkel."

"Sure, but we already figured that out."

"We *thought* that. We *assumed* that. But now there's proof. Torkel took off his own ring and put it on Magnus's body." He leafed through one of the folders until he came to what he wanted. "Here. 'Also under the decedent's right hand was a signet ring made of white gold or similar material, with a ruby or similar stone set in a circular, braided border. This ring was subsequently identified by decedent's family as belonging to him, an heirloom gift from his father when decedent joined the Swedish merchant marine.' "

"So you think Torkel planted it to fake the identification."

"Sure, Doc, it's obvious. What else could it be? He wanted everybody to think he was dead."

Gideon shook his head. "John, I don't know anymore . . ." He lifted one of the pictures and gazed at it for a while. "Maybe it *is* Torkel."

John had a habit of suddenly flinging out his arms when he was excited, and he did it now. Gideon knew enough to anticipate it and was just able to get his head out of the way of a flailing right hand. "Doc, don't start with me! Why do you do this? Jesus! First the guy in the plane is Magnus, positively. Then it's Torkel, absolutely. And now you're telling me *this* guy—"

"All I'm telling you is that I concluded the body on the plane was Torkel's because of the amputated toes—a reasonable conclusion, you'll agree—but now, according to Fukida, this guy here was missing the same two toes, which I can't confirm or refute from these pictures. And when you tell me that Torkel's ring was found with the body, how am I supposed to know what to think? Maybe somebody wanted everyone to think the body in the *plane* was Torkel's, when it was really Magnus's."

John's arms, still extended out to the sides, went to his temples. "Please let him tell me he's joking."

"I'm joking," Gideon said. "Well, I think I am."

"Doc—"

"No, I am, I am," Gideon said. "Joking. Nobody doctored *that* foot for effect. Resorption, remember? Osteoporotic atrophy, remember?"

"Right, right," John said, pacified.

"No, the man in the plane was Torkel Torkelsson, period. We can forget about him. But what we don't know is who the guy in the fire was. There's no way I can come up with anything solid from these pictures."

"It's Magnus," John said stolidly. "There's nobody else it could be. You heard Fukida."

"So what happened to his toes?" Gideon murmured.

"What happened is what Fukida said. Torkel cut them off himself. Or maybe the guy who did the autopsy let his imagination run away with him. Either or both—probably both, would be my guess."

"I suppose so," Gideon said.

John had calmed down enough to go back to leafing through the folders while he was speaking. "Hey, here's Auntie Dagmar's statement to the detective working the case. Want to hear it?"

"Sure."

"Okay, 'Statement of Dagmar Torkelsson, Date November 5, 1994, taken by Detective Paul Webster,' blah, blah, blah . . . here we are:

> DT: Yes, that's right. After dinner my brothers went back to the hay barn to do some work.
>
> PW: The hay barn? That's the building that burned down?
>
> DT: Yes, in the old days it was our hay barn, but now it's just used for storage space and the ranch offices. We still call it the hay barn. That is, we did.
>
> PW: Did they always do that? Go to the hay barn to go back to work after dinner?
>
> DT: Not always. Two times, three times a week.
>
> PW: Did you go with them?
>
> DT: No, I never do. I stayed home. I cleaned up the dishes and turned on the television.

"Yes, that's right," Gideon said. "They all lived together, didn't they?"

"Yup. In the Big House. It's Inge's and Keoni's now, home of Kohala Trails Adventure Ranch. Dagmar moved down to the coast after the fire. She has joint problems, so the weather's a lot better for her down there."

"Did they get along?"

"Like you'd expect two brothers and a sister in their seventies, living in one house, to get along."

"In other words, they didn't."

"No, that's not exactly right. Let's just say they were really tight, but at the same time they could get pretty crabby with each other. With anybody, for that matter. They were all one-of-a-kinds, Doc. No problem with weak personalities for that bunch."

Gideon laughed. "I'm starting to think you're right about that."

John began reading aloud again.

PW: And the next time you heard from your brother?

DT: I already told the officer—

PW: I know, but tell me again, please.

DT: Well, he called me . . . Magnus . . . and he said—

PW: What time was this?

DT: I don't know. I was watching *Hill Street Blues,* so it must have been—

PW: Okay, and what did he say?

DT: He said that Torkel was . . . that they'd killed Torkel and he had to get out of Hawaii before the same thing happened to him.

PW: Now, when you say he said "they"—

DT: I don't know who he meant. He said "they," that's all I know.

PW: He definitely said "they"? Plural? Not "him" or "her"? No names, no descriptions?

DT: He said . . . I think he said "they." I'm not sure, I can't remember.

PW: Did he say how your brother had been killed?

DT: (Shakes head.)

PW: Did he say there'd been a fire?

DT: I—I'm not sure. I don't think so. Maybe he did, I'm just not sure. It was all so—

PW: Okay. And what else did he say?

DT: He said he had to leave. He said he'd come back as soon as he could. He said he loved me. He was . . . he was very excited, I could hardly . . .

PW: Just take your time, ma'am. Would you like some water or—

DT: He said they were after him, too, and—

PW: Ma'am, why did you wait so long to tell us this? Why didn't you tell the police about it last night?

DT: He told me to wait.

PW: Your brother told you to wait?

DT: Yes, until today. Magnus said don't tell anyone what he was doing until today.

PW: Anyone? Or just the police?

DT: Anyone. I keep telling you, he was afraid they were coming after him, too, and he needed a chance to get away.

PW: Did he tell you that? That "they" were coming after him?

DT: No, he didn't say exactly that. Well, I don't think so. It was very quick, only a few sentences. He was so excited.

PW: And did he say where he was going?

DT: (Shakes head.) He was taking the plane, that's all he said.

At this point, Sarah returned. "Mission accomplished." She put another clasp envelope, a thinner one, on the table. "Autopsy photos. And here"—she waved a thick sheaf of paper in her other hand—"is the autopsy report itself. It was less hassle to copy it than to check it out, so I made you one you can keep. Don't tell anybody." She slapped it into Gideon's hand. "Enjoy."

Dr. Meikeljohn, the deputy coroner, might not have been the sharpest knife in the drawer, but he couldn't be faulted on exhaustiveness. Or wordiness. His problem was organization. There was no breakdown into *external examination* and *internal examination,* no *evidence of injury* section, no *evidence of medical and/or surgical intervention* section, no *pathology* section, no put-it-all-together *findings* and *opinion* sections, no explicit structure of any kind. The report was simply twenty-two pages (compared to the usual four or so) of disorganized, densely typed observations, along with many lengthy stream-of-consciousness detours into conjecture, speculation, and hunches that were usually—and for good reason—not found in autopsy reports. It was difficult for Gideon even to locate the part in which the condition of the toes was described. Looking for it, his attention was caught by a few pages that described in fastidious detail the courses and locations of the two bullets found in the body.

Despite the charred condition of the external remains, a five-by-three-centimeter gunshot wound is visible in the ventral aspect of the thorax at the level of the third intercostal space, four centimeters to the left of the lateral border of the sternum. Because of tissue destruction of the dermal layers due to post-mortem thermal injury, the forensically pertinent characteristics of the wound, e.g., the existence or lack thereof of marginal abrasion, soot deposit, stippling, and other adjunct features are not possible to determine.

Subsequent dissection shows that both projectiles entered through this entrance, penetrating the left pectoralis major and proceeding medio-dorsally, grazing the superior border of the fourth costal cartilage and perforating the superior lobe of the left lung. Entering the medial mediastinum, the projectiles transpierced the heart through the right ventricle and the left atrium, separated the descending thoracic aorta—

"No problem positively identifying the cause of death, anyway," Gideon murmured.

A few paragraphs before, he'd read that no soot or other carbon material had been found in the respiratory passages, proof positive that the victim had no longer been breathing at the time of the fire; he'd been dead when it started. And Meikeljohn's description of the bullets' horrific path made the reason for that crystal clear.

Gideon told John what he'd read, eliminating the jargon.

"Shot right in the heart, huh?" John said, looking up from the case file.

"Right *through* the heart. Twice. And if that wasn't enough, the bullets destroyed the aorta, too. You can't get much more killed than that."

"Two bullets," John mused. "Both in the heart. Well, there you go, see? You had a couple of shooters who knew what they were doing. The cops did get one thing right, Doc. These were professionals, not one old crank shooting another."

"Mm," Gideon said and silently went back to the report.

—separated the descending aorta, and lodged in the *corpus* of the eighth thoracic vertebra (T8), one above the other, three millimeters apart. The projectiles were found to be somewhat deformed, medium-sized, non-jacketed lead bullets of different calibers, with the inferior, smaller one showing some fragmentation. Among the interesting circumstances associated with them was the presence of a cartridge case partially embedded in the intervertebral fibrocartilage separating T8 and T9. Various possibilities come to mind to account for its presence there . . .

And off the good doctor went on another of his roundabout excursions into supposition and surmise. Gideon paged on until he found what he was looking for at the bottom of page thirteen.

"Here we go, John." He read aloud. " 'The right foot was naturally examined with especial care. External examination of the toes was not possible, inasmuch as the partially melted boot had fused to the skin. Therefore—' "

"Ah, there, you see?" exclaimed John, jabbing a finger in Gideon's direction. "He *was* expecting to find those amputations. He already had them in his mind. Why else would he 'naturally' examine the right foot with 'especial care'?"

Gideon nodded. "That's a good point." He continued reading.

> Therefore, a partial deep dissection of the anterior dorsum was accomplished to reveal the condition of the toes. It was found that parts of the second and third toes had been amputated, resection having taken place approximately one centimeter from the distal ends of the medial phalanges.

He turned the page, scanned the next one. "I don't believe it," he exclaimed, flipping to the following page, and then the one after that. "You're kidding me."

"What's the problem?" John asked.

"The problem? The problem is, that's it: 'On the right foot, parts of the second and third toes have been amputated, resection having taken place approximately one centimeter from the distal ends of the medial phalanges.' Here this guy takes pages and pages describing every sulcus and pimple on the bladder, but when it comes to something important, something that could make or break an identification, what do we get? 'On the right foot, parts of the second and third—' "

"Okay, okay, I heard you the first two times." John shook his head, puzzled. "But I don't get it. Isn't that what you were looking for? I mean, the toes aren't *there* anymore, what else is there to say?"

"There's a lot he could have—should have—said. Was

there any callus formation on the stumps? Was the medullary cavity open or capped? Was there any atrophy? All the things that would give us some idea of whether it was post- or antemortem." He stood up, slammed the sheaf onto the table, and stormed around the room.

"Gee, Doc, don't get yourself in a—"

"Was there anything to suggest whether it was a clean surgical procedure or some kind of amateur boondoggle? Was there—"

The door opened and Fukida walked in wearing a Colorado Rockies baseball cap and carrying a paper bag. "Problem?" he asked.

"Nah," John said. "He gets like this sometimes. Don't worry, he's usually not violent."

Fukida opened the bag and took out three lidded sixteen-ounce cardboard cups. "Here, I stopped on Ali'i Drive and got us some real coffee. I don't know," he said, looking hard at Gideon as he handed a cup to him, "I think I should have got *you* a decaf."

"This'll be fine," Gideon said. He laughed and dropped back into his chair. "Thanks, smells wonderful."

Fukida took a seat across the table from them, took the lid off his cup, crossed an ankle over one knee, and immediately started jiggling his foot. "I gather the autopsy report wasn't too helpful?"

"Not about those missing toes, no. It's the one place in the report where he decided to be concise."

"What about the photos?"

"No, there wasn't anything—"

"He means the autopsy photos, not the crime-scene ones, Doc. You haven't even looked at them."

"*Autopsy* photos! I forgot all about them!" He reached for the envelope.

"He's also a little absent-minded," John explained.

There were six black-and-white photographs: two pre-autopsy shots of the body from different angles, one of the entry wound, two taken during dissection that showed the bullets' trajectory . . . and one excellent-quality close-up of the right foot, post-dissection.

"Ah," Gideon murmured with satisfaction. He propped the photo against one of the case files that were now strewn on the table and settled back in his chair, hands clasped on his belly, to study it from three feet away. After a minute he leaned forward so that his face was twelve or fifteen inches from it. Finally, he straightened up.

"You were both on target," he announced. "This was faked. It's not Torkel. Those toes got hacked off after he died."

"I knew it. I told you." Fukida was pleased for a moment, but then he rolled his eyes. "Oh, boy, like I really need this."

"Or possibly right before," Gideon said, "but that makes no sense. Anyway, it was peri-mortem, not antemortem. It didn't happen years ago, that's for sure."

"You're positive about that?" Fukida asked dejectedly.

"Oh, yes. And it wasn't done by any surgeon, I'm positive about that, too. Or if it was, you better hope he never operates on you."

Whatever it was that had done the job, he explained, had been a sharp instrument, but sharp like a heavy chef's knife is sharp, not like a scalpel or a surgical saw.

"See"—he pointed to the photograph—"if you look at the cut ends of the bones, you can see that they're not clean. There's been some crushing at the margins."

Fukida wasn't at all sure he could see it, but John, who'd had more experience in this line, nodded. " 'Hacked' is the word, all right. An axe, that'd be my guess."

"I don't think so, John. Look at the second toe, right

above the cut—those striations running laterally across the bone? They're pretty clear."

These Fukida was able to make out. "Hesitation marks?"

"Right. The same kind of thing you get when someone's trying to cut his wrists and can't quite get up the nerve, or find the right spot. I think they were the first attempts to cut the toe off, and Torkel—or whoever did it—was trying to cut through the joint, which is pretty hard to find if you're not up on your anatomy, because the bases and the heads of the phalanges are wedged really close together; they kind of overlap, more so as you get older. So, on the next try he resorted to brute force and just chopped his way right through the bone; a single stroke each time, or maybe a single stroke to lop off both toes, but I don't think so. Almost certainly used a hammer or something like it to drive the blade through. The weapon itself was probably some kind of small, heavy blade, something like a heavy-duty box-cutter, maybe."

"Why couldn't it have been an axe?" John asked.

"If he'd had an axe to start with, why would there be any hesitation marks at all? When you swing an axe, you swing it. You're not looking for some delicate little joint to slip it through. Both toes would have come off with the first whack. Besides, you'd have to be pretty good with an axe, or with anything else big, to clip just those two and not damage the ones on either side; especially the big toe."

"That's true," John allowed.

"And the reason we know it happened after he died," Fukida said, "is because there's no—what did you call it, Johnny?"

"Osteoporotic atrophy. And resorption, let us never forget resorption."

"Also, the medullary cavities are wide open," Gideon

said. "No capping, no healing at all. This man had those two toes right up until he died. Ergo, whoever he is, Torkel Torkelsson he is not."

Fukida expelled a long, disgusted breath. "Wasn't there a ring? Do I remember right? Wasn't he wearing Torkel's ring?"

"Not exactly wearing," Gideon said. "There weren't any fingers, but the ring was near his hand, where the fingers would have been."

Fukida nodded. "So that was a plant, too; part of the scam. And we bought it. 'Screw-up' is right."

"Looks like it," John said. "Doc, you want to tell me something? All you had to do was take one look at the picture and you spotted this. This coroner, he had the real thing right in front of him, and he never saw it? I don't care how spaced-out he was. I mean, even *I* can see it—"

"Now that I've pointed it out."

"Well, yeah, but I'm not a medical examiner. Jesus, Teddy, what kind of coroners do you have here?"

"Hey, give me a break," Fukida said. "This isn't like it was in Honolulu. People are nice to each other here. We don't have a lot of homicides. We don't have a real forensic pathologist. We don't even have real coroners; the police are all deputy coroners, and the autopsies, when we do 'em, get done under contract, by local doctors. Meikeljohn was just a urologist from Waimea that was willing to do it, so we used him a couple of times. What would he know from bones?"

"True, not too many bones in the urinary tract. At least now," Gideon said, smiling, "I know why the bladder got all that loving attention."

"What about an ID?" Fukida asked. "The pictures tell you anything that indicates it's definitely Magnus?"

"Or definitely isn't?" John added.

A shake of the head from Gideon. "There's not much to work with. The sex is right, and the age is in the ballpark somewhere. That's about it, and that applies to a whole lot of people. So the answer is . . . I don't know, not for certain."

"So," John said to Fukida, "what now?"

"Now? Now I put an addendum in the case file to the effect that we screwed up slightly."

"And then?"

"Then what?"

"*Then* what do you do? Where do you go from there?"

Fukida twisted his baseball cap around so that it was backwards, leaned back in his chair, and clasped his hands behind his neck. "Beats the hell out of me. What do you suggest?"

John stared at him. "What the hell kind of—"

Gideon interrupted. "We thought," he said mildly, "that you might want to reopen the case."

Fukida rocked back and forth in his chair while he considered, his hands still clasped behind his head. "Nah, I don't think so."

"But—" John began.

"No, wait." He took off the cap, ran a hand through his thick black hair, and leaned soberly forward. "Look, Oliver, Johnny—you convinced me. The guy that was autopsied isn't Torkel Torkelsson. This guy pulled off the scam of a lifetime, making us—making everybody—think that the body in the fire was his, so he could get away without leaving a trail."

"Right!" John said. "So—"

"So does somebody here want to tell me exactly what crime I'm supposed to investigate? What section of the penal code applies?"

"I don't know," John said. "Maybe—"

"And what about statutes of limitation? This all happened ten years ago."

"Statutes of limitation don't apply," John said. "This was murder—a capital offense."

"Sure, but *he* didn't kill anyone. At least, we don't think so," he added in an undertone.

"Well, true, but—"

"More important, anybody want to tell me *who* I'm supposed to investigate? Everything that's left of Torkel Torkelsson is sitting in a shoe box on my desk. Even if he did do something criminal, I'd say that puts him pretty safely beyond the long arm of the law, wouldn't you?"

John and Gideon both nodded. "Guess so," John said.

Fukida sat still for a minute, snapping the rubber band against his wrist, then jumped up and shook hands with both of them.

"Great seeing you again, Johnny. Doctor, that was really something, what you did. I'm very impressed."

He walked them down the hall, through the lobby, and up to the front doors.

"Look, guys," he said as he saw them out, "I'm sorry I can't help, but I don't see anything for me to do. If there's a prosecutable crime involved here—and somebody to prosecute—give me a call when you figure out who and what they are."

TWELVE

"SOMETHING'S screwy," Gideon said.

John laughed. "You're telling me."

"No, I mean even screwier than it looks."

With Gideon behind the wheel of the pickup this time, they had just left Fukida's office, turning north onto the Queen Kaahumanu Highway to head back into the uplands, toward Waimea and the ranch.

"I know," said John, nodding. "Every time we find out something new, it just gets more confusing. Not supposed to work that way."

"It's the timing that doesn't make any sense, John. It's impossible for it to have happened the way we think."

"How so?"

"Well, when would Torkel have had the time to do what he did—cut off Magnus's toes, leave the ring, switch clothing with him, and the rest of it?"

"How do you know he switched clothes? That's not so

easy with a dead guy. You ever try to move a dead guy? Dead people are *heavy*."

"Well, at least we know Torkel got a boot back on his foot after the toes came off, and he wouldn't have been dumb enough to put *Magnus's* own boots back on him. I'm guessing he also dressed him in the rest of his own clothing."

"Yeah, I see what you mean. And he must have switched wallets and any other identifying things, too, but they probably got burnt up—except for the ring."

"Probably so, but *when* did he do all that? How could he get it done between the time of the shooting and the time they burnt the place down? Did they kill Magnus, then conveniently go away for an hour or two, leaving Torkel alone to tinker with his brother's body, and then come back later, at their leisure, and burn the place down?"

With his eyes closed and his face pushed out the open window to derive the full complement of pleasure from the oven-hot breeze, John thought about that for a moment. "Pretty doubtful," he agreed, bringing his head back in. His stiff, black hair was hardly mussed. "So what's your theory? I know you have to have one."

"Oh, hey, I'm not about to call it a theory. At best we're talking hypothesis or—"

"Yeah, yeah, whatever," John said, waving a hand. Finer academic distinctions were not his forte.

"Let's call it a speculation, I'd be more comfortable with that," Gideon said. "A supposition that's unverified to this point, but one—"

"Doc, I swear—!"

"Sorry, sorry. John, what I'm wondering is if the killers never burnt the place down at all. I'm wondering if Torkel's the one who came back and set the fire himself."

"You mean to cover the identity switch."

"Exactly."

"Yeah, could be." He nodded to himself. "Could very well be. Fits."

"It goes along with cutting off the toes, doesn't it?"

"It also goes along with putting his face right on that oil-soaked matting so there'd be nothing left to recognize." He turned things over in his mind for a moment. "And what about his fingers? Remember the photos? His fingers were—well, his hands; he didn't exactly have any fingers, did he?—his hands were positioned up by his face, too, where they'd get all that heat. No fingerprints that way."

"Well, possibly, but that just might be—"

"Oh, right, right, where the muscles tighten up ... the ... what do you call it again?"

"The pugilistic attitude," Gideon said. "The muscle fibers dehydrate and shrink, and pull on the tendons, so the forearms flex and the hands come up around the face like a fighter covering up. The knees bend and the feet come up, too. Remember how his feet stayed in the air when they turned him over?"

"Yeah, that's right. Okay, scratch that idea. But the rest of it holds together." John was getting into it now. His hands were starting to chop the air. Gideon shifted left to give himself a little more protection. "The shooters kill Magnus. Torkel gets away. He knows, or thinks he knows, that they don't know which one they shot. So after they're gone, he comes back, chops off his brother's toes, leaves his ring, and burns the place down. Everybody figures the bad guys did it, and the bad guys—and everyone else— think it's Torkel's body laying in the barn." He nodded, agreeing with himself. "I like it."

"That's one scenario," Gideon said gingerly. "I have another one, too. Another possibility."

"That nobody else was involved at all? That there never

were any 'bad guys'? That Torkel not only burnt the place down, but killed his own brother?"

"That's right," Gideon said, surprised. "Is that what you think?"

"No, that's not what I think. I just know the way *you* think. You got this bug in your ear. First it was Magnus who killed Torkel, and since that didn't work, now it's Torkel who killed Magnus. What have you got against these guys?"

"John, I'm just—"

"Doc, we've been all over this. There's all kinds of evidence against it. The slick, two-man execution, the statement from Dagmar—"

"Sure, but wouldn't Dagmar have lied if it helped her own brother get away with murder?"

"Of her own *other* brother? I don't know, but, yeah, okay, it's possible. Theoretically. But look, the main thing is—*why* would Torkel shoot his brother? Give me one possible reason."

"How would I know that? Because of the will, maybe? To get full title to the ranch?"

"No, how does that add up? If that's what he wanted, why pretend he was dead? How would that get him the ranch?"

Gideon nodded, worn down by John's more than reasonable arguments. "Yes, you're right about that, too. Okay, forget it. One more unverified supposition bites the dust."

"One more crackpot theory," John said.

They were climbing now. The breeze flowing in the driver's-side window was laced with pine and eucalyptus, and was refreshingly cool. John, finding the chill unwelcome, rolled up his window, leaned his head against it, and settled his body as comfortably as he could. After a few minutes he began to slip into a doze but then sat up with a sudden "*Damn!*" He turned with an earnest look at Gideon.

"Doc, maybe you're on to something after all. They *have* been lying to us. I just realized it. Well, holding back, anyway."

"Who are we talking about?"

"The family. The whole damn family. They knew it was Torkel in the plane all along!"

Gideon frowned. "How do you figure that?"

"Look, when we told them the body in the plane was Torkel's, how come nobody mentioned the ring? How come nobody jumped up and said, 'No, that's impossible, it can't be Torkel; we know the one that burned up was Torkel because he was wearing Torkel's ring'? Or at least brought it up?" He pounded his thigh with a fist. "Wouldn't *you* have said something? But there was nothing, not a peep. Why not?"

"Is it possible they didn't know about it?"

"No, it isn't. The file said it was family members that identified it, remember?"

"Well, yes, but it didn't say which family members."

"What's the difference? Even if it was only a couple of them, why would they keep something like that to themselves? No, I'm telling you, *somebody* should have said something."

"Somebody should have," Gideon agreed.

"What do you say we go talk to Axel about it?" John suggested. "I'd like to hear what he has to say."

For the next few minutes they retreated into their own thoughts. At the gate to the Little Hoaloha, it was John who got out to swing it open. When he climbed back into the truck, Gideon wore a look on his face somewhere between confusion and exasperation, with emphasis on the former.

"What?" John asked. He had the worried expression

that meant he knew in his heart that his friend was about to complicate things even more.

"None of that makes any sense either," Gideon told him.

John exploded. Out shot his arms. He banged an elbow hard into the doorpost and winced. "I *knew* you were going to say that. I *knew* it'd be too simple for you. What's the problem, not enough loose ends?"

"No, I'm serious. Look." He waited for John to settle down before going quietly on. "If they all knew what really happened—that Magnus wasn't Magnus and Torkel wasn't Torkel—then why would they ask me to look at the autopsy report? Why did they ask me to go out to Maravovo Atoll and check the plane in the first place? They'd have to be crazy to take chances like that. There was no reason they had to do that. They could have just let the salvage company bring the bones back, buried them, and left me out of it. None of this would have come up."

"Yeah, but . . . well, maybe they . . ." John sagged against his seat. "My head hurts."

"John, what do you say we forget about going up to see Axel? What do you say we turn the truck around and go back and talk to Fukida again? Tell him what we've been talking about, see what he thinks."

"Dump it in his lap, you mean."

"Absolutely. It's his baby, not ours."

Now John hedged. "All the way back to Kona? It's not like we have anything definite here, Doc. There might be a simple explanation for everything. We might be stirring up a lot of trouble for everybody for no good reason. These are good people, basically." He scowled down at his hands. "I *think* these are good people."

"Well, you're the cop. I'll leave it up to you. If you just want to drop the whole thing—"

"Nah," John said wearily, "you know better than that.

Okay, let's go. Imagine how happy Teddy'll be to see us again."

SERGEANT Fukida looked anything but happy. From across his desk, he eyed them with the wary expression of the barnyard rooster looking at a couple of smiling foxes come calling. He was wearing two rubber bands on his wrist now, wide ones, and was snapping them both with a forceful little twist of the thumb. That's got to hurt, Gideon thought. His baseball cap was still on, but no longer backward.

"I knew you guys would be back," Fukida said. "I could feel it in my bones. I just didn't think it would be *today*."

"This is serious, Teddy," John said. "There are some problems."

Fukida heaved a colossal sigh. "Okay, let's hear 'em."

The possibility that Torkel himself had set the hay barn fire to obscure his escape left him unconcerned and impatient ("You came back to tell me *this?*"), but the question of why no one had brought up the ring after Gideon had identified the body in the plane as Torkel's did catch his interest, and for few minutes they tossed possibilities back and forth. It didn't take long to narrow the likely explanations down to one: When the Torkelssons had learned that Gideon *knew* the body in Maravovo Lagoon was Torkel's, they realized that mention of the ring would make it clear that the confusion of identities had not been accidental, but purposeful; that Torkel had left his ring on Magnus's body in a deliberate, premeditated attempt to mislead the police.

And if they were afraid of bringing that out, didn't it mean that they'd been aware of the switch from the beginning? That they'd known all along that Torkel had actually outlived Magnus? That they had kept it to themselves because they much preferred their lives under the provisions of Magnus's generous will? (And who wouldn't?) If Torkel's will had gone into effect instead, the great bulk of the estate would have gone to the Swedish Seamen's Home.

Why they would have asked Gideon to look at the remains in the plane was still an unanswered question, but that didn't change the rest of it.

"And if it's all true," a glum-looking John mused, "then they're guilty of collusion to commit fraud for monetary gain."

"Even your friend Axel?" Gideon asked after a moment.

John rubbed his forehead and ran his fingers through his hair. "Whew, that's pretty hard to believe." But the cop in him came through. "I'm not ruling it out, though."

"They did more than that," Fukida said. He held out a pack of spearmint gum. When they shook their heads, he folded over two sticks, inserted them into his mouth, chawed them down to a single manageable bolus, and continued. "If they knew all along that Torkel got away and they've been covering for him all this time, then they've participated in"—he began counting off on his fingers—"one, falsification of public records; two, providing false information to the police; three, identity theft. And if Torkel set the fire and they knew about it and didn't say anything, then there's insurance fraud, too. And if they knowingly accepted property that should have gone to the Seamen's Home, that's not just fraud, that's theft."

"This is really getting ugly," John mumbled. "Are you going to reopen the case?"

There followed a period of gum-cracking, band-snapping, and general chair-jiggling while Fukida thought it through. "Wouldn't you?" he asked.

John shrugged. "I don't know. I guess so."

"Well, so would I. I'll have to talk to the lieutenant, but

I don't think there's much doubt. At least it's worth stirring things up. Maybe not a full-scale, official investigation at this point, no, but a look. Really sit down with the files, re-interview these characters . . ."

"What about the statutes of limitation?" Gideon asked. "With ten years gone by, are any of those things still prosecutable?"

"Who knows?" Fukida brushed the question aside and leaned forward in his chair. "I don't give a damn about fraud or identity theft, not from ten years ago. But if those people helped Torkel switch identities—if they knowingly participated in that faked ID—thereby misleading the police, then they just might be criminally responsible, at least as accessories after the fact, to Magnus's murder. That's worth looking at—and no statute of limitation to worry about."

"*Murder?*" John exploded. "Come on, Teddy, get real. You're stretching the hell out of—"

Fukida out-yelled him—not an easy thing to do. "They are also criminally responsible for making the Kona CIS look like a bunch of incompetent assholes, and laughing about it all the way to the bank!" The declaration was shouted into a vault of silence. The hum of conversation from other cubicles and desks had stopped entirely. Everyone was listening in. Everyone could hardly help it, Gideon thought.

John lowered his voice to a hiss. "That's what this is really about, isn't it, Teddy? They made you look like idiots, and now you want to get back at them."

Fukida glared at him, opened his mouth to shout some more, changed his mind, and settled back, shaking his head. After a second he sat up straight again, snorted, and angrily flung his cap into a corner. "I don't understand you, Lau. You walk in here uninvited, you rake up all kinds of dirty laundry, you tell me we got this wrong and that wrong, you raise a million questions . . . and then when I tell you, well, maybe there's something to it and we ought to reopen, you climb all over me. What do you want? Do you want us to investigate? Or do you want us to drop it?"

John had calmed down while Fukida spoke. He looked about as miserable as his open, cheerful face would permit. "Yes," he said. "And yes."

A beat passed before Fukida spoke. "What is that, zen? I don't get it."

Gideon did. It was what had been bothering John all day; the conflict between human being and lawman. By coming to Fukida, he felt, understandably enough, as if he were betraying his friends. But as a cop himself, he couldn't bring himself to pretend that all the equivocations, misrepresentations, omissions, and generally dubious behavior on the part of this family he'd known so long had never occurred.

"I have an idea," Gideon said. "For all we know, we're blowing things up way out of proportion. Basically, we're operating without facts. Maybe they didn't do anything illegal. Maybe we're seeing things all wrong. I know it looks bad, but maybe there's a simple explanation for everything that we haven't thought of."

John's and Fukida's faces showed that they believed this about as much as he did, but that they were willing to listen.

"So what I suggest, before you go barreling in in any kind of official way, Sergeant, is that you let us poke around a little more. Discreetly, of course."

"Like how?"

"Well, like the two of us—John and I—going back and having a chat with Axel. Informally. We were going to do that anyway, before we decided to come back here. Bring up some of these same questions and see what he has to say."

Fukida was shaking his head. "I don't think it's a good idea for civilians—"

"Who you calling a civilian?" John demanded. "And who dug up this stuff for you in the first place? Where would you be if not for us? Exactly where you were ten years ago—fat and happy and way out on a limb you didn't even know you were on."

"That's the truth," Fukida grumbled. "Happy, that's for sure. Okay, I won't do anything for a couple days. Go talk to Axel. Don't shake things up, though. Be discreet, you know?"

John put a hand to his heart. "Discretion is my middle name."

"THIS is good," John said as they headed to the truck. "I trust Axel. He'll level with us."

"I hope so."

John climbed in and buckled the seat belt. "Especially if we nudge him a little," he said under his breath.

THIRTEEN

THE old man didn't look up as John and Gideon climbed the steps of the front porch. He was moving slowly along on his knees, his mouth full of nails, hammering down the warped ends of the porch floorboards.

"Hey, Willie," John said. "I see they got you doing handyman jobs now, huh?"

"Got me doing everything," the old man muttered through the nails, still not looking up. "What else is new? You name it, I do it."

Then something about John's voice got his attention. He looked up, tipped back his curling, sweat-stained, flower-garlanded hat, spat the nails into his hand, and grinned. His good-natured face was as weathered, and almost as dark as the unpainted wood of the porch.

"What do you know, it's Johnny Lau, the kid that could never get enough to eat. You done growing yet?"

"I sure hope so," John said. "It's not easy finding shoes this big. How's it going, boss?"

"Not bad. Fine." He got to his feet, wincing a little as his knees straightened. A short, stubby man in old jeans and ancient, scuffed work boots. "You know, I saw you out here on the porch yesterday. Thought it was you. So how come you didn't say hello?"

"Well, you know," John said.

"Yeah, right. I'm Willie Akau," he said to Gideon. "Foreman here. I'm the guy that taught Johnny everything he knows. All the important stuff, anyway."

"Truer than you think," John said. "Willie, we're looking for Axel. Is he inside?"

"Naw, he's out at Paddock Number Four with the rest of 'em."

"They branding?"

"Branding, castrating, inoculating, the whole bit. Springtime, you know? Tell you what, I'm about done here and I want to see how they're doing anyway. Lemme get one of them Japanese quarter horses, and we'll go out and have a look."

"Japanese quarter horses?" a puzzled John echoed. "What're they?"

Willie grinned at him. "Things have changed since you worked here, brudda. A Japanese quarter horse—that's what we call a Honda ATV."

"ATV? What, you paniolos don't ride horses anymore?"

"Sure we do, most of the time. I was thinking about your friend. He don't look like no horseman to me."

Gideon laughed. "You're right about that." A few years earlier, in Oregon, he'd been thrown from a horse, fallen down a hillside, suffered a concussion, and almost gotten squashed flat when the terrified horse came within inches of rolling over him. Since then he'd been leery of getting on one again.

"Looks like some kind of professor or something."

"Right again." Good God, he thought, has it come to that? Have I started *looking* like a professor? "How can you tell?"

"It's your aura," John said. "Okay, Willie, let's get going."

"I'll get the ATV. You better sit in back, Professor. Easier to hold onto the roll bar back there."

THE ATV that Willie came back with wasn't a Honda, but a yellow, six-wheel-drive Argo equipped with caterpillar tracks; a cross between a beach buggy and a topless mini-tank, with room for six.

"Thought you'd be more comfortable in this monster, Professor. Safer, you know? Make sure you hold on tight to that bar now."

Muttering, Gideon got into the back as instructed but determinedly refused to grasp the roll bar, twice coming perilously close to tumbling out as a result. But once they got off the dirt trails and onto the grass-cushioned, rolling hills the ride smoothed out, and they made it to the paddock without incident. Willie went into the pipe-fenced corral to join his paniolos. Gideon and John stayed outside, leaning on the fence with Axel.

From his reading, and from what John had told him, Gideon expected—and hoped for—a colorful scene, with whooping paniolos roping the calves and throwing them, rodeo style, for the branding. But ranching, as he kept hearing, had changed. All it took was a little quiet clucking and nudging for the horsemen to urge the five or six dozen calves, one at a time, up a ramp and into the "squeeze box," a narrow, ten-foot-long wooden enclosure in which, Axel explained, they were inoculated against blackleg, branded with the Little Hoaloha "LH," had their ears notched for tags, and, if they were bulls, painlessly castrated—the method involved a rubber band that would cut off blood supply to the testes over the next few weeks; not a knife or a set of pincers, as in the old days. And everything was under the supervision of a veterinarian who was in there with them; another change from the old days.

There was no terrified baying or bellowing from the squeeze box. After a minute or two, the calf would simply emerge from the other end, snorting and shaking its head, but looking more offended than hurt or frightened. And in would come the next one.

"We don't castrate them all," Axel said. "A few of them are just vasectomized and kept around as teasers."

"Teasers?" Gideon said.

"We use them to determine when a cow is ready to be inseminated. See, the stud fees for good bulls are pretty scary, so we don't send for the big guys until we know the cows are willing to go along with it. Well, no cow will let a bull mount her except when she's in heat, so the way we know one of them is ready is when we see one of our vasectomized bulls mount her and go to work. That's why we call them teasers."

"Nice work if you can get it," John said. "Uh, Axel, we need to talk to you."

"Sure," Axel said, his eyes on the paniolos. "Go ahead, shoot. Willie!" he called. "The one that just came out. Take a look at that foreleg, would you? There's something the matter with it."

"No, let's go somewhere where you can pay attention," John said. "This is important."

The sudden change in tone made Axel blink. "All right. The tack shed."

They went to a tin-roofed, rough-hewn lean-to with ropes and rawhide straps hanging from the ceiling and the walls, and tools, sacks, and old saddle gear draped over racks, lying on work benches, or strewn about the dirt floor. The leather items were cracked and dusty, as if the shed hadn't been used as a workplace for years. Axel pulled three banged-up folding metal chairs from a stack that had been stored against one wall.

"Never mind the chairs, Axel," John said.

But Axel set them out anyway. There was something dogged in the way he did it, as if he sensed that nothing good was coming and he was trying to head it off as long as he could.

"What's the problem, John?" he asked when they'd sat down, the three of them facing each other somewhat awkwardly, three pairs of denimed knees almost touching. "Did you see the autopsy report?" He looked at Gideon. "Was it Magnus?"

"That I can't say for sure," Gideon answered. "It's impossible to tell from—"

"What we *can* say for sure," John cut in, eager to get started nudging, "is that, whoever it was, somebody chopped off two of his toes."

Axel was satisfactorily nudged. His face twisted in a grimace. "Somebody chopped off his *toes*—you mean on purpose?"

"I don't figure it was by accident."

"No, well, of course not. I mean . . . Jesus, that's horrible, that's disgusting! Are you sure?"

"Absolutely," Gideon said. "That's what made the autopsy doctor so positive he was Torkel."

"But who would . . . who would—"

"We're assuming it was Torkel," John said.

"Ah, no, that's crazy, that's—"

"We're also assuming it was Torkel who left his own ring on the body."

"What are you—" Axel began with a vehement shake of his head, but stopped in mid-sentence, his mouth open. "The ring!"

"So you did know about the ring?"

"Yes, sure, everybody knew about it." He took off his black-rimmed glasses and gnawed on the temple piece, thinking hard. Without them, his face was oddly blank and defenseless. He didn't have eyelashes, Gideon noticed. "You're right, you're absolutely right. Torkel must have left it there to fool everybody. Oh, this is too weird!"

"How come nobody mentioned it when we came back from Maravovo and said the body in the plane was Torkel?"

"Mentioned what?"

John sighed. "The ring, Axel."

"I don't know." He shrugged. "I guess we forgot about it. It was ten years ago."

"Did you?" John asked, sounding more like a policeman with every word. "You're telling me that every single one of you forgot there'd been a ring?"

Axel thrust out his unforgivable chin. "Well, *I* sure did."

"You, I can believe," John said, relaxing enough to let a smile come through. "You were probably thinking about all those macro-nutrients in manure at the time. But the others . . ." What was left of the smile slowly vanished. "Something's wrong, Axel. It didn't happen the way everybody said. People haven't leveled with us, and I don't think they leveled with the police either. I'm hoping you'll—"

Axel abruptly shoved his chair back and jumped up, raising a cloud of flour-like dust from the floor. "John, you're . . . you're pushing me." He stamped around in tight little circles, whapping his hat—a blue tennis hat with the names of the Hawaiian islands on the band; the kind every ABC store carried—against his jeans. Dust flew with every whap. "I mean, I appreciate that you're concerned, and I certainly appreciate what *you've* done, Gideon, but . . . look, no offense, but I really can't see how any of this is your business, either of you. I don't see why you're so damn interested in this, and I don't like it that you're trying to get me to say something against my own family. I don't know what Torkel did or didn't do, but I can tell you that nobody here, nobody in this family, did anything wrong!"

He had let most of it out in one breath, his voice rising to a squeak, and now he gulped air, staring down at them, pop-eyed and agitated. There were tears in his eyes.

"Sit down, Axel," John said calmly.

"I mean . . . it's just that . . . you come here, you act like—"

"Sit down, Axel."

"Well, I'm just—" Axel sat.

"Put your glasses back on."

He knuckled at the corners of his eyes, sniffled, and put on his glasses.

John put a hand on his knee, an extraordinary gesture for him. "Axel, listen to me. You're my friend, you have been for a lot of years. But more than that, your family has meant a lot to me. Torkel and Magnus especially, those guys really straightened me out, they taught me to . . . well, to grow up. The second best thing that ever happened to me was when Magnus fired me my first day on the job because I didn't show up on time. The best thing was when Torkel hired me back. And Dagmar—she bailed me out of trouble a hundred times. She was the first one that told me I ought to go into police work, did you know that?"

"Of course I know all that," Axel said uncomfortably, "and it's not that I don't—"

"So sure I'm interested. There's trouble on the way, Axel, and if there's some way I can help, I want to do it. We've just come from a long talk with a sergeant at CIS. He says—"

Axel's jaw dropped. "The police? You told them all this?"

"Yes, we did. Fukida wants to reopen the case—"

Axel's hand flew to his forehead. "Oh, mercy."

"—but he's not going to get on it for a couple of days. We said we wanted to talk to you first, and he said okay. So if you know something you haven't told us—or didn't tell the police back then—now's the time to do it, trust me. You're a lot better off—you're *all* a lot better off—if you come forward with it now than if you make Fukida dig it out on his own. I know this guy, Axel. You don't want to tangle with him. This is one hard-nosed sonofabitch, and he's already ticked off."

Axel had listened intently, growing mulish and frightened-looking. "But I *don't* know anything! There isn't anything to know!"

"We think there is," John said. "For example, we think that Torkel was the one who set the fire, too."

"You mean, to get away? To cover up the . . . the switch?"

Gideon thought he was going to deny it, to argue, but after a moment he nodded jerkily. "Okay. Okay, I see where you're going with this. Maybe he did. Maybe that's possible, I don't know. I mean, how would I know? But I still don't understand why the police would want to get involved after all this time. What difference does it make now?"

"Oh, I can tell you why it makes a difference," John said impassively. "It makes a difference because a scam was perpetrated ten years ago, and the result of that scam was that you, your brother Felix, your sister Hedwig, and your sister Inge"—he was speaking very slowly now, emphasizing each word—"all inherited big, valuable chunks of land that shouldn't have gone to you. If the truth'd been known about who really died first, it wouldn't have happened that way. Torkel's will would be the surviving one, and you'd each have come out with a few thousand bucks apiece, period. And the seamen's home would be the one that was rolling in dough."

"Oh," Axel said wretchedly, "I see."

"And listen to me now—if any of you knew about this—"

"We *didn't!* I swear! The first I heard it was Torkel was after you two—"

"—and failed to tell the police, then you've committed the crime of fraud, or at least you'd be accessories after the fact."

"John, you have to believe me!"

"Axel, did Torkel kill Magnus?" Gideon asked. It wasn't something he could honestly say he believed, but he figured it was his turn to do a little nudging and see what came of it.

On the other hand, it was interesting, the way his mind kept coming back to the question.

Axel stared bug-eyed at him. "Where did *that* come from?" Apparently unable to sit still, he jumped out of his chair again, jammed on his hat, and wandered distractedly outside, squinting in the bright sunlight. "I can't believe I'm hearing this," he said to the empty air. "I can't believe this is happening."

"Axel, take it easy," John called. "We're floundering here. We're just trying to make sense of what happened."

Axel's stooped shoulders rose and fell. He came back, flopped down in his chair again, and spread his hands. "I don't know what to tell you. I just don't know what to tell you."

John shook his head. "Well, between us, I'm not sure where the hell we go from here." He glanced at Gideon for help, but all Gideon could do was shrug. He wasn't sure either.

"Can't we just leave it alone?" Axel pleaded. "It was ten years ago."

"Well, I know, but this whole thing is too bizarre—"

"John, I am *not* going to lose my ranch! I swear to God, I didn't do anything wrong. Not knowingly. None of us did."

John hesitated. "Axel . . . I'm your friend, you know that, but I'm also a sworn officer of the law. I have an obligation to, to"—he flushed, something he did when he thought he was being pompous—"Well, not technically, but . . . I mean . . . I guess . . . oh, hell, I don't know. I guess we just leave it to Fukida. I don't know what else to suggest."

For a few seconds the three men sat without speaking. The smells of dust and worn-out leather seemed to be coming from their skin by now. At the rear of the shed a couple of flies buzzed listlessly and intermittently against a window pane. John continued to shake his head silently.

What a rare thing it was, Gideon thought, to see John Lau look irresolute. "Look, this whole thing really *is* none of my business," he said, "but I have an idea."

John and Axel looked up hopefully.

"Before Fukida comes in, maybe somebody should have a talk with Dagmar."

Axel frowned. "Why Dagmar?"

"Because if anybody knows what really happened that night, it's Dagmar."

"Oh, that's really ridiculous," Axel said hotly. "I'm

sorry, but this is really over the top. I can't believe you're accusing that fantastic old lady who's been through so much—"

"I didn't hear anybody make any accusations," John said stiffly. "Go ahead, Doc."

"Frankly, I'm not sure if I'm making any accusations or not, but if you think about it, everything we know, or think we know, about that night came through Dagmar: the story about Torkel's telephoning her, pretending to be Magnus; the whole business about how 'they' killed his brother and were threatening him—every bit of that came out of Dagmar's deposition. There was no other source for it, no independent verification."

"That's so, but—" Axel began.

"All I'm saying is that it would be good to hear what she has to say about all this."

"Well—"

"Doc's right," John said. "We ought to talk to her. Better us than the police, to start with. If we can't head this whole thing off, then maybe at least we can soften it."

Axel gave in. "I guess I can see that. Look, don't think I don't appreciate what you're trying to do."

"When would be a good time to see her?"

"Well, she has cinnamon buns and coffee on her terrace every morning and sits there for an hour or so. She's always in the best mood of the day then. That'd be a good time."

"What time in the morning?" John asked doubtfully.

"Nine, nine-thirty."

John brightened. "Oh, that's fine. We'll do it tomorrow."

"Not tomorrow, she'll still be in the hospital for her tests. She doesn't get out till three in the afternoon."

"Okay, the day after tomorrow, then—what is that, Tuesday? We can hold Fukida off that long. Doc and I could just sort of stop by in the morning, say we were in the neighborhood—"

"No, count me out of this one," Gideon said.

John was surprised. "It was your idea."

"Yes, but I only met the woman a couple of times. She hardly knows me. How can I come barging in uninvited with a bunch of questions?"

John understood. "Well, that's okay, I'll do it myself. No problem."

"I could go with you if it'd make things more comfortable," Axel offered. "I drop by for a cup of coffee every now and then anyway, if I'm on my way to Kona."

"No, that's all right. Auntie Dagmar and I are old pals."

Axel hesitated. "You're not going to *grill* her, are you?"

John laughed. "No, Axel, I'm not going to grill her. I'll leave my rubber hose back at the house."

"WE worked your friend over a little hard," Gideon said when Willie Akau had dropped them off in the equipment yard near the ranch house. "I feel kind of bad about it."

John nodded. "Had to be done. We'll make it up to him. How do you think it went? Do you buy what he said? About none of them knowing?"

"I don't know, John. It's pretty hard to believe that the reason nobody spoke up about the ring is that every single one of them just conveniently forgot about it."

John nodded. "You're right about that, but as far as Axel himself is concerned, whatever else he is, he's no con artist. With Axel, what you see is what you get."

FOURTEEN

EVEN with the cell phone jammed against her ear, Inge could hardly hear him, what with all the *yee-ha-ing* and *ki-yi-yi-ying,* let alone the mooing and stamping of the cows. She was riding postern on the afternoon's Cattle Drive Adventure ("An honest-to-goodness cattle drive in which you will ride trained cow horses as you help the wranglers drive our mini-herd of Angus crossbreeds over the open range"), and she had been lucky simply to hear the phone beep.

She pulled her horse to the side and cantered away from the tumult.

"Axel, calm down. Say again?"

"I said I think they know everything! Or they're about two inches away from it. John and Gideon, they were just here. You should have heard their questions. And . . . and . . ."

"Axel, take a deep breath. Now, what the hell are you

talking about?" She took a breath herself and closed her eyes. *Don't let this be what I think.*

But it was. Through his babbling she managed to make out the gist of what he was saying. No, she thought, they hadn't figured out everything, but they were close. At the least they knew that the accepted version of events had some holes, big holes, in it. She'd feared this might happen from the moment they'd came back from Maravovo with the news about Torkel, but by that time there had simply been no way to head them off. *Think,* she told herself. *Think.*

Axel was just repeating himself now, in stuttery, fragmented phrases, like an old-fashioned record with a needle stuck in a groove, and she interrupted. "What did you tell them?"

"I didn't tell them anything. Inge, they kept talking about the wills, and how the wrong one went into effect, and how we could be accomplices—I mean accessories—"

"How did you find out there was a ring?"

"I don't know. Maybe they—"

"What did you say when they asked why nobody mentioned it?"

"I said . . . I don't remember what I said. But I know I didn't tell them anything."

"But you don't remember what you said," Inge said wryly.

She'd dismounted now and was wandering about with the reins in her hand, letting Betsy nibble at the coarse grass. She could hear him clearly now. The whooping Indonesians and the disgusted cattle had moved off a hundred yards.

"No, but I know I didn't tell them anything that . . . Inge, I was so flustered, I hardly knew what I was saying. They kept talking about how the will might be invalidated if we knew all along it was Torkel in the plane—"

"Okay, Axel, shh, it's all right, you did fine. It couldn't be helped."

What rotten dumb luck that they had picked him to come to with their questions. If it had been her, she might have . . . well, what?

"Inge, they asked me if Torkel killed Magnus!"

That stopped her. "They asked you *what*?"

"They asked me—"

"I heard you, I heard you! Where would they get that idea?"

"I don't know! It was Gideon—"

"And what did you say to that? Or don't you remember that either?"

"What do you mean, what did I say? I told them it was ridiculous. But the fact that they would even come up with a question like that . . . what does it mean?"

"It means they were fishing. They know something's wrong, but they don't know what. This isn't good, Axel."

"You don't . . . you don't think . . . I mean, nothing could *happen*, not after all this time, could it?"

"Nothing serious, only that we might all go to jail and lose our inheritances," she snapped.

She heard his gasp. "But what should we do now?" he whispered.

"Let me make sure I have this straight. This Sergeant Fukida wants to look into it, but he's given John and Gideon a couple of days leeway before he gets started, and John is going to see Dagmar Tuesday? The day after tomorrow?"

"In the morning, yes. I think he wanted to head right over from here, but I told him she was in the hospital till tomorrow afternoon and it'd be better—"

"All right, that was good. Now be quiet, let me think."

He continued making agitated little sounds, as if he were walking around in a circle talking to himself, which he probably was. "Christ," she muttered, sticking the telephone in a saddle bag. She placed her hands on Betsy's rump, leaned her forehead on her hands, and thought. When she got the telephone out of the saddlebag again, Axel was still chattering away.

"But there have to be some kind of statutes of limitation. Felix would know—"

"All right, here's what we do," she said, and Axel fell instantly silent. "This is not something that we want Dagmar to have to deal with on her own. You saw how shaky she was the other day. She'll need some propping up."

"I know, I know. That's exactly what I was thinking— that we all better be there when John arrives—"

"No, how would that look? Axel, for a smart guy, you can be the most . . ." She sighed. "What we need to do is talk to Dagmar *first,* but, yes, everybody should be in on it. This concerns everyone, and everyone has a right to have their say. Here's the way it'll work: I'll run down to the hospital tomorrow morning to drive her home."

"She doesn't get out till the afternoon."

"Axel, for Christ's sake, they're not holding her prisoner! We don't have a lot of time; we'll cut the tests short. I'll tell them to have her ready early, and I'll explain everything to her on the way back. She'll be tired, and this is going to upset her—"

"It's sure upsetting me," Axel mumbled.

"—so we'll give her a few hours to rest and get herself together. We'll all meet at, oh, one o'clock. Can you have everybody at her place by then?"

"Wouldn't it be easier to meet up here, maybe at your place?"

"Axel, will you please try and use your head for once? We don't want John and Gideon to see us all getting together with her first, do we?"

"Oh. Well, I guess—"

"Don't guess. Just get hold of the rest and have them there by one."

"Everybody? But Felix is in Honolulu."

She clenched her teeth. "I *know* that, little brother, but he is fully capable of catching a plane and being on the Big Island an hour after walking out his front door. We're going to *need* him. He's our lawyer."

"All right, I'll get right on it. 'Bye, Inge."

"Axel?"

"Inge?"

"When I said 'everybody,' that didn't include Malani. Don't bring Malani."

She could tell he was holding the phone away from his ear and staring at it. "Well, holy cow, Inge, I'm not *stupid*."

" 'Bye, Axel."

WHEN Gideon and John got back to the house, they found Julie sprawled on one of two porch chairs, watching them and looking tired but contented. On a table next to her was a pitcher of iced orange-guava juice and two glasses.

"Pull up a couple of chairs. Malani's in the house, putting together something to nibble. The glasses are in the dining room, in the cabinet over the—"

"I know where they are," John said, going in to get some.

"You look happy," Gideon said as he dragged over two more chairs. "Have a good day?"

"Very," Julie said. "Malani showed me over the ranch. It's huge. We rode for three solid hours. It was wonderful." She rubbed her thigh and winced. "But I doubt if I'll be able to walk tomorrow. I used muscles I forgot I even had."

Gideon nodded. "Oho, the good old medial rotators.

You don't put much stress on them day-to-day, but you need them for hanging onto the horse with your knees. The adductors would have gotten a workout too: the *brevis,* the *pectineus . . ."*

"See? Didn't I say he gives lectures?" John said, coming back with the glasses.

"I assumed she'd want to know," Gideon said. "I know it will come as a shock to you, but some people are intellectually curious."

"I most certainly did want to know," Julie said loyally. "I'd been just about to ask." She smiled affectionately at the two men, picked up the pitcher, and poured for them. "So how did it go at the police station? Did you come up with some good answers?"

"No, but we sure got some great questions," John said. "I'm hoping Dagmar can help with the answers. I'm gonna go see her Tuesday morning."

"Why Dagmar?"

By the time John, with Gideon's help, had finished explaining, they were on their second glasses, and the three of them were covering the same ground and arriving at the same dead ends that they'd reached with Axel and with Fukida.

"John, aren't you putting yourself in an uncomfortable position, talking to Axel, and now to Dagmar?" Julie asked. "These are your friends, not just some anonymous suspects."

"Tell me about it. I *am* uncomfortable, Julie, but I already said I'd do it."

"To Axel, right? Dagmar isn't expecting you, is she? Are you sure you don't just want to leave it to Sergeant Fukida? In the long run, it might be better."

John hesitated, debating within himself. "Maybe I do, at that," he said softly. "It's not as if I really think there's anything I can do for them. I can call Fukida and let him know the ball's in his court, I'm out of it. Somehow, I don't think he'll complain."

"I'm uncomfortable, too," Gideon said. "It's been bothering me all day."

"What do *you* have to be uncomfortable about?" John asked.

"I'm uncomfortable about accepting these nice people's hospitality at the same time I seem to be doing everything I can to sic the police on them, and totally upsetting their lives, and maybe losing them their inheritances. I can't keep riding around in their pickup, eating their food, acting as if . . . well, as if everything is all right, when it's clearly not. And most of it is my fault."

"And the rest is mine," John said.

"Obviously, this is not turning into much of a vacation—for any of us." Julie said. She set down her glass with a thump. "I have a suggestion. I think we should all check out of Chez Torkelsson, go on down to one of those gorgeous resorts on the coast for a few days, forget about all this, and have ourselves a real vacation. Swim, sightsee, take in a luau, eat ourselves silly, and just relax in the sun. How does that sound?"

"Terrific," said Gideon, brightening.

John shrugged. "Nah, I think I'd probably just go on home if you guys do that."

"Have you seen the Seattle weather?" Julie asked him. "Let's see, I think I remember: tomorrow, low clouds and scattered showers; Tuesday, showers in the A.M., increasing to steady rain, sometimes heavy, in the afternoon; Wednesday, cloudy with likelihood of heavy—"

John threw up his hands. "Okay, okay. Sounds awful."

"And what about Meathead? You can't forget Meathead," Gideon said.

John laughed. "All right, you convinced me." He sobered. "But how the heck do we tell Axel and Malani? That'll be a little awkward."

"That's women's work," Julie said. "It takes a sensitive hand. You leave it to me. I'll square it with Malani after dinner tonight, and we can leave tomorrow. I guarantee: no hurt feelings."

As if on cue, Malani came out with a tray of crackers and mixed cheeses. "I thought I heard your voices," she said cheerfully. "Good, let's plan dinner." She set the tray down and took a chair. "I want us all to get away from the ranch and go into town for a meal for a change. I don't know about you, but if I have to look one more overdone steak in the eye, I . . . will . . . barf."

"How about pizza?" John suggested hopefully. "We passed a Domino's in Waimea."

"We'll eat Chinese," Malani went on, as if he hadn't spoken. "I know a place."

"Yes, ma'am," John said.

"And now," Malani said, putting a hand to her forehead and pretending to peer up at something through the surrounding tree branches, "the sun is over the yardarm. Who wants a glass of wine?"

In the kitchen, she got a bottle of Chardonnay out of the refrigerator and put it on the counter. Gideon, with the corkscrew in his hand, suddenly recalled something. "Malani, remember that box you couldn't find the other day?"

She looked up from setting out four big wine glasses. "Box?"

"Yes, with the effects from the plane. You said it'd been on the counter, but—"

"Oh, that's right, the one . . . well, I forgot to ask." She put her head in the doorway to the living room. "Kilia!"

Kilia—short, fat, and energetic—trotted into the dining room with a cleaning cloth in her hand. "Yes, missus?"

"Kilia, remember the box those young men brought the other day? With the cup and that little ceramic map—"

"Sure, missus."

"Did you put it away somewhere?"

"No, ma'am!" Kilia declared with a shudder. "That box and the one with the skeleton bones—I wouldn't touch them things."

"Thank you, Kilia. Well, not to worry," she said to Gideon. "It'll show up."

AUNTIE Dagmar was getting old.

The thought hit Inge like a blow when she peeked through the open doorway of Dagmar's room at Kona Hospital. She had certainly seemed depressed for a couple of days, but this was different. She was *old*. Old, and shrunken, and . . . frail. The ageing and shrinking had been going on for a long time but the *frail* was something new. So even Dagmar was not indestructible, she thought with a tiny, unanticipated catch in her throat; even Dagmar, who had seemingly been here since the beginning of time, was not permanent in this world.

The old woman was sitting hunched on the side of her bed, fully dressed in a black pant-suit, legs hanging down with her feet not reaching the floor, holding onto a small, blue, hard-sided suitcase that was set upright beside her. She'd put on lipstick and rouge for once, and her jet-black wig was actually on straight, but with her white, papery skin the effect was somewhere between clownish and ghoulish. She was like an ancient, wizened child—an unwanted wartime orphan—dumped in some deserted train station with her pathetic belongings, and waiting pitifully, hopelessly, for someone to come and get her.

"It's about time," she snapped when she saw Inge. "Rush, rush, rush, so I'm ready to be picked up, then wait, wait, wait. They didn't even give me a breakfast. Help me down from here. I don't suppose you thought to bring any schnapps?"

Inge smiled. That's what she got for getting sentimental about Auntie Dagmar. "Never mind the schnapps, Auntie. It's eight o'clock in the morning. We have a problem, a big problem."

"I hate problems," Dagmar said.

"Don't worry, I have it all worked out." She took Dagmar by one elbow—her arm was like a dried twig—and helped her down with the aid of a stepstool. "We just need to talk it over. Let's go somewhere and get something to eat."

"Now you're talking. Island Lava Java? Cinnamon rolls?"

"Anything you want. But I don't think they have schnapps."

DAGMAR cut her cinnamon roll precisely in half and lathered one portion with the extra butter she'd ordered, but didn't raise it to her mouth. Her coffee had been likewise creamed and sugared while Inge spoke, but otherwise untouched. She stared out at the tourists exploring Ali'i Drive, and at the sea wall on the other side of the street, and at Kailua Bay beyond. A white Norwegian Line cruise ship lay anchored a few hundred yards offshore and Kona was swarming with curious, tentative sixty- and seventy-year-olds in tank tops, flip-flops, and sunglasses. Even from their table, Inge could smell the sunscreen.

"No," Dagmar said.

Inge stared at her. "*No?* No, what?"

"No, everything. I'm not going to sit there with people pulling me this way and that way, telling me what to be careful about and how to act and what to say when I talk to John, and what not to say. And I'm not talking to John either."

Inge sighed. It was Dagmar's nature to be recalcitrant; there was no point in becoming impatient. "It won't be like that, Auntie," she said kindly. "We can just come up with a few guidelines—topics to steer clear of—"

"It *will* be like that. Felix will order me to say this, you'll order me to say that, Hedwig will lecture me on karma." She picked up the piece of cinnamon roll only to put it down again. "No," she said again, more firmly still. "I can't remember what I told the police before, it was so long ago. They have a record of it. I'm bound to contradict myself. John would catch me. Isn't he a detective or something now?"

"He's an FBI agent."

"Well, he used to be a detective."

"He used to be a policeman in Honolulu—"

"Don't keep changing the subject. That's a bad habit you have. The point is, I can't go through any more of that, where they harp on every word I said before. Impossible."

"But what do you suggest, Auntie? You can't avoid seeing him tomorrow."

"I most certainly can."

"How?"

"By going to see this Sergeant what's-his-name and telling him the truth today."

Inge was stunned. She didn't know what she'd been expecting, but it wasn't that. "But if you tell him the whole truth—"

"I didn't say the *whole* truth, I said the truth."

Confused, Inge jerked her head. "I don't—"

Dagmar grasped her wrist. "Inge, think about what you just told me. What do they know? They know that Torkel changed identities with Magnus. What do they suspect? They suspect that I—that we—were aware of it and lied to protect him."

"No, they also think we lied to protect our inheritances. Well, not you, because you got the same under both wills, but—"

"Yes, all right. So, do you think they'll simply drop it now? It's only a question of time until they ferret out what really happened. Isn't it better to come out with it voluntarily, than to be caught in one lie after another, like rats in a trap?"

"But you're not saying you'd tell them . . . ?"

"Everything? Of course not. I may be getting a bit senile, but I'm not crazy yet."

"I see," Inge said reflectively. It just could be that Dagmar had the right idea. The old lady might be getting frail, but not in the head. Still, there were problems. She leaned closer and lowered her voice. "Auntie, there may be criminal charges involved. And . . . what *about* our inheritances? We could lose them."

"Pooh, I don't believe that for a minute. Not after so much time. There are statutes about such things. Felix can straighten out any problems."

That was what Inge believed, too, but it was good to hear Dagmar say it. "But how will it look?"

"It will look as if everything possible was done to protect my dear brother and your dear uncle from the vicious assassins that threatened his life, even if the law did happen to be slightly violated in a technical sense. People will understand."

Not so technical, Inge thought, and yet, the more Dag-

mar talked, the more convinced she became that this was
the best course. People *would* understand. "The rest of the
family, though—they might not like it," she said. "This af-
fects all of us."

"Then they'll have to lump it, won't they?" Dagmar
said cheerfully. Sensing Inge's incipient agreement and
satisfied with the way the conversation was going, she finally took a bite of the roll, smacked her lips, and licked
butter from her fingers. "Now, Inge, dear, I imagine you'd
like to argue with me about it for a while. Will fifteen minutes do? If it's going to be longer, I'll want another cup of
coffee."

"I'm not going to argue," Inge said, laughing. "You
have my complete support. Would you like me to be with
you, or do you want to see him alone?"

"Suit yourself, dear," Dagmar said. Her sharp gray eyes
glinted happily from their parchmentlike folds of skin. She
no longer looked frail. She was, as always, looking forward
to stirring things up.

FIFTEEN

SERGEANT Fukida was in no mood to be trifled with. His annual mock-orange pollen allergy attack, late this year, had finally caught up with him as he'd gotten home from work the previous day, smiting him with itchy, runny eyes, headache, sinus congestion, achy joints, and all-around misery. With Chiyoko staying at their daughter's on Oahu overnight, he'd had to fend for himself, which meant not only an absence of much-needed wifely care and sympathy, but a pathetic, solitary dinner of scrambled eggs over rice, representing the extreme limit of his culinary virtuosity. He'd taken a couple of allergy tablets at eight and gone to bed, another two at midnight, and two more at three A.M. when a stuffed nose had strangled him out of sleep. He'd awakened to the alarm at seven with a vicious antihistamine hangover and nasal passages that felt as if they'd been cleaned out with a paint-scraper.

Headachy, dull-brained, and generally mad at the world,

he'd driven to work on a breakfast of microwave-warmed, leftover scrambled eggs and rice and three cups of tea. His plan was to tell Sarah, "No visitors, no phone calls," to barricade himself in his cubicle, and to spend the day on paperwork, of which he had plenty to catch up on, sleeping through lunch, if at all possible. This was not a day on which he should be expected to deal with living, speaking human beings. Fortunately, there were no appointments or meetings on his calendar.

His plan did not work.

"Morning, Sarge, couple of ladies waiting in there to see you," was Sarah's gratingly cheery greeting. "They were sitting in the lobby when I got here."

He stifled a groan. "To see me in particular, or anybody?" he asked, but without any real hope.

"Sorry," Sarah said with a grin. "To see you. I checked with the lieutenant, and he said it's you, all right."

"You know what it's about?"

"The Torkelsson thing."

"I knew I shouldn't have come to work," he said bitterly. "My head is in no condition to deal with the Torkelsson thing."

"Do you want me to—"

"No," he said, drawing himself up and looking for the first time into the opening to his cubicle. He could just see a pair of black-pant-clad legs, the feet of which barely touched the floor. "I'll deal with it."

"Brave sergeant," Sarah said. "Good sergeant."

HE disliked them right off the bat. The old woman sat as if she owned the place, barely turning her head to cast a beady, disapproving eye on him as he entered his own office. The younger one, in jeans and Western shirt, sprawled in his other visitor's chair like a man, legs akimbo, one booted ankle on the other knee. He didn't much care for that either.

"We've been waiting some time," the old woman told him.

Tough. He squeezed around the desk, took his seat, and looked at them inquiringly, his expression neutral.

"I am Dagmar Torkelsson," the old lady said. "This is my niece, Inge Torkelsson Nakoa. Do you know who we are?"

"Yes. What can I do for you?"

"You are familiar with the Torkelsson matter of some years ago?"

Fukida nodded.

"Excellent. We are here to correct certain misapprehensions that the police may have in regard to those events."

You are here, Fukida thought, because Lau and Oliver had gone about their "discreet" inquiries like a couple of bulls in a china shop, rattling the teeth of the entire Torkelsson establishment. They were now aware that the lies they had told ten years ago had caught up with them, and unless he was mistaken he was about to hear some bogus, newly concocted version of events that would supposedly explain away the old contradictions and ambiguities. A little more fancy dancing by the doyenne of the clan to once again boggle the minds of the credible, gullible, Hawaii County PD. Well, let 'em try. Irritable as he was, he was genuinely curious to see what they'd come up with. His headache, he found, had receded. He rearranged himself more comfortably in his chair and pulled a pad and pen to within easy reach.

"Misapprehensions?" he said.

The niece, Inge, spoke for the first time, doing her best

to look helpful and remorseful. "You see, we weren't entirely truthful before."

No! Really? he thought but didn't say. "In what way would that be, Mrs. Nakoa?"

After the briefest of glances between the two women, it was Dagmar who picked up the ball. "The fact is that we—all of us—have been aware from the beginning that the body in the hay barn was not that of my brother Torkel."

He tried not to show his surprise, but an outright, unforced admission of this central, critical fact was not what he'd been expecting. What game were they playing? He felt himself suddenly off-balance. His headache stabbed at him again. "You were—?"

"Young man," Dagmar said harshly, "will you kindly stop that wiggling? It makes it difficult to concentrate."

"Wiggling?"

She made a series of irritated gestures toward the ballpoint pen that he was inarguably clicking open and shut, toward his tapping foot, toward the base of his chair, which creaked with every little bobbing movement of his body. Angrily, he made himself be still, but who the hell did this old—

It was time, he decided, to retake the initiative. "Do you also happen to be aware of who chopped off two of his toes to make us think he was Torkel?" he asked brutally.

"Yes," Inge responded. "That was me."

"THAT was you," Fukida repeated stupidly, mostly because he couldn't think of anything else to say. Was he supposed to believe her? What were these two up to? Damn those allergy pills; the inside of his skull felt as if it were crammed with cotton balls.

"Uh-huh," he went on. "You cut off the toes. And what did you use to do that?"

She replied without hesitation. "I used a Swiss garlic-chopper, a sort of tiny little cleaver. And a paperweight—it was the business end of an old branding iron—as a mallet, to drive it through." She held an imaginary handle in one hand, pretending to tap it with an object in her other hand.

It has to be true, Fukida thought. Who could make up something like that? A Swiss garlic-chopper, for Christ's sake.

"I think we better get this on the record," he said. "Let's go someplace a little more comfortable."

HAPPILY unaware of what had been unfolding at the police department, Julie, Gideon, and John spent Monday morning acting on their decision of the day before. As Julie had promised, the previous evening she had extricated them from their awkward position at Axel's and Malani's without seriously raising anybody's hackles. And early today they had checked in at the Waikoloa Outrigger, left their bags with the concierge, and breakfasted at the poolside grill with a guilty but welcome sense of freedom. Then they had rented a Ford Taurus and driven down the South Kona coast to visit a few of John's favorite places: the hidden-away black sand beach at Ho'okena, the Captain Cook Monument at Kealakekua Bay, the evocative and beautiful Pu'ohunua O Honaunau—the Place of Refuge Historical Park, a city of stone where ancients who had broken laws against gods or kings (who were much the same) could find sanctuary and avoid the all-too-frequent death sentences of the old days.

In the town of Captain Cook, they stopped at a farmers

cooperative to watch the processing of macadamia nuts and pick up a few gifts to take home. Never once had the words "Torkel," "Magnus," "toes," or "ring" come up.

On the way back, at Gideon's urging, they stopped in Kona to visit a place that even John didn't know about: a lovingly restored Hawaiian compound on a grassy tongue of land on the grounds of the King Kamehameha Hotel. From an anthropological point of view, Gideon told them, this was perhaps the most important site in Hawaii, the Ahu'ena Heiau, where the kind of event beloved of anthropologists had taken place over a century earlier; that rarest of occasions on which an entire society had changed literally overnight. It was here, in the largest and most impressive of the thatched structures, that Liholiho, son of Kamehameha, had sat down to dine in the company of women, thereby turning convention on its head and ending with one stroke a long-standing, strictly enforced tabu, and—eventually—totally changing the relationship of men and women in Hawaii. Gideon wandered about, enchanted: *This would have been the* lele, *where subjects left gifts. Look, this must have been the oracle tower, this must have been* . . . Julie and John trailed patiently along among the buildings and carved statues, making respectful noises until Gideon had his fill.

At a little before one, they were leaving the hotel's parking lot, looking for a likely place to have lunch, when John, sprawled sidewise in the Taurus's back seat and reading something that he'd brought along with him from the ranch, let out a yell.

"*What?*" He sat straight up and excitedly read aloud from the sheets of paper in his hand. " 'Among the interesting circumstances associated with them was the presence of a cartridge case partially embedded in the intervertebral fibro . . . fibrocartilage separating T8 and . . .' " He shook the papers and practically moaned. "Doc, Doc, how could you not tell me about this?"

"John, what are you talking about? Is that the autopsy report? How'd you get it? I thought we weren't supposed to—"

"This is a copy that clerk made. Sarah. She gave it to us, remember?"

"And you've had it ever since?"

"Yeah. Why didn't you tell me about the cartridge case?"

"The case?" He barely remembered reading about it. "It didn't seem important. Meikeljohn thought it was just some kind of freak accident. I didn't want to bore you."

"Okay, okay, never mind. Let's get back on the highway. We gotta go see Fukida."

"I thought you were all done—"

"So did I, but I was wrong."

"Do we have to go right this minute?" Julie said. "I was just thinking that Greek restaurant up on the corner, with the outside balcony tables, looks very appealing."

"Forget lunch, will you? We can eat later. We gotta go to the CIS."

"Forget lunch?" Gideon murmured. "We can eat later? This must be serious."

"You got that right," John said.

SIXTEEN

"TEDDY, you got a forensics library here?"

They had left Julie in Kona—where she wanted to see the old church and royal palace—and barged in on Fukida, who was having a tuna sandwich on rye and a can of Diet Coke at his desk. He had a mound of files spread out in front of him, was wearing his Colorado Rockies cap, and he was thinking hard, staring out the window with a dreamy, thoughtful look on his face. Although the sandwich was in his hand, he wasn't eating. Gideon and John's entry snapped him out of his reflections and into a more characteristic temper.

"What is this, more Torkel-Magnus crap? What do you people think, I don't have enough to keep me busy?"

"You got a forensics library?" John repeated.

"Sit down a minute. I got a little news for you two."

"I got news for *you*, Teddy," John said. Hands on his hips, he shifted from foot to foot, while they stared at each other. "So, I guess you're not gonna tell me if there's a forensics library?"

Fukida sighed and slapped down his sandwich. "*Sarah!*"

"My master's voice," floated over the partition from the clerical bullpen and in a moment Sarah herself followed. "You bellowed, sire?" She'd been having lunch, too. She was still chewing.

"Take this guy to the library, will you please?"

"Uh . . . the library?" she said doubtfully. "It's lunchtime. The boys have their poker game going."

"I'm not gonna bother them," John said. "Oh, and I also need the report from ballistics, if there is one, Teddy. On Torkelsson."

"What do you mean, *if* there is one? What kind of outfit do you think we run here?"

"I'm starting to wonder. So, can I look at it or not?"

"Give the man whatever he wants," Fukida said with a magisterial wave. "*Mi casa es su casa.*"

As John left, Fukida motioned Gideon to a chair. "Sit, chief. You want a Coke or something?"

"No, thanks."

"So what's the big guy all excited about?"

"I have no idea, Sergeant. But it was important enough to skip lunch, so, whatever it is, hold on to your hat."

Fukida went back to his sandwich. "May as well call me Ted," he mumbled.

"Thanks, Ted."

"As long as you're going to be coming in here every day."

"Not *every* day, I hope," Gideon said, smiling. He saw now that the folders spread across Fukida's desk were from the Torkelsson file. Now that was interesting. "You said there was some kind of news?"

"Plenty, but wait'll Lau gets back. I don't want to have

to go through it twice." He swiveled his chair to look out the window and chomped methodically, as if he were counting chews. "I wonder what he wants the ballistics report for."

"Beats me. I don't know if you know it or not, Ted, but one of John's specialties at the Bureau is ballistics. He really knows his stuff. He lectures on it in Quantico every couple of years."

"No, I didn't know. I'm impressed. That's a good outfit, the Academy. I took a fingerprint technology course there a little while ago; learned a lot. The kid's come a long way. I knew he would. Don't tell him I said that."

At which point John came barreling into the room with an open book in one hand and a green folder in the other. "Here it is. Listen." He held up the book so they could see the cover. "This is Di Maio, *Gunshot Wounds*. He's talking about this case where this guy got shot in the knee, okay? Here's what he says—"

"The *knee?*" Fukida exploded. "Who gives a shit about a guy who got shot in the knee?"

"The point is—"

"Sit down, Lau," Fukida commanded. "I got something important to tell you."

"Well, this is important, too. You think I—"

"Johnny, for the last time—"

"Okay, okay," John said, taking the remaining chair. "You want to tell me? Tell me. See? I'm sitting down." One conspicuous fore-finger remained in the book, marking his place.

"And *listen*."

"I'm listening." He closed the book and held up the finger for inspection. "See?"

"Okay. Now. Dagmar and Inge Torkelsson were in to see me a little while ago. Apparently, you two guys scared the bejesus out of Axel with that 'discreet' interviewing, and Axel called Inge, and Inge talked to Dagmar, and the two of them decided the best thing was to make a clean breast of it right now, before they got in even deeper."

He folded his hands, started his thumbs circling around each other, and leaned back. "The brunt of it is, they all knew about the Torkel-Magnus switch from Day One—all of them, the whole damn family, and they all conspired to cover it up. They sat right here and admitted it."

He sat back expectantly, waiting for their reactions.

Gideon wasn't sure what his own was. Was he surprised? No, not really; not after the questions he and John had been raising the last few days. Did that mean he'd been expecting this? No, he couldn't say that either. He'd known that a lot of the Torkelssons' story was bogus, but he couldn't say that he'd explicitly formed the theory that they were *all* involved in the switched identities. At the same time, he was conscious of a curious sense of anti-climax, as if he'd been anticipating something more, something worse, but what that might be he wasn't sure.

Aside from that, did he feel exploited by them, made a fool of? Well, yes. They'd trundled him off to a humid, fly-infested atoll to do his thing when they'd already known perfectly well who was in that plane. On the other hand, he couldn't deny that he'd enjoyed the day, and Waikiki had been a pleasant interlude, so what was there to be angry about?

There was one other thing. When John had suggested visiting Dagmar at home that morning, hadn't Axel said she'd be in the hospital till three in the afternoon, two hours from now? But obviously, she wasn't. What was that all about?

But mostly he was confused, wondering once more why, if they knew about the Torkel-Magnus switch and wanted to keep it to themselves, they would have encouraged him, first to go to Maravovo, and then to examine the autopsy report. Surely they would have realized he might come up with the truth about the identities. Had they really thought he'd fail to notice the chopped-off toes?

John's reaction was more defined. His face had darkened, his well-fleshed cheeks had flattened, and his chin had settled almost down to his chest. He was angry and he was hurt. "All of them knew?" he asked. "You're including Axel in that?"

"Oh, yeah. They were all in on it, every last one of them."

"Hell."

"Well, listen to the story before you get too tough on him," Fukida said. "Here's the way they say it happened."

The first part of Dagmar's deposition was accurate, she had said. Torkel and Magnus had gone to the hay barn after dinner to put in some work, and there they had been attacked by two gunmen. That was so. But everything after that had been a lie. There had been no telephone call from Torkel pretending to be Magnus. Instead, he'd shown up at the house, dazed and cradling his bloodied hand. He'd explained to his sister that Magnus had been murdered, but he himself had managed to escape into the darkness, although one of the shots they'd fired after him had gone through his hand. He'd hidden on the roof of a nearby shed until well after they'd left, then walked the half-mile of dirt track back home.

"Who shot him?" Gideon asked. "Did he tell her, or was it just 'them' again?"

"She says he saw them, but he was pretty sure he didn't know them. Had no idea who sent them. They just showed up out of nowhere. Two guys, both white, both on the small side, both with revolvers—"

"Revolvers?" John interrupted. "She said 'revolvers'? Not just 'pistols' or 'guns'?"

Fukida frowned. "She said 'revolvers,' but I'm not sure she knows the difference, or that Torkel was quick enough to see what they were carrying in the dark. She probably just meant handguns. Why, what's the big deal?"

"Forget it," John said. "Go ahead." But Gideon caught a little tilt of his head that told him that he knew something they didn't and was reserving it for later.

"Anyway," Fukida said, absently getting a couple of thick rubber bands from a cup on his desk and slipping them over his wrist, "Dagmar telephones Inge, and Inge runs right over, and they doctor him up a little and try to tell him that the best thing to do is to go to the police right then and there, but he doesn't want to hear it. The guy is in shock, and he's scared to death they're coming after him, too, and all he wants to do is get the hell out of there. Only where's he supposed to go?"

"He had no idea who they were or why they were there, and yet he was positive they were coming back for him?" Gideon said. "Doesn't that seem a little strange to you?"

"Guy was in shock," Fukida repeated with a shrug. "That makes you strange."

John held his counsel, looking more inscrutable by the minute.

Fukida continued: "At that point, they call the others over—Hedwig, and Axel, and the one that lives in Honolulu now—"

"Felix," Gideon said.

"Felix, right. Felix the Cat. And they hold a war council. Everyone tells Torkel the best thing for him to do is to go straight to the police—"

"So they say now," John said.

"So they say now," Fukida agreed.

But nobody could convince him, Fukida continued. They couldn't shake his certainty that he was next on the list. They finally gave up and, putting their heads together, came up with what would be their plan. Torkel would flee, heading for the tiny landing strip on the privately owned island of Tarabao, where Hedwig's ex-husband, an osteopath turned beachcomber, now lived, and there he would stay until it was safe to return; they hoped, with luck, that it would be a matter of a few weeks or months. The idea of exchanging identities with Magnus was all Torkel's. They had argued vociferously against it—

So they say now, Gideon thought.

—but had finally gone reluctantly along when they were unable to sway him. The leaving of the ring, the removal of the toes, and the burning of the hay barn were cover-ups following from that. And they decided that, if it was going to be done at all, it would be best if the responsibility for the deception was shared by everyone. So each niece or nephew had taken on a specific task. Inge and Hedwig had gone back to the hay barn, where Hedwig set the fire and Inge had forced the ring on his finger and removed the offending toes.

"What'd she use?" John asked.

"She used a Swiss garlic-chopper," Fukida said.

"Come again?"

"A Swiss garlic-chopper. Like a miniature cleaver. With an old branding-iron paperweight as a mallet."

John glanced at Gideon. "Score one for you, Doc."

Gideon modestly shrugged it off. "Easy when you know how. I wonder what she did with them—with the toes."

"I asked her that," Fukida said. "They had pigs at the time. She said she tossed them in the trough."

Gideon shuddered. "Tough lady."

Axel's job had been to drive the fainting Torkel to the

airport, get the plane out of the hangar and gassed up, and get his uncle into it to await the arrival of the pilot. Felix had stayed the night with Dagmar to provide moral support and assistance once the fire and the body were discovered and the police and fire departments got into the act.

As soon as the Grumman had taken off, everyone but Felix had gone back to their homes. The spouses—Malani and Keoni—had been kept in the dark and fed the same story that the police were shortly to hear. Torkel was to call Inge the next day to let them know he was safe, but of course that never happened.

Fukida, now chewing a couple of sticks of spearmint gum, tipped his chair back and clasped his hands behind his neck, signifying that he had come to the end.

"It all fits," John said half to himself. "It all goddam fits."

"I don't quite get it," Gideon said. "Were they ever going to tell the police what really happened, or did Torkel plan on being Magnus for the rest of his life?"

"At the time, I don't think they had it all worked out," Fukida said. "They weren't exactly doing a lot of long-range planning. They were all scared, not just Torkel."

"And what about the wills?" John asked sourly. "Don't tell me it didn't occur to them that they were whole lot better off if Torkel was supposedly dead, gone, and out of the picture, and Magnus's will would be the one that counted. They all profited from the switch."

"I don't know. They say that didn't have anything to do with it."

"And you buy that?"

Fukida stretched the thick rubber bands on his wrist. Gideon braced himself for the snap, but the sergeant just eased them back. "I think I do, yeah. I'd guess it didn't cross their minds at the time."

"Well, then, you have more faith in people than I do."

"Not much. Because I would also guess it damn well did cross their minds later on, especially when they never heard anything from Torkel—and that it had a whole lot to do with why they stuck to their story. Right up until today."

"Another reason being," John said, "that it also occurred to them they'd committed all kinds of prosecutable offenses, jail-time offenses."

"That, too."

"What's going to happen with the wills now?" Gideon asked.

"Not my worry. Question for the lawyers."

"Are you going to reopen the criminal case?"

"Counsel's checking the various statutes of limitation now. If there's anything still actionable, you bet we are. I don't like being jerked around like that."

"They did come forward on their own," Gideon pointed out, wondering why he was defending them.

"Yeah," John said hotly, "but only because they were scared. And there's something still actionable, all right. There's no limitation on murder."

Now rubber thwapped against flesh. "You see these people as accessories after the fact now?"

"Maybe before the fact."

Fukida eyed him. "Now wait a minute. Are you saying you think they had something to do with the murder itself? I thought these were your buddies."

John sighed. "Teddy, are you done? Can I tell you what I came here to tell you?"

Fukida crossed his arms, uncrossed them, turned his cap around backward, which made a boyish shock of black hair pop ridiculously out of the opening, and crossed his arms again. "I wish you would, already, instead of sitting there like the goddamn cat that ate the canary."

"Okay, then, let me read what I was going to read before."

"About the guy that got shot in the knee," Fukida said with a sigh. "Sure, what else do I have to do today?"

"Just shut up and let me read." He found his place in the book, cleared his throat, and began to read aloud, something he did clumsily.

> . . . on surgical exploration there were found to be two bullets and a cartridge case in the knee joint. All three missiles entered through one entrance wound. The bullets were .32 ACP and .380 ACP caliber and the case was .32 ACP.

He looked up, scowling. "You guys following?"

"No," said Fukida through his sandwich. Gideon had never seen anyone take such small bites, or work his way around the edges the way he did. The thing looked as if it had been nibbled by a family of rabbits.

"I'm following," Gideon said. "It's pretty much the same situation described in the autopsy report."

"It's the *exact* same situation."

"Well, I wouldn't say that. Two bullets through the knee is not the exact same situation as two bullets through the heart."

John brushed this aside. "I'm talking about the situation with the bullets and the cartridge case. That's the same."

"Okay, so?"

"So this." He went back to the book.

> It was hypothesized that a .32 ACP cartridge was inadvertently put in a .380 automatic. The cartridge slipped forward, lodging in the barrel. A .380 ACP cartridge was then chambered. On firing, the .380 bullet struck the .32 ACP primer, discharging the cartridge. The whole complex of two bullets and one case was swept down the barrel, emerged from the muzzle, and entered the victim.

He slapped the book closed, tossed it onto the files on the crowded desk, and loomed over Fukida. "In other words, piggyback bullets!" he yelled, arms spread. "Tandem bullets! You ever hear of those before?"

"*No!*" Fukida yelled back up at him.

"Me neither," Gideon said slowly, as John's point sank in, "but I see where you're going with this. You're saying—"

John dropped back into his chair. "Right!" he said, still shouting. "I'm saying that it's *all* baloney, the whole cockamamie story. There weren't any hitmen, there wasn't any execution, there wasn't any—"

"Whoa-whoa-whoa," Fukida interrupted. "Slow down, sport. Control yourself, breathe deeply." He made calming motions with his hands. "Look, I'm just a simple island cop, I don't know from piggyback bullets. You want to explain what the hell you're talking about?"

John made a visible, not-altogether-successful effort to contain his agitation. "I am talking," he said with excruciatingly precise diction, "about the old Walther semi-automatic that they had in the Big House back then. It was—"

"What big house?" Fukida asked.

"*The* Big House. It's where Inge's dude ranch is now. Back then, it was where Torkel, Magnus, and Dagmar lived. They built it—"

"Wait, goddammit! They had a gun right in the house?" Fukida made a disgusted gesture at the files. "I was just looking at the early interrogations. Dagmar was *asked* if they had one." He poked irritably among the folders, looking for the right one to prove his assertion, but gave it up and batted them aside. "She said no, definitely not, except for some old varmint rifles that the section managers had."

John shrugged. "She lied. What else is new?"

Fukida slowly shook his head. "These people."

"John," Gideon said, "is this the pistol you and Felix were talking about in Waikiki? I thought it didn't work."

"They *said* it didn't work. Obviously, it worked, all right, only not real well. That's exactly my point."

Fukida swiveled in his chair to look at Gideon. "That's his point? *What's* his point, do you know?"

"I think so, yes," Gideon said, and to John: "You're saying that both of the bullets found in Magnus may have come from one gun—just the way they did in the guy that was shot in the knee. Right?"

"Right."

Fukida considered, energetically cracking his gum for a few seconds before arriving at his conclusion. "Nah, I don't think so. That's too crazy."

John sighed. "Jeez, Teddy, and you used to be so sharp. Look, the Walther was an old World War II job chambered for 9mm. short bullets. Now, what do we call 9mm. shorts in the States, or wouldn't a simple island cop know that?"

"We call them .380 ACPs," Fukida said slowly, and Gideon had the impression that he was starting to think that John just might be onto something after all.

"And what were the two bullets found in Magnus's body?"

"Let's see . . ." The tiny part of the tuna sandwich that was left was put aside again on its bed of waxed paper. "One of them was a .380 ACP. I forget what the other one was, but I got this hunch you're gonna tell me it was a .32."

John tossed the green folder he had with him—apparently the ballistics report—onto the desk. "I am. See for yourself."

Fukida sat there. "Just like in your book."

"Just like." He patted the book.

"Okay," Fukida said, "either I'm losing my mind, or you're starting to make sense." He paused and thought of something. "Or are you . . . ?" He reached for the ballistics report after all. "Let me see that thing."

There were three sheets in the folder. Fukida found what he was looking for on the second.

"Here, listen":

Comparison microscopic examinations were made involving the submitted .32 and .380 ACP bullets. Based on the total dissimilarity of rifling class (the .32 was free of rifling marks; the .380 ACP was deeply and distinctively marked) and the absence of individual characteristics common to the two missiles, it is the conclusion of the examiner that the bullets were fired from different weapons.

In the case of the .32, the absence of rifling marks suggests that the weapon was either a zip gun, a smooth-bore pistol or rifle, or a revolver, the barrel of which had been removed to prevent the imparting of such marks. In the case of the .380, the weapon was most likely a semi-automatic pistol.

"The lab guys in Honolulu are good, Johnny," he said, closing the folder. "You know that. If they say two different guns, I have to accept it. They don't make that kind of mistake."

"Well, this time they did, but it wasn't their fault. The rifling didn't match, that's true, but there was a reason. See, the .380 would have gotten grooved when it went down the barrel, just the way it was supposed to. But the .32 would have been too small for the Walther's barrel. It just slipped on through without getting grooved."

Fukida leaned back and nodded. "You've really thought this through."

John was transparently pleased at the closest thing to a compliment he'd gotten from his old superior. "Thanks,

Teddy. It makes sense if you think about it. Doc here doesn't think so, though."

Gideon hadn't realized his doubts were that apparent. John was getting to be as good as Julie at reading his face—a sobering thought. "No," he said, "what you're saying makes a whole lot of sense. I'm just wondering why the crime lab was so off-base. Why didn't they come to the same conclusion?"

"Simple," John said. "First of all, this kind of thing doesn't happen every day of the week. Second, all they had to go on were the two bullets. They didn't know about the cartridge case. It was never forwarded to Honolulu. And without that, there's no way they'd come up with what really happened. I wouldn't have, either."

"We didn't forward—?" Fukida leaned over, snatched the folder back from John, leafed furiously through the three pages, and threw it back down with a groan. "It's true. They never got it. I can't believe it." He tore off his cap and tossed it onto the desk as well.

"Ah, these things happen," John said kindly.

Gideon knew that they did indeed, and a great deal more often than most people realized. Some clerk or officer down the line, reasoning that Ballistics' job was to examine bullets and weapons, had decided, probably without giving it any conscious thought, that cartridge cases, being neither bullets nor weapons, were not to be sent on to the ballistics lab. Many an otherwise solid prosecution had fallen apart as the result of similar innocent, reasonable errors of judgment and omission.

"Not on my watch, they don't," Fukida said grimly. He stood and went to the window. Leaning on the sill, he watched a white airliner lift off over the lava fields, wheel overhead, almost directly over the police station, and head for Honolulu. "You sure had it right, Johnny," he said;

shaking his head. "This whole thing has been a royal screw-up right from the get-go."

"But it's not like it's your fault, Ted," John said. "You weren't even on the case."

An awkward period of silence followed while Fukida continued to stare blindly out the window. "So," he said quietly, "the hitmen were bullshit after all. So who killed Magnus?"

"Gotta be Torkel," John said. "Why else would he run? Why else would he change his identity? Besides which, the gun was in his house."

"It was Dagmar's house, too," Fukida said. "She must have known where the gun was. And anyway, couldn't any of them—Axel, Inge, the whole bunch—have gotten to it if they wanted to?"

"Yeah, but 'any of them' didn't secretly take off in the middle of the night and run for it. 'Any of them' didn't change identities with his brother. That's not something you do—give up your whole life, give up who you are—unless you've got a hell of a reason for it. Nah, Torkel's our man."

Gideon saw it that way, too. "And the others have been covering for him ever since—to protect him." A moment later he added: "And their inheritances."

"And themselves," said Fukida. "If even half of this is true—"

"It's true," John said.

"—they committed a bookful of crimes. Add that to what they told me today—"

"Yeah, but I wonder if any of *that's* true," John muttered.

"Oh, yeah, some of it is, all right. They told me exactly what the accelerants were and where they were placed. It squared right down the line with the arson report."

"And the garlic-chopper," Gideon added. "That fits the facts, too. A lot of other things wouldn't have."

"Besides which, who could make up something like that?"

"It looks like the only thing that slipped their minds was who actually killed Magnus," John said wryly.

"You don't suppose it's possible that they honestly didn't know?" Gideon wondered aloud. "That Torkel hoodwinked them, too?" He looked at their expressions. "No, I guess not."

"Get real," John said.

"All right, then, isn't it possible that Torkel and Dagmar *together* hoodwinked the rest of them? If the two of them came up with the hitmen story, then got on the phone to the nieces and nephews, how would any of them know any better?"

"Well, now, *that's* possible," John said.

"That old lady, she's a piece of work," Fukida said almost admiringly. "One way or another, she's in it up to her hips. I think I'm gonna go have another talk with her tomorrow."

"Teddy, I was planning to talk to her tomorrow morning, too," John said. "Can I go with you? I know her pretty well. Maybe I could help."

"I thought you weren't going to—" Gideon began.

"That was then. This is now. I'm not crazy about being jerked around either."

"Sure, you can come," Fukida said. "That'd be good. You're at the Outrigger? I'll pick you up at a quarter to nine. I hope you weren't thinking of coming, Gideon. I'd have to say no to that."

"No, sir, count me out. I'm on vacation."

Fukida laughed. "That's right, screw everything up for

everybody else, then opt out and say you're on vacation. Very nice."

"Always happy to be of help."

Fukida played a quick rat-tat-tat on his thighs and reached for the phone. "Okey-doke, I'm gonna get a warrant."

"What for?" John said. "You don't need a warrant to talk to—"

"Not for Dagmar. A search warrant. For the Big House. I thought I'd see if that old Walther just might still be around."

"You think they'd have kept it all these years?" Gideon asked doubtfully.

"Probably not, but it can't hurt to look. I'm gonna send a couple of guys out right now."

"Right now?" John said. "You can get a warrant just like that?"

"Watch me," Fukida said and punched a button on his phone.

SEVENTEEN

"DON'T be greedy, Einar," Dagmar said absently, watching the largest of the sea turtles nudge its fellows aside in pursuit of a fast-sinking gobbet of bran-raisin muffin. "You've had your share."

As had they all. This was an unscheduled feeding, the result of an abundance of leftovers from the pastry basket she'd ordered when that horde of nephews and nieces had unexpectedly descended on her, exuding concern for her welfare and consideration for her feelings.

God damn them to hell.

For once, the lovely cove and her old friends the green turtles had failed to work their magic. Her mind, far from being calmed, strummed like tightened wire with what seemed like a hundred emotions: frustration, shame, disgust with her spineless, selfish family—so strikingly different from her own generation—anger at being exploited by them, anger at being a weak old woman . . .

At first, the meeting had gone as well as could have been expected. Of course, there had been the predictable eruptions from the weak ones—Hedwig and Axel—on hearing that she'd gone to Fukida. How could she have taken it upon herself to do such a thing? What would happen to them now? Would they all go to jail? What did this mean for their inheritances? Would everything now go to the Swedish Seamen's Home?

But Felix, all puffed up with noisy self-importance like the lawyer he was, had overridden and pacified them. If they thought about it for a moment, they would see that Auntie Dagmar had done nothing so terrible. Statutes of limitation made it unlikely that the police would find it worth their while to reopen the investigation or begin a new one. As to the Swedish Seamen's Home, there was little to fear, due to the delightful legal principle known as adverse possession: Once property had been held without challenge for a prescribed period of time, the courts would frown upon the bringing of new suits. And, as fortunately happened to be the case, that period of time was almost always considered to be . . . ten years. So in order to challenge the Torkelssons' right to their land, the Seamen's Home would have to prove—not merely assert—intent to defraud. That they might try to do so was of course possible, but given the passage of a decade, the imponderables of proving anything in court, and the enormous hassle and legal costs of mounting such a suit, Felix would be very surprised if it were to come to anything.

And even in the unlikely event that it did, that a suit was actually brought, then the Seamen's Home would be up against the hoary old concept of *res judicata:* A thing, once settled by a competent court (as in probate), was not to be subject to future litigation . . .

The sludgelike flow of verbiage had soothed them.

Everyone had settled down. Then came the call from Keoni. Inge, who took it, came back as pale and frightened as Dagmar had ever seen her. The police had been to the Big House—were even at that moment in the house—with a search warrant: They were looking for—Inge closed her eyes as if she were wishing the reality away—a World War II model Walther PPK semi-automatic pistol.

After the first mute shock, all hell had broken loose. Even Felix was at a loss to put a good face on the clear meaning of this development: The police had somehow concluded that the story of the unidentified assassins was a sham; that Magnus had been killed with a weapon that had been in his own home. Of course, they wouldn't find it; the gun had been rusting in fifty feet of water off Upolu Point ever since that night. But that didn't change the horrific implication: The police knew.

They had all turned on Dagmar at that point, even Felix, even Inge. Why couldn't she have left well enough alone? What had she told Fukida that could have led him to this?

Nothing, nothing, she had bawled back at them—Inge was there, Inge knew! To her dismay, her voice had cracked and spiraled into a witch's shriek. At that point, Felix had outshouted them all and taken control again. This was no time to panic and hurl accusations at each other. More than ever, they had to stick together, be a family. They were most certainly in serious trouble now. Their inheritances, their very freedom, were in jeopardy. Still, all was not lost. Fukida couldn't know what had really happened, he could only suspect. There was still time to avert disaster, but they had to put on their thinking caps . . .

It was Axel, of all people, who had come up with a plan. If Dagmar was willing to bend the truth just a little more— what little truth still remained to bend—she could save them all. If not, it was all over. Their futures, their very lives, were in her hands, in the hands of their dear Auntie Dagmar.

No, it was impossible, she had told them. She had borne the brunt of this for too long already. She couldn't remember what she'd told the police before, and now, with this new trumped-up story they were thrusting on her ("tweaking the facts a tiny little bit," Axel called it), how did they expect her to keep everything straight? How could she avoid tying herself in knots? They weren't stupid, these detectives, they were bound to see through her, and then where would everybody be? And she was sick to her soul of bending the truth and said so. But in the end, worn out by the ceaseless prodding, by the endless self-justifications and airy reassurances, she had knuckled under to them, too old and too tired to fight any more.

Yes, she understood how much more important it was to all of them than it was to her, but by God, it had stuck in her craw. What about *her?* What they were asking her to say, if she understood it correctly (and she wasn't at all sure she did), was tantamount to admitting to the police that she'd been guilty of committing a crime, a serious crime. What would happen to her? But Felix had pooh-poohed this, blandly assuring one and all that the authorities would never prosecute an eighty-two-year-old woman, an island legend, for a few transgressions committed ten years before in an effort to protect the life of her one living brother and to help her beloved family through a difficult time. Besides, there were statutes of limitation that applied, blah blah blah. No, no, nothing at all to worry about there.

Easy for him to say.

The last of the pastries had been thrown to the turtles now, and she abstractedly wiped her fingers on the linen napkin. The turtles, not so different from her nieces and nephews, turned and swam off the second they saw they had nothing more to get from her. She filled the cap of her flask with aquavit, drank, and refilled it. It had been a long time since she'd been really soused, but if this wasn't a good day to get soused, she didn't know what was. Tomorrow would be time enough to deal with her problems.

There were a few crumbs left on the liner of the pastry basket and without knowing it she lifted them to her mouth with a moistened finger. She had lit a cigarillo earlier but had let it go out after one puff; her throat was too tight and raw to smoke. A few more tipples would take care of that.

When she heard a footstep on the gravel path behind her she instinctively reached for her wig, but then changed her mind. The hell with it, it was far too early for the good-looking kid with her dinner, and who else did she need to put on any pretenses for? She was eighty-two years old, she had a right to be going bald if she wanted to. If whoever it was didn't like it, that was too bad for him, he could just keep going.

So deeply was she mired in resentment and recrimination that his presence didn't register again until she sensed it just behind her. Her neck prickled. He was standing too close. She didn't like that, didn't like anyone looking right down at the top of her scalp. She should have slipped the wig on, damn it.

He was so close now that she felt his belt buckle brush against the back of her head. Repulsed, she pulled angrily to one side to get away from him. "Now see here—"

But when his hand clamped on her shoulder from behind like some terrible talon, the air went out of her, as much from astonishment as pain. What . . . what . . .

Too quickly for her to absorb, his other hand closed on her wrist, and she was somehow no longer in contact with the earth, but flopping wildly in the air, dropping like a stone toward the sharp, black rocks that rimmed the cove. She goggled at them, and then at the cloudless blue sky as she tumbled, mouth open, eyes wide with incomprehension.

What . . . what . . .

EIGHTEEN

THE needle-sharp bisection of the North Kohala lowlands into parched lava fields and huge, lavish coastal resorts is stunning. On one side of the coast highway is a brown, dusty, lifeless plain of *a'a* lava. On the other is the lushest landscape that can be imagined: thick, soft grass, palm trees, frangipani, jacaranda, glorious masses of wonderfully fragrant blossoms—red, orange, white, purple. Two people could walk along the border, practically hand in hand, for miles, with one in a moist, green land of tropical plants, bright colors, and verdant lawns all the way, and the other never leaving a blasted, barren moonscape of jagged, dun-colored rocks.

Taking the turnoff for the Outrigger and the other Waikoloa area resorts, John, Julie, and Gideon turned abruptly from the latter into the former, heading down a broad, curving parkway lined with lush trees and redolent with every sweet smell of the tropics.

"I've been thinking . . ." Julie began.

"Uh-oh," John said. He'd been in one of his funks ever since the session with Fukida, and this was as close as he'd come to a coherent sentence in a while. They'd picked up Julie, had a late lunch at the Greek restaurant, and headed back to the hotel, all without any notable input from him.

Gideon looked over his shoulder at him. "John, do you know that whenever anybody says, 'I've been thinking,' you say, 'uh-oh'?"

"Not anybody. Mostly just you two." He laughed and sat himself up straighter in the back seat, signs that he was ready to rejoin the world. As his funks went, it had been a long one.

"What have you been thinking, Julie?" Gideon asked.

"Well, you know how you keep wondering why they let you get involved with this thing in the first place? I think I know."

That surprised him. "Why?"

"Well, who exactly asked you to go out to that atoll?"

"They all asked him," John said.

"That's right," Gideon agreed.

"No, that's not what you said when you first told me about it. You said Malani asked you."

We did? Gideon thought.

"Umm . . ." said John, thinking.

"Yes, you did. You said she was the one that called the salvage company, and when she came back from talking to them, she said—"

"She said they didn't know how to handle skeletons," Gideon remembered, "and she volunteered me."

"That's right, and why wouldn't she? From what Inge and Dagmar said, she didn't know anything about the cover-up. She didn't know there was anything to hide."

"That's a good point, but look, they all agreed to it, no

objections. Why would they do that? Felix even put us up in Honolulu."

"What choice did they have?" Julie countered. "Think about it. How would it have looked if they said no you couldn't, after the salvage company said they wanted you and you said you would?"

"But how could they not have worried that I'd find out it was Torkel in that plane? You'd think they'd have come up with some excuse, any excuse, to keep me from—"

A snort of laughter came from the back seat. "They didn't worry because you told them there was nothing to worry about."

"*I* told them?"

"You said—and I pretty much quote—that with any luck you could maybe tell the age, the sex, the race, and, um . . ."

"The approximate height," Gideon supplied. "All of which would have fitted Magnus as much as it did Torkel. I think you've hit on it, Julie. Malani didn't know she was putting her foot in it—"

"Or Torkel's foot," John said, throwing up his hands. "Sorry."

"—but when she did, the others went along with it because they thought they were safe. Good thinking, Julie. That'd explain it."

"Amazing," John said. "She wasn't even there and she remembers it better than we do."

"Thank you," Julie said happily. "Shall I go on?"

"There's more?"

"Oh, yes. Who was it that got you to look at the autopsy report after you got back from the atoll?"

John and Gideon looked at each other in the rearview mirror. "Malani?" they both offered.

She nodded crisply. "Yes. And I *was* there for that one."

"You're right," Gideon said, thinking back to the gathering on Axel's porch. "Malani was the one who forced the issue . . . again."

"That's right, she was," John said. "Malani's like that. If she gets an idea in her head, she doesn't hang back."

"But this time the others did," Gideon said. "Remember? Hedwig wanted to put me in a lotus leaf instead, and Axel didn't want to stir things up, and Inge wanted to let him rest in peace—"

"But then the two of you convinced them they'd better have you do it, right?" Julie said. "So it was like the first time. How could they say no without making it obvious they were covering something up—even if they thought you might find out about the ring?"

"Ah, ah!" John exclaimed; he was completely back in form now. "But they *didn't* think we were going to find out about the ring. The ring wasn't in the autopsy report, it was in the case files! And as far as they knew, we weren't going to be looking at the case files!"

Gideon slowly nodded. "It all makes sense."

Julie tapped her mouth, covering a yawn of mock boredom. "Anything else I can help you boys with, you just let me know. Oh, look, here's the Outrigger. Swimming pool, here I come. And I'm for another moratorium through tonight. Tomorrow is another day."

"Me too," Gideon said.

John raised his hand. "Count me in. Enough is enough."

FAUSTINO Parra arranged the place-setting the way the old lady liked it on windless days like this: on the round, glass-topped table at the foot of her terrace, with the Spanish-tile fountain behind her and the big blue Pacific spread out in front of her. He removed three of the four chairs—they made her feel lonely, she said—and opened the zipper of the thermal carton a couple of inches more so that her dinner wouldn't continue to baste in its own juices. Oyster stew, grilled moonfish with black-olive polenta and shiitake mushrooms, and, in a separate cooler bag, a half-bottle of Sauvignon blanc and a macadamia-nut torte topped with currants, whipped cream, and toasted coconut for desert. For a woman who couldn't weigh more than ninety pounds, she could certainly put the stuff away, he thought respectfully. Not that a lot of it didn't go to the turtles, of course.

He stood back, took one more look at the setting, straightened the silverware so that it lined up perfectly with the bottom edge of the bamboo place mat, nodded with satisfaction, checked his bowtie to make sure that it was straight, and went to find her at her cove, looking forward to bringing her back.

He hadn't always looked forward to it. At first, he'd actively disliked her. It didn't seem right to him that a woman—let alone a woman of that age—smelled morning and night like the inside of a bar after a hard day: booze and cigars. And the way she waited for him to offer his arm, as if she was the queen of Hungary or something. That wasn't part of his job and he'd resented it. She hadn't made things any better when he handed her her first bill to be signed. "Now Raymond," she'd said (sometimes it was "Raymond," sometimes "Steven," once in a while "Faustino"), "let's get something clear right at the start. I can't be bothered with calculating percentages every time I sign for something, you understand? So you keep track of what you bring, and whenever the amount comes to four hundred dollars, you tell me and I will tip you accordingly. Is that satisfactory?"

What could he say but yes? But in his heart he simmered. Why should he have to *ask* for his tip? It was demeaning. More than that, he assumed it was her way of getting out of tipping him at all, in hopes that he wouldn't have the nerve to bring it up. But he had, and two weeks later when he told her that her bill to date had been $405.24, she smiled and handed him two crisp fifty-dollar bills that she'd had all ready and waiting—over and above the automatic eighteen percent that had already been added for service.

It had blown him away. And it was in *cash*, that was the best part. Nothing to go into the service pool, nothing to be declared as income. It had made all the difference in the world. He still didn't like the way her breath smelled, and he still didn't like the way her fingers dug into his arm like hard little toothpicks, but she was good for a minimum of $200 a month, his best customer by a mile; he'd come to depend on it. More than that, he'd eventually come around to actually liking her. After you got to know her, you began to see her good side. She was generous, she was funny, she had a lot of good points.

And now he had another $400 to report; $418, actually, but nowadays he returned her generosity by regularly rounding down, something that made him feel good. Besides, he suspected that she kept a more accurate account than he did, so it was another way of staying on her good side. His money had really been due that morning, when he'd brought the pastries, but she'd had company and he didn't like asking in front of them.

As he approached the curve that opened onto the promontory he paused to scuff his feet a bit on the gravel so that she'd have time to get that pathetic wig on, but when he rounded it he came to an abrupt stop. She wasn't there waiting for him; something that had never happened before in all these months. There was an empty, overturned pastry basket on the ground next to the bench, and on the bench itself there was something black, silky . . . the wig.

His throat constricted. This wasn't right. Something was wrong. He crossed himself without knowing it, held his breath, took two quick steps to the rim of the promontory, and looked over.

"*Oh, my God,*" he said and turned his face away, retching.

"CALL for you on two," Sarah told Fukida over the telephone.

"Who?"

"Two people on the line. Ms. Sakado, the day manager at the Mauna Kai, and a waiter named Faustino Parra—who's a little hysterical, so be gentle with him."

"What's it about, do you know?"

"Something about the Torkelssons again."

He laughed a little wildly. "Of course. What else could it be? Why did I bother asking?"

"You can handle it, boss. I have complete confidence."

He punched the button for line two. "Sergeant Fukida," he said, doodling horses on his note pad, "how can I help you?"

Five seconds later the doodling had stopped. The pen had been thrown down. "Jesus. We'll be right there. Don't let anyone within fifty yards of her."

ARRANGED neatly over a low glass table on the broad, columned terrace of the Outrigger on a sunny morning, overlooking an agreeable panorama of man-made streams, waterfalls, and exquisitely tended tropical gardens, the lurid photographs seemed wildly out of place: blood and trauma and violent death.

Julie and Gideon had met John for morning coffee while John waited to be picked up by Fukida on the way to Dagmar's house just a couple of miles up the coast. They had gotten lattés and muffins at the lobby coffee bar and carried them out to the terrace to enjoy them in the fresh air. When Fukida hadn't shown up at 8:45, as agreed, they'd gotten seconds on the lattés. At 9:05, he arrived.

"Hey, you're late," John began, "I thought you were the one who always—" But the look on Fukida's face stopped him. "What's the matter?"

Fukida hesitated, looking at Julie. "And this lady . . . ?"

"My wife, Julie," Gideon said. "Julie, this is Sergeant Fukida."

Fukida nodded a curt greeting and sat down. "Dagmar's dead," he said.

He was wearing a shapeless tweed jacket, trousers that almost but didn't quite match it, and a nondescript tie. No baseball cap. He seemed diminished, like an over-aged, undernourished department store clerk.

The three of them stared at him and he quickly explained. Her body was discovered by a waiter from the Mauna Kai at five o'clock the day before, at the base of a twenty-foot cliff near her house.

John closed his eyes and lowered his head. "Ah, no."

"The doc says death occurred somewhere between noon and four yesterday, resulting from severe injuries to the head, apparently from the fall."

"An accident?" Gideon asked. "Or—"

That was when the photographs came out. "You two are good with pictures. You tell me." But he held on to them, looking at Julie before laying them out. "These are pretty graphic, ma'am. You might not want to—"

"That's all right, I'll stay," Julie said, which surprised

Gideon. "I want to know. There was something about her," she said to him by way of explanation. "I liked her. . . ."

"Yeah, and if you're married to *him,* I guess you've seen this kind of thing before," Fukida said, fanning the photos out over the table. "So where do you get the coffee?"

They pointed him toward the coffee bar, and as he left they began going through the color photos. Fukida had apparently brought only a select few; six altogether. Gideon lifted the first one. It had been taken at the top of the promontory, an overview of the bench and the area around it.

"What is that, her wig?" Julie asked.

"Looks like it," said John. "So we know one thing it wasn't, anyway."

"Right, we know it wasn't suicide," Gideon agreed. "People like to look nice when they kill themselves. She'd never have done it, letting strangers find her without the wig."

"Not Auntie Dagmar, that's for sure," John said.

The rest were photographs of the body, going from full-body shots to close-ups of Dagmar's bloodied head. Julie swallowed and looked away once or twice, but stuck it out. One of them had been made after unbuttoning the top two buttons of Dagmar's blouse and pulling it down over her right shoulder.

"It seems . . . indecent," Julie said. "A dignified, private old woman like that—dead, helpless—exposed to public view like a . . . like a . . ."

"It has to be done," John said softly. "And not many people see these."

"I know that."

"Ah, look at this," Gideon said. He tapped the area just to the right of her bared neck, where even Dagmar's scrawny trapezius muscle created a triangular cushion of flesh above the collar bone. "These three blueish spots . . . you can hardly see two of them . . . that's extravasated blood just under the skin."

"Would that be 'bruises' in English?" Julie asked.

"Yes, bruises."

"Fingermarks," John said.

Gideon nodded. He poured a little coffee onto a napkin, wet his index finger, middle finger, and ring finger with it, and grasped the edge of the table, his thumb underneath, pinching hard. When he lifted his hand, there was a curving row of three spots on the glass, to all intents and purposes exactly like the bruises on Dagmar's shoulder.

"Somebody grabbed her from behind—hard—maybe while she was sitting on the bench." He gently placed his fingers on Julie's shoulder to illustrate, his thumb in back.

She shivered. "And pushed her over the edge?"

"Looks like it."

"So what's the verdict?" Fukida asked, coming back with his cardboard cup of coffee; the four-dollar *vente* size.

"Murder," John said. "You agree?"

"Sure, no question about it. Also—and this you probably can't tell from the pictures—she was laying a good four feet from the base of the cliff. No way did she just fall off, or even jump. Somebody shoved her, good and hard."

"Or threw her," Julie said. "How hard would it have been? She's nothing but skin and bones."

"That's true, too."

"Fingerprints?" John asked.

"No."

"Did you check the bench? The paint might have been soft from being out in the sun, there might—"

"Johnny, for Christ's sake! Of *course* I checked the bench. We dusted everything. Give me a little credit, will you?"

"Sorry."

"Anyway, whoever did it wore gloves."

"How can you know that?" Julie asked.

"We picked up some glove-leather impressions. One on her watch, one, maybe two, on the bench."

"Glove smears," John said. "That's not gonna do you much good."

Fukida shrugged. "Yeah, well."

"What about suspects?" Gideon asked, handing back the photos.

"Oh, yeah, suspects, we got suspects." He sucked coffee through the opening in the lid, made a face, and twisted the lid off to get a healthy mouthful. Gideon could smell the sprinkling of chocolate on top. "The kid that found her, the waiter, he was there earlier, too, delivering pastries to her at about one—"

"One?" John interrupted. "Wait a minute, that means the noon end of the TOD range is wrong. It had to be after that."

Fukida put a finger to his temple and looked archly at him. "Whoa, not too much gets by this guy."

"Duh," John said, not taking offense.

"And the kid told us she had company. Guess who."

"Inge?" Gideon answered on the spur of the moment.

"Hedwig?" John offered. "Axel?"

"Right, right, and right. Also Felix the Cat, all the way from sunny Waikiki. The whole sorry bunch of them."

"Felix?" John repeated. "Must have been important to bring him over. Do you know what it was about?"

"No. The kid says he didn't hear anything, but they looked like they weren't having any fun. He thought they were fighting about something and shut up when he came in. He said Dagmar looked really upset."

"What do you *think* it was about?"

"What do *you* think it was about?"

"I think they were having a strategy session," John said bluntly. "Figuring out where they go from here, coming up with whatever new cockamamie story they were going to befuddle you guys with."

"That's what I think, too."

"And so those are your suspects?" Gideon asked. "The nieces and nephews?"

"Who else? Last people to see her alive . . . fighting about something . . . all kinds of nasty, threatening things popping on the old case . . . sure, they're my prime suspects, you bet. Well, and the two spouses, too—Malani and what's his name, Keoni. They've got a stake in this, too. My guess at this point is that one of them—who knows, maybe more than one of them—wanted to make absolutely sure she never told anyone what really happened."

"Yes," Julie said nodding, "I remember, the other day when we were all talking on Axel's porch, she looked really depressed, really tired. She talked about being ready for it all to come out."

"Well, there you go." Fukida was impatiently twirling the cup lid on the table, leaving little rings of foam. He was ready to leave. "Well . . ."

"And at this point, we think the real story is that Magnus was murdered by Torkel?" Gideon suggested.

"That . . . or by one of the nephews—or nieces."

John looked hard at him. "Are you serious about that, Teddy?"

"I'm serious about it as a possibility, yeah, you bet." Fukida tipped the cup all the way up to finish his coffee, sucking up the last of the foam, and stood. "Everybody's being interrogated today, this morning. I'm on my way to talk to Inge now, and I've got two of my detectives going to see Axel and Hedwig."

"What about Felix?"

"Honolulu PD is helping out there. We gave them a list of questions. I want everybody talked to at about the same time so they can't compare notes ahead of time."

"That's good," John said.

"I'm glad you approve." Fukida paused before leaving, leaning on the back of his chair. "I'm not asking you along, Johnny. You've done great, but I think maybe it's time for you to step out of this."

"You're not gonna get any argument from me on that. If I never see any of that lousy bunch again, it'll be too soon."

When Fukida had gone, the three of them sat looking out over the gardens toward the sea. "What awful news," Julie said, following which there was a long silence.

"I have to get away from here," John said, still staring out to sea. "I just don't want to hang around here anymore."

"You're ready to go home?" Julie asked sympathetically.

"Not if I can help it, not while Meathead is still loose. But my sister Brenda wants us all to come down to Hilo. You guys interested?"

"That's your sister who's a park ranger?" Julie asked. "I'd love to meet her."

"Right, at Volcanoes. You two would have a lot in common. So I've been thinking—"

"Uh-oh," Gideon said.

John responded with a fleeting smile. "—that we could head down south today, maybe get rooms at Volcano House for a couple of nights—it'll be a whole lot cheaper than the Outrigger, I can tell you that. We could go up into Hilo for dinner with Brenda and her family tonight, and then maybe tomorrow Brenda could show us around the park. What do you say?"

"Sounds good," said Gideon.

"I'd love it," Julie said.

NINETEEN

IT was a view that the pony-tailed old man in the gold-braided captain's hat never got tired of—that, as far as he knew, no one had ever gotten tired of: the island of Tahiti, rearing up before him in the morning, the upper slopes of its green mountains and hanging valleys glowing like fire, the heavy mists that had clung to the bottoms of the deep ravines all night slowly separating into feathery tendrils as the sun hit them, the sky itself still a pellucid aquamarine, not the pale blue it would turn later on. Behind him, nine miles away across the Sea of the Moon, was the even more lushly exotic island of Moorea, where he lived and from which he'd just motored.

God, what a place.

With a sigh of self-satisfaction, he slowly steered *Cap'n Jack's Reward*, a converted fifty-foot Danish fishing trawler, through the ships anchored in Papeete Harbor and then, edging it forward and back as deftly as if it were a twelve-foot dinghy, slipped it into its space along the concrete bulkhead that edged the long waterfront quay. Good. Done.

Nine-thirty, according to the clock on the cabin wall. That left him over an hour before the day's clients, six Hemingway wannabe's referred to him by Tahiti Nights Travel Agency (for the usual fifteen percent), showed up to spend a manly day on the high seas in pursuit of marlin and mahi-mahi. He just hoped nobody threw up on his beautiful, newly stained but not yet polyurethaned teak deck.

"Mornin', Cap'n Jack, toss me a rope, I'll tie you up."

Teoni, waiting for him on the quay, was his one-man crew; reliable, competent, and unfailingly good-humored, even with problem customers—of whom there were many. Cap'n Jack had often wondered what it was about deep-sea fishing that brought out the worst in so many men. In Teoni's opinion it was the result of the temporary absence of the civilizing influence of women, and Cap'n Jack thought it was as good a theory as any.

A final check of the ice chest (ham and cheese sandwiches, taro chips, beer, bottled water, fruit juice, apples and oranges, Twinkies, chocolate chip cookies), a quick look in at the head to make sure the toilet paper and paper towels were out and that it was generally ship-shape (by the end of the day, it sure wouldn't be), a few unnecessary instructions to Teoni, and after flipping down his eye patch so as not to disturb squeamish passersby, he was off on his two-block walk to the Tiki Soft Internet Café for his morning coffee and a little surfing of the twenty-first-century variety.

Half an hour later, with a chocolate croissant and a heavily creamed and sugared coffee under his belt and a fresh cup on the table in front of him, he had checked and responded to the meager collection of e-mail in his inbox, had ordered two new rod-holders from Pomare Marine, and had opened his Favorites folder to relax for a final few minutes with "Upcountry Doings, Your E-News Update for North Hawaii."

As usual, there was little in it of concern to him, but reading it was an ingrained habit by now and he scrolled dutifully through it, looking for names and places that rang a bell. He had already hit the PAGE DOWN key to scroll past "Sad News from the North Kohala Coast"—there wasn't anything on the coast that interested him—when his mind registered a glimpse of the name "Torkelsson" in the body of the article.

Now *that* interested him.

He scrolled back up the page and read intently, his hand rhythmically stroking his beard, his coffee forgotten.

Sad News from the North Kohala Coast

The body of Dagmar Birget Torkelsson, one of our true pioneers, was discovered yesterday afternoon on the beach near her home at Hulopo'e Beach Estates. Ms. Torkelsson is believed to have died of injuries suffered in a fall. Kona police are investigating the matter.

Dagmar Torkelsson was eighty-two years old. She had lived on the Big Island since arriving from Sweden with her three brothers in the 1950s. Over the next forty years, this remarkable family created and slowly developed the Hoaloha Ranch above Waimea. Now broken up, the Hoaloha at one time represented a cattle empire second only to that of the Parker Ranch.

Ms. Torkelsson is survived by her nieces Hedwig Torkelsson and Inge Nakoa, and by her nephews Axel and Felix Torkelsson.

A private memorial service will be held Friday at the

Waimea United Church of Christ, followed by an RSVP reception at the Waimea Community Center for family and close friends. Others wishing to pay their respects to the deceased are cordially invited to a public memorial and reception at the Center on Saturday at two P.M.

The old man finished his coffee, paid ten cents to print the article, put the gold-braided captain's hat back on his head, and went thoughtfully back to his boat.

TWENTY

UNLIKE the West Hawaii police station in Kona, the headquarters of HPD—the Honolulu Police Department—are on a busy street in the heart of downtown. There is not a garbage dump or compost heap in sight. The building itself is large, handsome, and imposing: a white, four-story structure with banks of concrete steps leading up to the pillared entrance, thirty-foot palm trees at the corners, and a gleaming red-tiled roof. The lobby buzzes with activity and purpose, as in any big-city police department.

But two floors below the lobby, on Level B-2, where the Scientific Investigation Section—the only police crime lab in the Hawaiian Islands—is quartered, you wouldn't be aware of any of this. There, white-coated criminalists, in their brightly lit but windowless quarters, go quietly about their work, bent over microscopes, spectrographs, and computer screens.

One such, Benjamin Kaaua, stared fixedly at the screen

of his fingerprint-comparator, on which two magnified images were projected side by side. On the left was a print—not a fingerprint, but a greatly enlarged print from the base of the thumb of a left-handed leather glove—lifted from the face of a watch on the wrist of the old woman that had been killed. On the right was an equally enlarged image of a small portion of the same area from one of the four left-handed leather gloves that Fukida had obtained from two of the suspects in the case. The image on the left was steady. The one on the right changed as Kaaua periodically moved the card on the focusing platform below the screen. On the card were twelve tiny photographs of different parts of the glove's surface. This was the second of three such cards for this glove, and he was now on the last of its twelve images. A similar process on the three cards for the other three gloves had produced nothing. Altogether, he had been on the machine for two hours without a break. The final image on the card didn't match either, and the card was pulled from under its clip and set to the side.

Before inserting the last one, Kaaua stood up to get the blood flowing to his legs again, stretched, and walked around the table, working his head from side to side and squeezing his eyes shut. Time for a break, really, but with one card to go he was eager to finish up.

What he was doing—what criminalists spent most of their time doing—was applying the First Law of Criminalistics: No two objects in the universe are exactly alike. Even mass-produced objects or things made in a mold, while they might be extremely similar when new, would quickly become different. No two things ever wear in exactly the same way. No two things ever tear, or break, or get used, or rust, or get nicked in exactly the same way.

The leather of any cowhide glove, coming as it did from the skin of an animal, was different from every other cowhide glove that had ever been made or would ever be made. And once it had been used, there would be flexure creases, tension lines, wear-furrows, and scuffs that would make it even more observably unique.

So if this glove was indeed the same one that had left the print at the crime scene, there would be a visible match somewhere on the final card.

In theory.

The original print, the one from the watch face, was unusually clear, barely smudged, not at all the usual fuzzy smear. And Fukida, thanks to the course he'd taken at the FBI Academy, had known enough to look for it, and to realize it might be important when he saw it. He'd done a good job of lifting it, too, using superglue and dye stain. He'd lifted another print from the back of the bench Dagmar Torkelsson had been sitting on, but it was too indistinct for comparison.

Kaaua took his stool again, wrapped his feet around the base, rubbed his eyes, put on his glasses, refocused on the final card's first photo, and caught his breath. To be sure he was seeing what he thought he was seeing, he increased the magnification all the way up to twenty-seven times, then way down to three so he could look at a wider area. He flicked off the light and hummed happily to himself.

We have a match.

FOR once, Sergeant Fukida was motionless. His hands lay quietly on his desk, his feet flat on the floor. His Colorado Rockies cap was on his head in thinking position (backward). He was cogitating.

Dagmar wasn't the only Torkelsson who had been a piece of work. In all his career he'd never encountered a bunch quite like this one. It was as if they had an unlimited number of versions available to answer anything they were asked. Catch them in a lie, and out popped another one, like sausages out of a sausage machine, to explain the first one away. When he and his detectives had compared notes at the end of the day yesterday, it was as if they'd all been working on completely different cases.

But today things had turned around. Obviously, the family members had compared notes, too, because early this morning Felix had called from Honolulu; they had concluded it was past time to set the record straight.

"Mm," a skeptical Fukida had replied. He'd heard this before.

Yesterday, Felix explained, they had been in a state of shock on learning of Dagmar's death—of Dagmar's *murder*—and had been frightened and off-balance, hardly knowing what they were saying. Now they wanted to clear the air and do whatever they could to demonstrate their innocence in her murder and to help in finding her killer. They had designated him as their spokesman, and if it was all right with Fukida he would like to meet with him as soon as possible.

Would he be acting as their lawyer, Fukida wanted to know. Felix said he would not, but merely as their representative. Indeed, he hoped that, when all was known, there would be no need for a lawyer. There had been an implied question mark at the end of the sentence, to which Fukida had not responded.

"Come on over," was all he'd said. "When can you be here?"

Two hours later, they were sitting in the most spartan of the interrogation rooms, a running tape recorder on the scarred table between them. No coffee, no soft drinks. Despite the austere surroundings and the chill in Fukida's greeting, Felix was annoyingly self-assured and at ease, as if he were there to do a favor for a friend. Fukida had a

strong sense of another load of bullshit on the way to being
shoveled up.

He pressed the start button on the recorder. "All right,"
he said with no preamble other than stating their names
and the date for the record, "first I want to know why you
all got together with her at her house yesterday morning.
What it was *really* about," he added as Felix opened his
mouth. "I don't want to hear the same crap about 'moral
support' and 'shoring her up' that I heard yesterday. They
didn't need to fly you in from Oahu for moral support."

Felix threw back his head and laughed, as if Fukida had
told a joke. "Actually, I think it would be better if I started
at the beginning."

Fukida was stone-faced. "I think it would be better if
you answered my questions."

Felix responded with an accommodating shrug and carried on, unflustered. This, Fukida thought, was a very cool
guy, probably a hell of a lawyer. "The fact is, the meeting
was supposed to be about moral support, in a way—you
know, let's all stick together and keep things close to the
vest—but when we got there we found out she'd already
been to see you and told you some things, and then when
Inge's husband called to tell us your men had just showed
up at their place with a search warrant for the old gun—"

Fukida's interest quickened. At yesterday's interviews,
no one—including Felix—had mentioned such a call. Was
he actually about to get some reliable information here?

"—everything changed. We knew that tired old story
about the hitmen couldn't stand up any more, but we
couldn't afford to let the real story come out—"

"Because of your inheritances?"

Felix showed his first sign of unease. "Yes."

"But now you feel you *can* let the real story come out?"

"That's right. Somebody murdered our aunt—I mean,

this is Auntie Dagmar, for God's sake. That changes things. It took a while to sink in, but it finally did. So did the idea that it pretty much had to be one of us."

"I wouldn't say—"

"Come on, Sergeant, I'm leveling with you. You can level with me."

"Go ahead," Fukida said. "You couldn't afford to let the real story come out . . ."

"No. We wanted her to . . . well, to lie—to tell a *new* lie—all of us did. Including me. And we would back her up."

"And that lie was . . . ?"

"That Torkel murdered his brother Magnus."

"That—" The puzzle pieces that Fukida had all poised and ready to press into place fell apart. "You mean that he *didn't?*"

"No, he didn't."

"Then . . . who did?"

"Nobody murdered him, Sergeant. The whole thing was an accident."

"Dammit, Torkelsson, don't jerk me around. I've had it with you people. If it was an accident, what was the problem with letting it come out? Why couldn't you . . . why would you . . ." He shook his head. "I think maybe you *better* start at the beginning, Counselor."

THE story Felix told took an hour and a half, and, bizarre as it was, it had a ring of authenticity to it that none of the other umpteen constantly evolving versions had ever had. And it fit the known facts.

The two elderly bachelor brothers, Felix said, had increasingly gotten on each others' nerves over the years. Seemingly once a month they decided they'd be better off living apart, but Dagmar had always smoothed things over.

The three of them had lived together for forty years, after all, and the prospect of breaking up—"divorcing," she called it—in their seventies was just plain ridiculous. Unseemly. So they stayed.

But it wasn't only the annoyance of constantly being in each others' way. The two men had different philosophies of running the ranch. Magnus's attention was focused on the bottom line, on expenses and debits and cash flow. Torkel was more the dreamer, and the older he got the more cockeyed and expensive his schemes became. On the night in question they had been quarreling throughout dinner over his grandiose plan to collect run-off water from the higher elevations of the Kohalas into a concrete-lined catch-basin, from which it would be piped by gravity-feed to a dozen reservoirs and then sent on to five hundred giant troughs placed at strategic locations on the ranch. It would have cost millions. They had consumed a few glasses of wine, as they usually did at dinner, and Torkel, pushing things, pulled out a checkbook and said he'd write a check for the digging of the catch-basin right then and there.

Infuriated, Magnus had gone to get the gun—

"Wait a minute," Fukida said. "Are you telling me Magnus tried to kill Torkel for pulling out his checkbook?"

"No, no, not kill. Look, that gun had been there forever. Nobody knew it had any bullets in it. Nobody thought it *worked*. The clip was so rusted you couldn't get it out."

"So why did he get it?"

"Because that's what he *did*. He'd done it before; it was an old routine."

"It was an old routine to threaten his brother with a gun?"

"You don't understand. It was a game they played."

"That's some game."

"Nobody took it seriously. He'd wave it around, and Dagmar would say, 'Oh, put that thing away,' and he'd put it away, and they'd all go to bed mad at each other, and the next morning it'd be forgotten."

"But not this time."

Felix shook his head. "No, not this time. He *would* have put it away, but when he waved it in Torkel's face, Torkel made a disgusted grab at the barrel and sort of bent Magnus's arm back . . . and bang. The bullet—bullets, rather, although nobody knew it at the time—went through Torkel's hand and into Magnus. Magnus dropped dead on the spot. The other two were pretty well stunned, as you can imagine."

"Mr. Torkelsson, how do you know all this? Were you there?"

"No, only the three of them. But Dagmar told us later. Torkel, too, although he was barely coherent by the time we arrived."

Dagmar again, thought Fukida. *The only living eyewitness. Only she was no longer living.*

Other than the fact that Inge and Hedwig, with Felix's help, had loaded Magnus's body into a pickup truck and taken it to the hay barn before they lopped off his toes and set the fire, the remainder of the story—how Torkel had been desperate to leave, how they'd gotten him to the airport, etc.—fit perfectly with what Inge and Dagmar had told him the day before.

Which hardly proved it was true, but Fukida was increasingly inclined to accept this latest retelling. The gun's neglected condition—rusted, loaded with the wrong bullets—made the idea of an accidental killing highly believable. More than that, if there was anything self-serving about this version, he couldn't see it. Telling the story opened them all up to a ton of legal problems, some of them criminal.

Still, there was a lot about it that didn't compute. "Look,

if it happened the way you said, if there weren't any hitmen to worry about, what the hell was Torkel so desperate about?"

"He was desperate because he figured it would *look* like murder and he couldn't face the idea of jail—or even of a trial—not at his age. Dagmar kept telling him not to do it, that if he ran he'd *really* look guilty." Felix shook his head. "But you couldn't reason with him."

"So who came up with the idea of switching identities?"

"That was Torkel, but, you see, the idea wasn't to *switch* identities, not at first. He wasn't interested in *being* Magnus. He just wanted to make it look as if *he* was dead. He figured that'd make it a lot harder for the police to find him, since they wouldn't be looking for him."

"It wouldn't make it any easier," Fukida agreed.

"So we all went along with that. But then we started talking. If you people bought the story that it was Torkel's body in the barn, you were going to want to know what happened to Magnus . . . for instance, where was he? And how the hell were we going to handle that? So we started throwing around ideas and the best thing we came up with—I honestly forget who came up with it first; Hedwig, maybe, or maybe it was me—was to pretty much tell the truth . . . with a twist. One brother got killed, the other one flew away. Only we'd reverse them."

Fukida nodded. "Since Magnus was now Torkel, Torkel would become Magnus."

"That's about it."

"I'm surprised he went for it. That's a hell of a decision, to become somebody else. Especially your own brother."

"Yeah, but you see, it wasn't that cut-and-dried, Sergeant. At that point nobody was thinking about who Torkel would *become*. We were just thinking about the story we were going to tell the police. Anyway, all he was interested in was getting out of there and covering his tracks, so he jumped right on the idea and we all went along with that, too. After that—"

"Why?"

Felix was startled. "Uh . . . why?"

"Yeah, why'd you all go along? It wouldn't have anything to do with the fact that you'd all come off filthy rich if everybody thought Magnus was the last one alive?"

For the first time Felix showed a flash of anger. "In the first place, none of us are 'filthy rich'—"

"Don't yell. It screws up the recorder. It also irritates me."

"I'm sorry." He lowered his voice to what he thought was a whisper. "In the second place, Torkel wasn't supposed to get himself killed in a plane crash. He was supposed to be back in touch with us as soon as he could. The idea was that I was going to explain things and straighten everything out with you guys and with the prosecuting attorney, and then, assuming I could get it all taken care of, he was supposed to come back and be Torkel again." He folded his arms and glared at Fukida. "So you want to tell me how was that going to make us filthy rich? I think you know what Torkel was going to leave us—zilch."

Fukida responded equally heatedly. "Yeah, right, but then, after he didn't show up, and you all tossed things around some more, you figured, well, why not just leave things the way they are? I mean, it was a lot simpler than stirring everything up again, and you'd all come out of it a lot better, and who would it hurt? Except for that seamen's home, of course."

Felix sagged, unfolded his arms, and dropped his eyes. "I guess that's about right," he said wearily. "I'd want to put it a little more . . . positively than that, but . . . that's about right. We acted in our own selfish interests. And we broke the law."

We're getting there now, Fukida thought. *Maybe not quite the whole truth yet, but close, and getting closer.* "Listen, Mr. Torkelsson, you might want to have a lawyer of your own here before we talk much more. I don't want to be accused of—"

"No lawyer," Felix said firmly. "Unless I'm under arrest."

Fukida shook his head. "Not at the moment."

Felix laughed and relaxed. "All right, what else do you need to know? And if there's really any coffee in that machine, I'd appreciate some."

"You're a braver man than I am," Fukida said, walking with him to the break room.

Felix put in his dollar and punched buttons—two sugars, two creams (no wonder he was able to drink the stuff)—and waited for the cup to fill with the resultant slush.

"So tell me," Fukida said, "who came up with the idea of these mysterious hitmen? You?"

Felix laughed. "No, you." Standing at the machine, taking short, rapid gulps of the too-hot coffee, he explained.

When Dagmar had first talked to the police about what "Magnus" had supposedly said on the telephone, she'd used the word *they*—"they" killed Torkel, "they" were coming after him—but it was just a figure of speech; she hadn't meant to suggest that there was more than one person. But when the autopsy was performed and two different-caliber bullets were found in the body, the police had understandably taken the "they" seriously. With both bullets right through the heart, the leap to "professional, anonymous hitmen" had been easy and logical. Of course, the family had embraced the idea as a godsend that temporarily took the pressure off Torkel. Later, after he hadn't been heard from again and was presumed lost, it had simply been easier all around to stick with it than to change their story. And so the police had spent months on a pointless wild goose chase.

A royal screw-up, Fukida thought, shaking his head. That was the term for it, all right.

Back in the interrogation room, he had Felix repeat the story for the recorder. "That about it?" Felix said when he'd finished.

They were both getting tired now. Fukida's sinuses ached and Felix looked as if he might be thinking that the coffee hadn't been such a hot idea after all.

"Almost. Let's go back to the meeting with Dagmar the day she was killed. You said you all wanted her to lie and say Torkel *murdered* Magnus?"

Felix nodded. "Right."

"I don't get it. What was that about?"

"The wills again, the goddamn wills. See, if the truth came out—that it was an accident—then Torkel, as the last survivor, would be the one with the valid will, right? And the seamen's home would be the big beneficiary. But if Torkel *killed* Magnus—murdered him—then—"

"Then Magnus's will would be the one that counted, because you can't inherit from someone you murder—so the money couldn't go to Torkel in the first place, and he couldn't leave it to the home. It'd go straight from Magnus to you."

"That's it, I'm afraid."

"Yeah, but—you're a lawyer, you tell me—would the courts really turn everything upside down and reverse a ten-year-old will?"

"Sarge, I don't think I have to tell you about the courts. Anytime you go before a judge or a jury, you're in a crapshoot. You never know. My guess is that if the home didn't bother to bring suit, things would stay the way they are. But if they did . . ." He raised his hands and flicked out his fingers, shooting untold possibilities into the air.

"And Dagmar wouldn't go along with it? That's why you think someone killed her?"

"Well, she went along with it, or said she did. But anybody could see her heart wasn't in it. She was on the edge, she just wanted to be done with it. Whoever killed her just couldn't risk it. That's what I think."

Fukida smiled crookedly. "This whole thing gets weirder and weirder," he said slowly. "I know about cases where someone got killed to keep them from telling the police that someone else was a murderer. But killing somebody to keep them from telling that someone else *wasn't* a murderer? Now that's different."

Felix smiled in return. "We've always been an innovative family," he said, softly for him.

AND that had been the end of it. Felix had hung around while the tape was transcribed for his signature and had left. Now Fukida, with the transcription in front of him, was mulling things over. He was inclined to believe what he'd been told, and it was all very interesting and explained a lot, and so on, but did it put him any closer to finding Dagmar's murderer? All four of the nieces and nephews—he was by no means excluding Felix—would have had exactly the same motive for killing her. As to opportunity, none of them had a solid alibi for the time of the murder, but none of them needed one. She'd apparently been killed not long after the meeting at her house broke up, and any of them could have done it before heading home—they'd come and gone separately—and still have been back up in the mountains well inside of an hour. So—

The telephone's buzz broke into his thoughts, which hadn't been going anywhere anyway. "Yup?"

"Line four for you, Sergeant," Sarah said. "It's Ben Kaaua from Honolulu."

"Hello, Ben, I sure hope you have something for me."

"Well, what we have," Kaaua said smugly, and paused for dramatic effect, "is . . . a . . . match!"

"You're positive? You could say that in court?"

"Say it, and mean it, and prove it."

Fukida banged his fist on the desk. "Ben, that's fantastic. Next time I see you for lunch, I owe you one steak sandwich."

"Hell with that, buddy. You owe me a steak dinner."

TWENTY-ONE

WILLIE Akau stood motionless, one arm raised straight above his head, his dusty, garlanded hat in his hand, as the last of the trailer trucks was backed up, inch by inch, to the long, narrow, high-walled loading ramp that fed into the hold of the *Philomena Purcell,* the old Corral Line cargo ship that had been taking Hoaloha Ranch cattle—and more recently, Little Hoaloha cattle—to Vancouver for the last fifteen years. In air-conditioned comfort, no less.

At just the right moment, the hand holding the hat flashed down and the truck stopped instantly. "Okay, Somoa, open 'er up," Willie yelled to the young paniolo standing at the ready.

Somoa hopped up onto the truck bed and tugged on the pull-chain, hand over hand. The perforated metal door clattered up, Somoa jumped out of the way, and the cattle, bawling uncertainly, but docile and cooperative, headed onto the ramp, their hooves drumming satisfyingly on the wooden floor.

"Eh-hoo! Ehhhhh-hoo! Hoo!"

Willie had been hearing that call as man and boy for going on sixty years now. Today it came from the two additional paniolos he'd stationed on either side of the ramp with pole prods to urge the cows along in case any of them needed coaxing.

But they didn't need the poles this time, and in fact, they rarely did. They didn't really need the *eh-hoo*s either. When it came down to it, they didn't much need Willie Akau.

In the old days, it was different. The trip to the Kawaihae docks had been a wild and woolly affair then, a full-fledged, old-fashioned cattle drive from the mountains to the sea. They had to start at one in the morning to get the cows there on time. And then when you got to the docks, you had to ride horseback right into the water and *swim* every damn cow out to an anchored ship, one at a time, then struggle to get a belly band around the frightened animal (he'd gotten his hand broken once and his nose twice doing it) so the deckhands could haul it up in a sling. You had to know what you were doing every step of the way.

Now they just walked them onto the trucks before ever leaving the ranch, and walked them off when they got to the dock. And they started at nine, not at one.

Willie had gotten $1.50 a day on his first cattle drive—which was exactly what Somoa had plunked into the nearby vending machine to get the super-sized chocolate milk he was working on. Now Willie made damn near a hundred times that for doing about a hundred times less work.

It was getting to be retirement time, he thought with a

sigh. He'd done a good job training the hands, and Somoa was more than ready to take over. It was time, all right. The Torkelssons had done right by him when it came to a pension, but he wasn't going to live forever, and if he kept this up he'd wind up dropping dead in the saddle—or more likely at the wheel of an ATV. Not that that'd be so bad, but it'd be kind of nice to get to spend some of that pension, to kick back, do some fishing, do some traveling, do some hanging around the docks, schmoozing and drinking beer in the afternoon, like so many of the old ranch hands turned beach bums.

He watched one of them now, coming down the dock toward him with a rolling, limping gait. Sunburnt and bearded, shaggy gray hair caught in a pony tail, shapeless old captain's hat on his head, black patch tied over one eye. Interesting-looking guy. Not a ranch hand, though. An old salt, a tough, gristly old pirate, really; nobody he remembered seeing around before.

"How you doin', buddy?" Willie said. "Can I help you with something?"

"Oh, I expect you can, Willie," the old man said, and his lean, leathery face split in a grin.

Willie did a double-take, then peered hard at him for a good five seconds. The *Philomena Purcell* did a short test-burst of its powerful foghorn, startling the cattle into a round of jostling and stamping, and bringing a chorus of *eh-hoo*s from the hands.

Willie heard none of it. "Oh . . . my . . . gawd . . . ," he said.

"YOU know, I bet my Uncle Jake would like that," Julie said.

"Absolutely," John said. "How could anybody not like a

topless dashboard hula dancer that plays the Hawaiian War Chant while she jiggles?"

"I don't know, it's pretty hard to beat this coconut piggy bank carved into a monkey head," Gideon said, fingering it. "I think it's meant to be a guenon, or maybe a mangabey. One of the Cercopithecinae, at any rate."

"Well, obviously," John said, yawning. "Cercopitheci-nae, for sure."

They were in Hilo Hattie's in Kona. The two-day getaway to Hilo and Volcanoes National Park had done its work. They had put the Torkelsson affair behind them. The subject of Dagmar's murder had naturally come up a few times, but only in a desultory way. Talking and surmising had led nowhere and had been depressing, and, in any case, they now understood and accepted—even John did—that it was Fukida's baby, not theirs.

Besides that, their thoughts had naturally enough begun to turn toward home. They had seats on a Hawaiian Airlines flight the following afternoon and they had stopped in the giant store on their way back to the Outrigger, where they planned to spend their last night, to pick up presents for friends and family. The "serious" purchases had already been made—a handsome coral belt for John's wife Marti, and a Tommy Bahama Aloha blouse for Julie's sister. Now they were meandering down the souvenir aisles, searching for a few less formal gifts. John, done with his shopping and getting bored, called the Outrigger to see if there were any messages.

"Call from Inge," he told them when he'd hung up and they were in the checkout line. "We're invited to a memorial reception for Dagmar. Casual dress. Just family and close friends."

"I doubt if Julie and I qualify as close friends," Gideon said.

"No, she made a point of saying they'd like to have you. She sounded like she meant it. I guess they really don't want there to be any hard feelings."

"I don't think so," Gideon said doubtfully. "I've stirred up a lot of trouble for those people." He swiped his credit card through the machine on the counter.

"I think we ought to go," John said.

"When is it?" Julie asked.

"Two o'clock, at the community center in Waimea. We'll be a little late, but we can make it. I think it'd be a nice thing if we showed up. For a few minutes, anyway."

"I think so, too," Julie said. "To pay our respects."

"Yes, but—"

"Good, it's settled," John said. "Let's get going."

Gideon gave up with a sigh. "Okay, I'll go along." He signed the $57 receipt and tucked a copy in his wallet.

"I still think we should have gotten him the monkey head," he muttered as they left, just to prove he did have a mind of his own.

HEDWIG, Inge, Axel, and Felix, forming a ragged reception line, seemed genuinely grateful when John, Julie, and Gideon made their appearance. Hedwig, reeking of jasmine and splendidly draped in a shimmering silk muu-muu of royal blue threaded with gold, hugged them all to her soft bosom. A teary-eyed Inge energetically pumped their hands. Axel, also showing emotion, hugged John and Gideon, but shyly shook hands with Julie. Felix went the other way, throwing wide his arms and bear-hugging a startled Julie—it was the first time they'd met—but cordially shaking hands with John and Gideon. Malani and Keoni beside their respective spouses, politely nodded and murmured appreciation for their coming. All very hospitable and sincere and gratifying.

And yet, thought Gideon, there was something surreal about it all. If Fukida was right—and he, Julie, and John agreed with him—then one of these people, these warm, nice, decent people (if you made a few allowances for fraud, theft, and one or two other little transgressions) was the murderer of the woman they were all there to memorialize.

Not that there were so very many. The Torkelssons, it appeared, did not have many friends. In addition to the four siblings and the two spouses, there were perhaps a dozen people who looked as if they were probably ranchers and their wives, and about ten Hawaiian and Asian men, some old, some young, but all with a compact, athletic grace that marked them as current or retired paniolos. Gideon recognized Willie Akau and a couple of the others he'd seen around the Little Hoaloha. The paniolos, some of whom still had range dust on their work clothes, were gathered in two clumps near the refreshment table, most of them clutching tiny paper cups of pink lemonade and looking thoroughly ill at ease.

The refreshments were ample—punch, lemonade, coffee, trays of cookies and fruit breads—but the room would comfortably have held a hundred—a plain, linoleum-tiled, echoing space, far too large for the two dozen or so people in it, so that the affair had a forlorn quality, with guests whispering rather than talking, to keep from making too much noise.

Until Felix took over. "I think we're all here now," he honked from the middle of the room. "On behalf of my family, I want to thank you for coming. My aunt would have really appreciated knowing you were here."

"She does know," Hedwig said with a wise smile.

Felix looked pained. "You all know my sister Hedwig, who is now going to lead us in a . . . in a what, Hedwig?"

"In a Circle of Karmic Energy."

With a theatrical half-bow, Felix stepped aside and turned the floor over to Hedwig. "Whatever," Gideon heard him mutter out of the side of his mouth.

Hedwig spread her massive arms, bringing silence. In the full, gorgeous, blue-and-gold muu-muu she looked immense, the Mother Goddess herself.

"It must be hard to get that big being a vegetarian," Gideon mused.

"Be good," Julie warned him, but she was smiling.

Hedwig lowered her head and waggled her outstretched fingers. "We will hold hands and form a circle."

A circle was duly formed. John held Julie's left hand, Gideon her right. On Gideon's other side, he grasped the callused hand of a wiry old paniolo, making both of them uncomfortable.

Hedwig looked up to see that all was proper and again lowered her cropped blonde head and began to intone.

"Let those who form this circle be here in peace and love, and may it be a protection against any negative energy that may come to do us harm. We are here to honor a beloved person who has moved to another plane. By the formation of this circle we make thinner the veil between the worlds, so that we can call to those who have gone on before us and they will hear us . . ."

Although his head was bowed, Gideon managed to throw a pointed look across Julie and at John. *This is your fault, pal, and don't think I'm going to let you forget it.*

"I ask you now," Hedwig went on, "to sense the presence of the entity we knew as Dagmar Torkelsson among us, and to allow the energy and love she brings us to build and grow. Visualize the energy circling round, gathering strength." She paused for the space of three long breaths, visualizing. "And now I want you to bask in this energy a moment longer, and then divide yourselves into groups of three or four, and to share with each other your memories and reflections. In that way, we release this positive energy back into the universe . . ."

Gideon, his mind wandering, found himself looking into the community kitchen at one end of the room. Something there—something important, he thought—had fleetingly engaged his attention, but whatever it was, he'd lost it as suddenly as it had come. He scanned the stainless-steel sinks, the counter, the two big stainless-steel refrigerators, the electric coffee percolators, the open shelves of dishes and utensils. His eyes went back and focused on the refrigerators, both of which were covered with little notes attached by a colorful multitude of refrigerator magnets. There were surfboards, pigs and penguins in grass skirts, hula dancers, palm trees, martini glasses with olives—

He froze. "*John!*" The exclamation popped out on its own. Fortunately, the circle was now breaking up into its smaller groups, so he didn't disrupt the visualization in progress.

John looked curiously at him. "What?"

He began to point into the kitchen, then said: "Come on, you two. I want to show you something."

"My goodness," Julie said as he grabbed her wrist, "what's all the excitement about?"

Once in the kitchen, he pointed at one of the magnet-laden refrigerators. "Take a look at that."

"Look at what?" a puzzled John asked. "What's so—"

When he realized which one Gideon was pointing to, it stopped him in his tracks. "I'll be damned," he whispered and plucked it from the metal surface. "Holy cow, am I nuts, or is this the same . . ."

"I think it's exactly the same."

"I think so, too."

"John, do you realize what this means? It must—"

"I know," John said, running his hand over the irregular surface. "It's almost too fantastic, but—"

"I know."

"I can't tell you what a thrill it is to observe great minds in action," Julie said dryly, "but if one of you could manage a coherent sentence, I would be endlessly grateful."

"This thing is a ceramic map of the Big Island," John said, offering it for her inspection.

"Ah. Well, as a matter of fact, I did manage to grasp that much on my own."

"It's also a magnet, Julie," Gideon said. "A big one, for a refrigerator magnet."

"Uh-huh. And . . . ?"

"You remember that box of stuff from the plane that nobody could find? One of these was in it."

"We figured it was a coaster," John said, "or a . . . what do you call it?"

"A trivet," Gideon supplied, shaking his head. "We should have realized."

"How could we realize?" John protested. "We had no idea what was going on."

"Well, I guess those would have to qualify as coherent sentences," Julie said, "but I still don't—"

"Julie," Gideon said, "what would a magnet be doing in the cockpit of a small plane? Think what it'd do if it got anywhere near the compass."

"Are you saying—" Suddenly aware that she was nearly shouting, she looked quickly around and dropped her voice. The three of them moved their heads closer together. "Are you saying that someone *purposely* tried to make the plane go off-course—"

"Tried and succeeded," John amended. "Maravovo's a long way from Tarabao. And there isn't much other land out there."

Julie jerked her head as if to clear it. "But wouldn't that be murder? Doesn't it mean that someone *murdered* Torkel?"

"And the pilot, Claudia," Gideon said, nodding.

"But why would anyone—"

"And, hey, remember," John said, "it was all tangled up in a wad of duct tape. It must have been stuck somewhere where they wouldn't see it—under the console, I bet, right near the compass. The compass would have been all screwed up and they'd never know it. And they were flying in the dark; so they wouldn't have been able to tell from—"

"Stuck by *whom?*" Julie demanded, her voice rising again as her frustration increased. "And why?"

John and Gideon looked at each other. It was Gideon who answered. "I can't vouch for the why, but I think we can make a pretty good guess as to whom."

"More than a guess," John said grimly. "Only one guy went to the airport with Torkel. Only one guy got the plane out of the hangar and waited around till the pilot showed up. Only one guy was *there*. And he used to be a pilot himself, don't forget that. He knew all about compasses and planes." His eyes, narrowed now, roved the room and focused. Julie followed the direction of his gaze. Her hand went to her mouth.

"Axel," she breathed.

"The miserable sonofabitch," John said.

JOHN wanted to go over to him right then, put him under citizen's arrest, and drag him off, preferably forcibly, to the Kona PD, but Gideon convinced him things would go more smoothly all around if he called Fukida instead and let him make the arrest. John, sagging a little after the first wave of anger passed, agreed, but suggested that Gideon make the call. "It'll go over better if he thinks you figured it out for him, not me."

"Besides," he added with a half-smile, "you *did* figure it out."

"It sure took me long enough. Okay, I'll call from out in the hall. Julie, keep this guy"—he gestured with his chin at John—"in check. Don't let him get his hands on Axel. It'd be better if he's still alive when the police get here."

USING one of the pay phones in the hallway, Gideon called the CIS only to learn that Fukida was out on a call.

"This is pretty important, Sarah. Isn't there any way I can get hold of him?"

"I'll have him radioed," Sarah said. "He'll call you right back. What's your number?"

It took less than a minute for Fukida's call to come through. "How ya doin', sport?" he practically chirped. "What's so important?"

Gideon had never heard him so upbeat. "Where are you?" he asked. "What happened, Ted?"

"Where I am is in my car. And where I'm going is to the Waimea Community Center. And when I get there I'm going to collar our killer. The CIS has done it again, chief. We got our man!"

"Axel," Gideon said.

Gideon heard him whoosh out his breath. "Now how the hell do you know that?"

"The magnet. How do *you* know?"

"The glove." And then, after a few seconds: "What magnet?"

"The magnet that . . . uh, Ted, I'm not sure we're track-ing here. What glove? Who are you talking about?"

"Who am I . . . I just told you. Axel—Axel's glove. He's our murderer, he killed Dagmar. I thought you agreed with me."

"No, I'm talking about the other murder."

"The other . . . ? You mean Magnus? Are you telling me Axel also—"

"No, not Magnus. Torkel. Look, I'm at the Center myself—"

"*So now Torkel was murdered, too?*" Gideon winced and held the receiver away from his ear. "You guys are driving me nuts!"

And with that, Fukida hung up, but a few seconds later he called back. "Don't go away," he growled. "I'm gonna want to talk to you."

UNDER the stunned and recriminatory stares of his rela-tives and friends, a drooping, unresisting Axel Torkelsson was cuffed, read his rights, and led away by Fukida and a uniformed officer. Malani, dry-eyed but too dazed to speak, was enfolded in Hedwig's warm, fragrant arms. People looked at one another but mostly said nothing.

After a few seconds, Felix took charge with his usual élan.

"I guess that's it for the reception, folks," he announced. "Thank you all for coming."

"ALL right, I understand why he killed Dagmar," Julie said. "Sergeant Fukida explained that. He was afraid she was going to break down and tell the police the truth; that is, that Torkel was *not* a murderer, which would have meant there was a real chance—especially once the seamen's home found out about it—that Magnus's will might be thrown out and Torkel's implemented instead. Whew, do I have that right?"

"That's the way I understand it," John said. "Of course I'm just a simple federal cop."

"All right. Fine. What I don't understand is why he wanted Torkel's plane to go down. Why would he want to kill *him?*"

"Well—" Gideon began, then paused as the cocktail waitress put down their drink orders: iced tea for Julie, a Mai Tai for John, and a glass of Chardonnay for Gideon. They were in Hawaii Calls, the Outrigger's wall-less restaurant, at a tree-shaded outdoor table in the rear, toward the beach. They clinked glasses and took their first welcome sips.

"Well," he continued, "that's something we don't know for sure yet, but at a guess, it was probably pretty much the same reason. Axel must have realized that if Torkel ever did come back and explain that he *wasn't* Magnus—which he was supposed to do, eventually—it would turn out the same way: goodbye, Magnus's will, hello Torkel's."

"Goodbye, Little Hoaloha," John said, "hello, nothing."

Julie slowly shook her head. "And so he murdered two people—took away their lives because they got in the way of getting something that wasn't really his anyway . . . that pleasant, harmless-looking little man."

"Three people," Gideon said. "Don't forget Claudia."

"You two ready to order dinner?" John asked restlessly. He was more than ready to change the subject.

"Sure, I guess so," Julie said, then suddenly shuddered, the shiver running visibly down her body.

"Cold?" Gideon asked. "Do you want to move in under the roof?"

"No, it's beautiful out here with the ocean, and the sun

going down. I think I could use a pullover, though. The tan one in the closet to the right—would you mind?"

Gideon, with the pullover over one shoulder, was closing the door to their room behind him, when he heard the phone ring. On the line was Fukida.

"Hey, chief, I'm glad I caught you. Listen, have you people had dinner yet?"

"No, we were just thinking about it."

"Great. How about if I join you?"

"Well, sure," Gideon said, puzzled. He and John were scheduled to be deposed by Fukida the next morning at CIS. What couldn't wait until then? And *dinner?* Why the sudden sociability?

"Um, fine, Ted. We'll wait for you. We're at Hawaii Calls, in the resort."

Fukida heard the ambiguity in his voice and laughed, rather merrily for him. "Ah, don't sound so worried. My wife's in Honolulu this week. I just thought it'd be nice to have some company, and eat some decent food, too. See you in a few minutes."

"Fine."

"Oh, also . . . there's somebody I'd like you to meet." And with an improbable final happy chuckle he hung up.

TWENTY-TWO

"HE'S got something up his sleeve, that's all I know," Gideon said. "He was chuckling."

"Chuckling?" John said. "There's something wrong there. Snicker, I could see. Sneer, for sure. But chuckle? Whoa, this looks bad. I'm telling you, Teddy can be . . . Teddy can be . . ." The words trailed off. He was staring into space, apparently at nothing. ". . . He can be . . ."

"John, what is it?" Julie asked.

But John was at a loss for words in the most literal sense of the phrase. He had jumped up, knocking over his chair, and all he could do was point.

Gideon turned to see Fukida coming toward them through the restaurant with an old man wearing a captain's hat with faded gold braid, a yellow T-shirt with some kind of logo on it, and rumpled khakis. Not much taller than Fukida, he had the look of an old rake, bearded and pony-tailed, with a black patch over one eye and a rolling limp.

When they got closer, Gideon was able to read the T-shirt logo: *Old Fishermen Never Die, They Just Smell That Way.*

"Hello, everybody," Fukida said, grinning.

John, still staring at the old man, found his voice again. "Mr. T! How did you . . . we thought you were . . . we were *sure* you were . . ."

"Well, as you can see, I'm not," the old man said. "I'm hale and hearty and crabbier than ever. It's nice to see you, boy."

"And this is Gideon Oliver," Fukida said, "the one I've been telling you about."

The old man laughed delightedly. "Oh, yeah. You've been working on my case, I hear."

As he got to his feet, Gideon's mind was whirling at top speed, teeming with what seemed to be impossibilities. Who was this guy supposed to be? Could he actually be Magnus Torkelsson, whose body, after all, was never positively identified? But if so, whose burned body had been left in the hay barn? Or could it be . . . what was his name, Andreas, the oldest brother, who had supposedly died decades ago? But if so, what did "you've been working on my case" mean?

"You're—you're Magnus Torkelsson?" he asked, choosing the less improbable impossibility.

The old man threw a glance at Fukida and laughed, both of them looking pleased with themselves. "Magnus? No, I'm not Magnus." He sat down at the table. "Me, I'm Torkel."

Gideon was flabbergasted. "You *can't* be Torkel. I examined your remains myself," he said stupidly. "I identified you from your right foot. It's in a . . . it's in a box at the Kona police station."

"Oh, so that's where it is." Smiling, he pulled his right cuff up above his white sock and rapped with his knuckles on the almost-flesh-colored plastic shell that substituted for his right lower leg.

HE had seen the lights when the Grumman was fifty feet above the surface of the lagoon, he told them, but he hadn't known what they were—a pair of whale-oil lanterns hung on posts at the front ends of two dugout canoes that had been night-fishing for rockfish and rays along the reef. Four men altogether, they had come from Tiku, the nearest inhabited island, and they had been flabbergasted when the plane fell without warning out of the sky and plowed itself into the water within a few hundred feet of them.

The last thing he remembered from that night was the wrenching screech of the wing shearing off as it hit the water. The next thing was waking up in a pandanus-roofed hut two, or possibly four, days later—he had never figured out their language well enough to know for sure. But what he did know for sure was that they had paddled to the downed plane before it sank. They had found the pilot dead and Torkel unconscious, with his foot caught inextricably in the twisted metal under the console. Using the tools they had brought for gutting and quartering the rays, they had taken his leg off at the knee, staunched the blood with a tourniquet made from his shirt, and taken him to Tiku.

There, with the stump bound up in pandanus leaves that had been soaked in an evil-smelling poultice, he slowly recovered, although one eye was damaged beyond repair. He remained on Tiku for five weeks, leaving with the first people to call there during his stay—a Japanese scientific team studying the effects of ocean currents on intertidal marine life. They had taken him to Tarawa, from where he'd gone first to Australia, then to Fiji, and then, a year after the plane crash, to the island of Moorea, part of French Polynesia. And there he'd stayed, living a lonely and isolated life, carving furniture and drums from the local milo and kamani woods, until he met and married a beautiful French widow, his "trophy wife" (she was seventy-one).

After that he'd given up the furniture shop, bought a boat (she was rich as well as beautiful), and set himself up in the fishing charter business, which he still worked at two or three days a week whenever he felt like it.

"And that's about it," he said. "The story of my life. Never for one minute did I regret leaving Hawaii and the ranch behind. The best decision I ever made."

"Is that a heck of a story, or what?" Fukida said with a delighted, almost proprietary air. "I've been on some pretty strange cases, but that has to be a first."

"It's a first for me, too," Gideon said slowly, still struggling to absorb what he'd just heard. "It's the first time I ever identified a living man from his skeletal remains." He couldn't help laughing. "It's probably a first for the science of forensic anthropology."

Torkel guffawed. He was really enjoying himself. "I never would have come back either, but then I read about what happened to my sister, and I knew it just had to have something to do with what happened back then, and the will and all, and I figured I owed it to her to come back and finally straighten things out"—he sobered—"and do what I could to help the police find out who killed her."

"And Mr. Torkelsson has been very helpful," Fukida said. "What he said jibed right down the line with what Felix told me."

"Were you surprised that it was Axel, Mr. Torkelsson?" Julie asked.

Torkel leaned back in his chair, lifted his cap, smoothed down his lank gray hair, and screwed the cap back on. *Cap'n Jack's Charters,* it said in faded gold braid. "Not really. The boy always seemed like a little apple-polisher to me. 'Yes, Uncle Torkel, no, uncle Torkel.' But I never knew until today that anybody tried to kill *me,* though. That was some surprise."

They hadn't thought to order food until well into Torkel's account, and now the waitress and a busboy showed up to remove their salads and set out the main courses. Since no one had wanted to interrupt his narrative by studying the menu, they'd all followed the waitress's recommendation: blackened tuna in a soy-mustard dressing.

Once the luscious-smelling plates were set in front of them, however, they seemed to realize how hungry they were, so for a few minutes they simply shoveled the food in, limiting their conversation, such as it was, to little more than appreciative grunts.

"Ted," Gideon asked when they'd slowed down a little, "what's going to happen to the nephews and nieces?"

"Well, Axel's gonna go away for a while," Fukida said, chewing.

"Of course. But what about the others? Inge, and Felix, and Hedwig?"

Fukida nodded. "You mean am I going to do anything about all the fudging from ten years ago." He laid down his fork. "I haven't made up my mind. There are a lot of extenuating circumstances. And a lot of problems with reopening."

Gideon looked at him, his head cocked. "Am I reading you wrong, or does that mean you're inclined to let it go?"

"No, you're not reading me wrong," Fukida said and went back to his blackened tuna.

"Wait, hold it," John said. "How can you just let it go? That's Mr. T's property they're living on, and he's sitting right here. He was declared dead by accident."

"Not quite by accident, Johnny. He was declared dead

because he went out of his way to mislead the police and everybody else to make it look as if he *was* dead—his own doing. I don't really know how the courts would feel about giving him back his property now."

"Mm. I see what you mean about extenuating circumstances," Julie said.

"Oh, hell, it's a moot point, anyway," said Torkel, who had cleaned his plate as if he hadn't eaten in two days. "I'm happy where I am, I've mellowed, and I have everything I want. No worries. Why would I want to be a rancher again? That was somebody else, not me."

"But what about the seamen's home?" Gideon asked. "You wanted them to have the money from the ranch."

"Now that's another funny thing. The Swedish Seamen's Home went kaput in 1997. There aren't enough old Swedish sailors around anymore to make it worthwhile; not indigent ones, anyhow." He shrugged. "So, what do I care who has the property? I like those kids all right, they're welcome to it. In my eyes, they didn't do anything wrong."

"See?" Fukida said. "Not much point in my resuscitating the case, even if I wanted to, which I don't. Who would benefit? No, let me get Axel put away, and I'm done with it. Seems to me I had a life before the Torkelssons, and it'd be nice to get back to it."

John mopped up the last of the soy-mustard sauce with a roll and sat back. "So what happens now, Mr. T? What's next for you?"

"Me?" Torkel said. "First, I'd sure like to see that box with my foot in it. I haven't seen that foot for a long time. Then I need to arrange for Dagmar's burial when the sergeant here releases her. And then . . ."

He took a deep breath, filled with contentment. "Then

I'm going to go back to my beautiful Tahiti, back to my gorgeous trophy wife, going to catch some marlin and mahi-mahi when I feel like it, live in sandals and shorts, and watch the sun go down over Mount Tohiea from my patio every single night of the week, with a cold gin and tonic in my hand."

John, Gideon, and Julie looked at each other. "Makes sense to me," John said.